Malevolent Nevers

By
Tom Rimer

This is a work of fiction. Names, characters, places and incidents either are products of the author's imagination or are used fictitiously. Any resemblance to actual events or locales or persons, living or dead, is entirely coincidental.

MALEVOLENT NEVERS

First edition. December 3, 2021.

Copyright © 2021 Tom Rimer.

Written by Tom Rimer.

Cover Art © 2021 Gemma Amor

Cover Design © 2021 Jessica Moon and Chad Moon

Formatting by Mandy Russell

Editing by Mandy Russell

This book is dedicated to the horrors that live out behind my shed.

And to the horrors that surely live out behind all of your sheds, too.

Table of Contents

One	1
Two	9
Three	14
Four	20
Five	26
Six	30
Seven	33
Eight	38
Nine	43
Ten	50
Eleven	58
Twelve	63
Thirteen	68
Fourteen	73
Fifteen	78
Sixteen	83
Seventeen	87
Eighteen	92
Nineteen	98
Twenty	103
Twenty One	107
Twenty Two	113
Twenty Three	119
Twenty Four	125
Twenty Five	130
Twenty Six	135
Twenty Seven	140
Twenty Eight	144

TWENTY NINE	146
THIRTY	151
THIRTY ONE	155
THIRTY TWO	161
THIRTY THREE	166
THIRTY FOUR	170
THIRTY FIVE	174
THIRTY SIX	181
THIRTY SEVEN	185
THIRTY EIGHT	189
THIRTY NINE	199
FORTY	206
FORTY ONE	211
FORTY TWO	218
FORTY THREE	230
FORTY FOUR	236
FORTY FIVE	240
FORTY SIX	245
FORTY SEVEN	254
FORTY EIGHT	258
FORTY NINE	266
FIFTY	271
FIFTY ONE	280
FIFTY TWO	287
FIFTY THREE	293
FIFTY FOUR	298
FIFTY FIVE	305
FIFTY SIX	310
FIFTY SEVEN	317
FIFTY EIGHT	322
FIFTY NINE	329

One

The glowing theater marquee floated above the two shapes huddled together on the cracked sidewalk. The sign flashed, intermittently, the title of that evening's featured horror flick: *Glitter Zombies*. The shadows beneath shivered in the frigid, midnight, fall air. It was far colder than a typical October month in Atlanta and probably didn't foreshadow as much about the ugly days ahead as it should have. The teens, bathed in a starry-eyed enchantment cast by the other, were far too bewitched to notice much else.

Simeon Ward, a bit of chipped black nail polish still visible on one pinky, reached into the large popcorn bucket and picked at the remnants. His greasy hair, once blond, was dyed black, and he casually relocated it from one side of his head to the other. He was in the process of dislodging a kernel from between his teeth, when a car—covered in stickers featuring the logos of what appeared to be local bands—revved its engine as it rambled past. A face hidden in the gloom shouted at him from an open window.

"Simi!"

The car didn't stop and he didn't bother attempting a wave before it rounded the corner at the end of the block.

"Who was that?"

Simi turned and looked into the large green eyes of his girlfriend, Mags Downing. A couple of meandering dreads hung down in front of her face, just barely reaching the dark skin of her cheekbones.

"No clue," Simi sighed. "Some asshole."

He had no memory of the car, but it wasn't a surprise to him he'd been recognized. Most people in this part of town knew him, knew Mags. Both had lived in the same neighborhood, just a couple of blocks over from where they were sitting, for their entire lives. Their houses, directly across the street from one another, made it easy for the two to regularly sneak out for late-night rendezvous, movies, and general insouciant shenanigans. They'd been doing so together for years, long before the official "dating" designation was ever uttered.

Feels like ancient history, man.

"Yeah," she yawned. "So, what'd you think? The movie, I mean." She reached out and snatched the last piece of popcorn before he was able. He squinted at her playfully and threw the bucket somewhere behind, vaguely in the direction of an overflowing trash receptacle.

Simi stretched his arms out in front of himself, the black jean sleeves of his jacket momentarily leaving his wrists exposed to the night. "I dunno," he said, shivering. "This one didn't scare me. Not really. A few good jumps, I guess. But, mostly, I just thought it was kind of dumb."

Mags looked disappointed. "Dumb? Come on, really? Maybe you're just getting harder to scare. I actually thought it was pretty good. I mean the whole glitter thing was—"

"Awkward," he interrupted. "And confusing. I didn't get it."

She rested her head on his shoulder. "Don't try and analyze it, Simi. You always over-think it. Movies like this one are just supposed to be fun. What'd you expect? It was freaking called *Glitter Zombies*."

Simi played, absentmindedly, with one of her dreads. "I don't think I'm over-thinking anything. I just want to know why the undead were all covered in glitter and shit. I mean, what was that even about? What were they going for?"

"Dude, it's art. You clearly just don't know art when you see it."

He scoffed. "*That* was art?"

Mags smiled up at him. "Mhmm," she said. "A. R. T." She leaned her face upward and kissed him quickly on the nose. "Art."

He shrugged. "If you say so."

For a few beats after, both Simi and Mags sat in silence. He staring up at the stars, she staring up at him staring up at the stars. When his gaze remained fixed for a bit too long, and the lasting silence encroached on maladroit, Mags reached up and gently poked him under his chin.

"Hey," she said. "You okay?"

Nope.

Simi didn't look away from the sky. "I'm fine."

Mags adjusted to get a better look at the contortion of his face. "Look, Buddy, I know you better than anyone and I can tell you're somewhere else right now. What's up?"

Simi hung his head in defeat. Mags always had a way of dragging it out of him and a knack for realizing when her first and only beau needed to talk. "It's just…"

She finished for him. "Him?"

Simi nodded. "And *her*. Definitely her too."

Mags nodded. "Anything new?"

It's never anything new, Mags. We keep doing this, having this same shitty conversation. I know you're trying to help but it's unfortunately never going to be new.

He shook his head. Another car drove by, this one hitting a small puddle that came close to splashing onto their outstretched sneakers. Neither flinched or was dislodged from their chat.

"Nothing new," he confirmed. "Hate that she's gone. Hate that she left me with him. Hate *him*. But, what're you gonna do?"

Mags sat up and interlocked her hand with his. They each wore a matching neon green cord around a ring finger. It was a childhood memory, a shared carnival trinket from a local fair long gone. Years before, each had placed the identical prize on the hand of the other in jest. Neither one had ever removed theirs. Though the rings themselves were fading and fraying, Simi and Mags' recollection of the moment was as brilliant as ever.

"When was the last time you talked to her?"

Simi hung his head between his knees. "Weeks ago," he said. "She's too busy, gallivanting around the world with that old, rich, silver-spoon. Too busy to talk. Too busy for her son."

Mags kissed his hand. "And... *him?*"

Simi laughed. "Who, my dad?" She nodded and he continued. "Ah, he's the same. Trying, I guess. But, as you know, none of this is really his jam."

Mags rolled her eyes at him. "This? You mean, *you?* You're his son. You're his only jam."

Simi kicked a crushed can he'd been toeing out into the road. "Yeah, well. He's still adjusting to being a functioning human again. Being a father's still a ways off. You know that."

Do you?

She bit her lip, unsure of how far to press. "And… the functioning adult stuff. That's going—"

"It's going fine. I mean, he's stayed sober. Nothing's changed there. Just passed a year. But, I'm sure you—"

"Oh, yeah, I didn't forget. That's so great, Simi. Really, it is. I hope you realize that."

Simi half-heartedly bobbed his head. "It is," he hesitated, not wanting to downplay his dad's success. "But I can tell it's still a struggle for him. He's still… *rough*. In more ways than one. And I can tell he just wants her to come back so he can take off and do his own thing."

Mags wrapped an arm around Simi's shoulders and squeezed. "You don't know that. It's just taking him some time. He practically had to start all over and hit the ground running as a father to a seventeen-year-old—"

"Look," he interrupted. "That's entirely his fault. No one told him to leave us. No one told him he needed to spend my entire childhood in pubs and at blackjack tables instead of with me."

Mags squeezed harder. "I know," she said. "I know. Trust me. But, he *is* back. He came back. He wants to be a part of your life."

Simi stood up and puts his hands in his pockets. Mags didn't move and still sat looking up at him from the pavement. "I guess. But, would he have if Mom hadn't decided to suddenly jet across the globe? Not like he had a place to stay anyways. She gave him a temporary roof over his head and a spot to park his truck. I hate to even suggest it, but—"

"Don't," she stopped him. "Don't suggest it."

The marquee flickered once more, winking at the lull

in their conversation. Simi paced a couple of times behind his girlfriend and was about to speak when a pair of headlights rounded the corner onto their street. The high beams flashed repeatedly and, even before the rusted seventies-era Ford came to a screeching halt, both Simi and Mags knew who it was.

Here we go.

Simi turned his back to the vehicle and Mags stood up to greet it. Reflecting the purple *Glitter Zombies* lettering, the passenger side window squealed as it was manually rolled down. A completely bald head, also catching a bit of the glow from the signage, poked itself out.

"There you both are," he said. "Been driving around for the past hour looking for you two. You know it's after midnight?" The man didn't seem at all worried, only mildly annoyed.

"Hi Abe," Mags said informally. She'd known Simi's dad, at least in theory, since she was just a kid. "We decided to catch a late movie."

Abel Ward smiled warmly. "No biggie," he said, in his best cool-dad attempt. "Should have figured." He glanced at the back of his son. "Hi, Simi."

"Why don't you use your phone? Texting is like a *thing* now, Abe."

Abe's expression darkened. Hearing his son calling him by his first name was not a preference. "Look, I'm sorry. I left it back at home. I'm going to get better at that. I promise."

Simi shrugged and walked over to the door. It groaned as he pulled it toward himself. Mags, having participated in the familiar song-and-dance many times before, hopped in first. Once she was settled in beside Abe, Simi followed and slammed their only escape shut.

The radio was on low, but Simi could hear the twang of a banjo quietly welcome them to the awkwardness of the tiny, crammed, cab as his father's truck lurched away from the curb. Bluegrass music, the constant soundtrack to Abel Ward's plodding, frequently disappointing, career as a parent played them off into the night.

As they slowly moved away from the theater, Simi mumbled under his breath. "One of these days, it's gonna fall right off of its hinges into the road."

Abe squinted. It was late and he was very tired. "The door?"

"Yeah, Abe. The door. Obviously."

Abe laughed, nervously, inexpertly attempting to maneuver around the tension oozing from his son. "Well, she's lasted this long, hasn't she?" He smiled at Mags, looking for some support, but she shrugged. It was clear she didn't want to get in between them, even though she physically *was*. "But, you're right. Definitely gonna be a lot of work to get her back into tip-top shape again."

Simi didn't respond. He only stared out his window. The ride, fortunately for them all, would be very short, but Mags still chose to fill the delicate silence. She almost always did.

"Hey, thanks for the lift, Abe. By the way, you should totally check out *Glitter Zombies*, it—"

"That's okay," he chuckled. "I'm good. Not exactly my jam, if you know what I mean."

Simi and Mags both exchanged glances. Abe was vaguely aware the two were making eyes at one another, but he ignored it. They usually were.

A minute later they braked in front of Mags' home, an elongated squeal accompanying their arrival and no doubt alerting the neighborhood of the late-night return. The kids got out and Abe pulled his aging truck into a driveway across the street that—technically speaking—belonged to Simi's mother, Tammy. Abe's ex-wife.

"'Night, Mags," he whispered as he stepped out of the truck. "Simi—"

"I know," Simi hissed. "I'm just gonna say goodnight. I'll be right in."

Mags grabbed Simi's hand and the two walked to her front door. They both waited for Abe's back to turn on them before leaning in for a quick kiss.

"Okay, okay," she poked him in the chest. "Enough for tonight. I'm sure my dad's awake, staring at us out of his bedroom window."

"Creepy," Simi smiled.

They hugged and, before she reached for the doorknob, Mags breathed through her teeth, "I hope you two have a good night. Remember, give him a chance. He's building himself back, one piece at a time."

Simi didn't respond, but his longtime girlfriend opened the door and disappeared within. Turning back to his own home, he could see the living room lights were on. His father was already inside. Unlike most dads, he undoubtedly wasn't ready for bed. Abe Ward was a certified night-owl; there'd be a good chance he'd just want to "talk" about "things" and "hang out" once he found himself alone with his son for the evening. But Simi didn't want to talk. He had no interest in hanging out. He just wanted to sleep.

I don't owe you shit, Abe.

Simi took another deep breath of the surprisingly chilly nighttime air and started his long trudge across their very small street.

Two

Abel Ward stood with his back toward the large bay window in his ex-wife's living room. If he'd turned, with the curtains spread wide, he'd have been able to see Simi and Mags across the street saying their goodnights. He wanted no part of any sort of accusation that he was spying on the two or not properly giving them their space. *Kids need their space.* He likely would've just headed upstairs to avoid the risk entirely, but he'd made it his mission to "be around" for Simi each night, once his son finally came home. For that reason, he lingered not far from the doorway, intentionally keeping himself turned away from the tableau outside.

Just to be on the safe side.

Everything with Simi was like walking on eggshells, (wobbling, already-cracked, eggshells) all while wearing an oversized pair of military-grade combat boots. Or, at least that's how it felt to Abe. His son bristled with each attempted sign of affection, with every seemingly harmless joke his father tried out. But none of that was a surprise, not to Abe. All of it, he conjectured, was warranted. All of it was the fault of one Abel Ward.

Every goddamn minute of it. I own this.

And he *was* honest with himself. He couldn't say for sure what the end game would be with him and Simi. It wasn't clear, and likely wouldn't be for some time, if they'd ever have a typical father-son relationship. In fact, he was betting they never would. Abe kept telling himself that if they, at least, could be friends and talk, if they could one day easily converse with one another, he might be forced to accept it.

Let's see if we can even get that far, though. Baby steps.

The door creaked open behind him and he stiffened. He heard Simi drop his keys into the small, rainbow-colored, ceramic bowl. Abe always assumed it had been made in elementary school art class, but his memory from that era of his son's life was foggy, at best. The initials 'S.W.' were scratched, clumsily, down the side facing outward. As Abe was opening his mouth to greet his son, Simi picked up a cell phone from beside the bowl on the antique buffet table. The freshly awoken screen illuminated the teen's face in blue light and he spoke first.

"Here's your phone," he said. "And it looks like you've missed, damn, like nine calls tonight."

Abe crossed the living room and gently took possession of the device. "Huh?" he said, immediately scrolling. "Who would be calling me at this hour?"

Simi shrugged and walked into the kitchen, only partly interested. Abe heard the fridge door open and then slam shut shortly after. "Funny thing is, only one of the calls was from me."

Abe squinted at the eight other missed calls. Though

many people often suggested he acted younger than most his age, the weakness of his vision revealed the truth behind the nearly fifty years he'd been alive. "Interesting," he mumbled.

Simi grunted through a gulp of milk, likely straight from the carton. When Abe didn't continue, Simi wiped the mustache from his upper lip. "Well, who was it?"

Abe shook his head and lowered himself to the couch. "Not sure. Not someone from my contacts. Just a Foxborough number."

Simi finished drained the milk carton and then placed it onto the counter. "Foxborough? As in—ah—"

"Massachusetts. Yep."

They both were motionless for an instant. Eventually, Simi broke the silence. "Isn't that where you grew up?"

Abe was nodding, staring off somewhere Simi couldn't himself see.

"Weird. Any idea who it could be?"

Abe continued looking ahead. His gaze was stuck on a deep crack that was slowly making its way across the wooden mantel. It was widening, he'd recently noticed, expanding with the winter or from water damage, or perhaps due to some other cause entirely. For some reason it started, right then, to bother him, and—in that moment—with his cell phone glowing between his hands, he could oddly focus on nothing else.

"Gotta fix that," he suddenly mumbled. "You know, before your mother gets back."

Simi followed his father's eyes to the fracture across the room. "Um, what? You mean…" he walked to the fireplace. "This thing?" He pointed to the large spider-webbing fissure that spanned the length of the beam just above the open mouth of the hearth. "This thing? It's been like this forever, Abe."

Abe scratched at his freshly shaven dome, slowly returning to the land of the living. "Really? Looks like it's getting worse, to me. In any case, I'm gonna see what I can do about it."

Simi rolled his eyes and turned himself toward the hallway. He began walking to his bedroom at its end. "Alright, well. I'm tired," he paused before adding, uncouthly, "See ya."

"Night," Abe called to Simi's back. A door opened and closed gently, in response.

Well, so much for "being around" tonight.

He looked down at his phone again. It was after midnight, but a few of the calls had come in within the hour.

Eight.

Despite the time, someone was (*desperately?*) trying to reach him. Someone from his hometown, a place he'd managed to stay clear of, and detached from, for nearly thirty years. Just before his twentieth birthday, he'd hitchhiked down the East Coast, intending to never look back. To never return. There'd been too much pain and not enough joy. As it turned out, moving south hadn't cured the majority of his ails. If anything, it'd merely relocated them to a warmer climate.

He unbuttoned his red flannel and pulled it off over his head. It might have been Georgia-cold outside that night, but inside was as Georgia-warm as ever. He flapped the Atlanta Falcons t-shirt he was wearing a bit to cool himself off and, after a brief hesitation, tapped the number appearing eight separate times on his call screen.

Apprehensively, Abe brought the phone to his ear and listened.

Riiiiing.

He breathed in through his nose.

Riiiiiiing.

He released the air building up in his lungs.

Riii—

"Hello?" a sleepy voice answered from the other end of the line before the phone could fully toll a third time.

Abe, who'd been in the process of taking another, anxiety-quelling breath, felt himself almost gag on his own oxygen. "It's, uh—I mean, this is—"

"Abe?" the voice nearly whispered, itself sounding almost out of breath. "Abel Ward?"

Immediately, he recognized the hushed, gentle, tone. It was one he hadn't heard since before his southerly departure. Her voice still held the grit and the gravel he'd known and laughed with and—

"D?" he stammered.

He could sense tears on the other end of the line. Happy ones. "Hey, you. Long time no—"

"Daisy is everything okay? It's so late. I can only assume—I mean, is everyone—"

He listened attentively as Daisy Peltzer, an old friend—

She was more than a friend.

—sighed deeply.

"It's Elma, Abe. She's... well, she hasn't got long and... well, she says she wants to go over some things."

Abe looked up at the wall clock hanging in front of his face. It was almost 1:00 am and he was talking to his high school crush for the first time in decades. There were more than a thousand miles between them, but the urgency in her voice, and the fluttering in his chest, forced him to disregard the hour and the distance.

"What kind of things?"

Three

"This is some bullshit, Abe."

Simi stood in the doorway to the bathroom, a toothbrush hanging from his incredulous sneer. His father lingered awkwardly in the hallway with one hand in a pocket and the other holding a steaming cup of morning coffee. His head drooped toward the floor.

"I know how much this sucks for you—"

"Oh, do you? Do you really? You just expect me to—what—just say 'peace out' to my life, my friends, my *girlfriend*? What about school? You do know I still go to school, right Abe?"

Abe lifted his head incrementally but didn't quite manage to bring his gaze to eye level. "Hey, if I had another choice, I'd make it."

Simi spat into the sink. When he returned to face the doorway, he noticed Abe eyeing the lightning bolt tattoo on his bare chest. Simi made no attempt to hide it and instead barreled forward in pleading his case.

"See, but you *do* have another choice. You really do. We don't have to pack ourselves into your old-ass truck and drive all the way up the East Coast, thousands of miles away from Mags—"

"Actually, it's more like one thousand. Just over a thousand or so."

"Whatever, Abe! Holy shit, what's wrong with you? I mean, you get what I'm saying right?" Simi stormed past his father, intentionally bumping shoulders with him as he moved into the hallway. "We do *not*, I repeat, we do not need to do this. Who is she again?"

"She's my great-aunt."

"And why haven't I ever heard of her before?"

Abe sighed deeply. He leaned back against the wall behind him and looked up at the glass sconce above his head. A moth was flittering into and around the lit bulb. Simi's voice jarred him out of his temporary trance.

"Hello? Earth to Abe?" He was standing inside of his room, pulling a black t-shirt—with a grinning skull emblazoned in the center of it—over his head. "Are you even listening? This is such a ridiculous thing you're asking of me. At the very least, you could wake the hell up and pay attention for once."

Abe straightened and faced his son, a wisp of strength revealing itself on his prematurely aging frame. "There's a lot I've failed at in my life, Simi. There's this like, fantastically long, dumb list of things I should have been better at. Things I should have taken the time to talk to you about and teach you. Where I grew up—our family— would've taken a long time to go over. And time is just something I've never had much of with you."

Simi threw himself down into a desk chair in front

of a computer monitor. Abe could just barely make out the game he was playing. Some sort of RPG where the participant had to do battle with an army of disgusting alien creatures as they burst through purple orbs that littered the ground. He'd seen Simi playing before but never dared to show interest or even attempt to ask what it was.

From the corner of his eye, without removing his gaze from the screen and the violet glow reflecting in his pupils, Simi could see Abe slowly entering the room. "Yeah, well. All that's your fault. I shouldn't have to suffer because you're deciding now it's time to play catch up. I have a life and was doing just fine until you came back." His fingers flicked, mindlessly, at the buttons on his keyboard. "I'm not going."

I don't want to spend time with you in general, never mind all the way up in New England.

"Simi," Abe started awkwardly, not having much previous experience putting a foot down with his teenager. "I'm sorry but, we have to. She's dying, my Aunt Elma, and there's no one else—"

Simi didn't look up. "I told you, I'm not going. Sorry to hear she's on the way out, but I don't even know her. Besides, she's one hundred and five years old. She's lived a good, *long* life. Sounds like it's her time."

Abe grunted and Simi could tell he was winning. There was no way Abe, himself, would be able to change his mind.

"Call your mother."

Simi hit pause. "Huh? Why? Why would I call her—?"

"Because you're my responsibility and, until she says otherwise, that's all there is to it. Call, if you want."

Abe was playing a card he hadn't yet had to. He knew Simi would do whatever his mother asked of him and the boy's hand hesitated near his cell phone. Before he even dialed, Simi knew he'd lost the argument.

Goddamn you, Abe. And damn you, Mom, for leaving me alone with this asshole.

He lifted the phone and selected "Mom" from his list of contacts. As it rang, he allowed his eyes to settle on his father's. The man stood sheepishly in the doorway, his tatted forearms crossed, waiting to hear the result of the phone call.

Riiiing.

Tammy Ward picked up the line immediately. "Simi, hon, you okay?"

"I — yeah, Mom. I'm okay. Well, er, sort of. Look, I'm sorry to bother you, but—"

Tammy laughed on the other end of the line at something. Simi thought he could hear seagulls and the clinking of glasses.

"Sorry honey, I'm on a boat—a really big boat. Technically a yacht, I guess. Can you believe that? Me? Anywho, we're close to shore, but the signal is fading in and out. What do you need?"

Simi looked up at Abe, who was still leaning with his arms folded in the door frame. He refused to remove his eyes from his shoes, but Simi could tell, by the grin his dad was trying to conceal, he'd known exactly how this conversation would play out.

"Mom, Abe wants me to go up to Massachusetts with him. Some family thing and—"

Again, there was laughter on the other end of the call. After a few pauses, the voice returned, distracted. "Hey, yeah, that sounds like a *wonderful* idea. You've never seen where your father grew up. Hell, neither have I, now that I mention it. This sounds like a sweet bonding experience—"

"Mom, you're not listening—"

"— and quite frankly, I'm shocked he even came up with this idea. Maybe Abel is finally turning that corner."

"Mom, please. I want to stay *here*, I just need you to tell him that I'm okay to be on my own for a while."

She cackled again; the sound of surf followed her shrieks. "Oh, no, no, no. Absolutely, not, Simi. I don't want you alone. Stay with your father. This will be good for you both—"

Shit, she's gonna hang up.

"Mom, don't hang up. Please, I can't leave—"

"Honey, I love you so much, but I can barely hear you. Let's talk again in a few weeks. 'Kay?"

"Mom—"

"Honey, I loooove you! Kisses!"

"Mom!" Simi yelled into the phone as the call ended. He flipped the glossy, rectangular device onto his bed and swiveled aggressively toward the door. "Happy now?"

Abe entered and attempted to put his hand on Simi's shoulder, but it was immediately swatted away. "Sim, look, I'm sorry. I can give you until tomorrow, but we're gonna need to leave super early. Before the sun's up. I wanna be outta here by 3:00—"

"3:00? AM? Are you high?"

"—Pack a bag, call Mags, do whatever you need to. I'll call your school and tell them… I dunno, I'll tell them you're going on a family vacation or something." When he didn't get a response, he added, "Simi, I'm really, really sorry."

Simi ignored him and after a few awkward beats, Abe sighed and made his way back toward the other end of the house. Simi listened for the call to the school and heard the promised "vacation" mentioned to the office secretary.

Simi stood up and rummaged through his closet for

an empty duffel bag. They weren't leaving until the following day, but he was too angry to focus on anything else.

Fun family vacation, huh? What family?

Simi chucked a few articles of clothing, haphazardly, into the bag. He looked out his door and could just barely make out Abe struggling to hang up his phone after ending the conversation.

This is going to be a goddamn family vacation from hell.

Four

They were nearly an hour into their drive and Abe still hadn't attempted to speak again to Simi. Abe spent only the briefest amount of time packing his small bag, before tossing it into the bed of his pickup and then sitting, with the engine idling, as he waited for his son to emerge. To his credit, Simi appeared from the house right at 3:00 am with his own duffel. He'd settled into his seat without a word, but did manage to slam the passenger side door in the most violently passive-aggressive way possible.

As the green highway signs danced past— in the blurry, hypnotizing, way that highway signs tend to—Abe looked to his left at Simi, whose head rested on a just barely-cracked window, his black hair flittering with a breeze that'd managed to breech the confines of their awkward, rattling, prison. His eyes were closed, but Abe was pretty sure Simi wasn't sleeping.

Gonna have to talk at some point, kid. Can't ignore me this entire trip.

He laughed momentarily to himself and then his face thought otherwise, tensing back up.

Can you?

He looked again over at Simi, his son—a walking, frustrating, mystery of his father's own making. Abe hesitated before, inexplicably, deciding to tap at the teen's temple with his knuckles. Simi immediately grabbed his father's weathered, calloused hand, his eyes springing open.

"What the hell, Abe?"

He pulled his arm back, chuckling. "Sorry, wasn't sure if you were awake."

Simi pulled one of his earbuds out. "You could've just asked."

Abe nodded. "Gotcha," he hesitated. "You awake now, then?"

Simi turned and looked out his own window, sighing. "How long is this gonna take again? Are you certain this piece of junk is even going to make it?"

Abe glanced at his watch, barely removing his eyes from the painted lines and the blacktop in front of the truck's hood. "Hopin' to roll in before dark. All depends on the traffic, though." He smiled widely. "You're gonna love Massachusetts, man."

Simi, seemingly giving up on his attempt at listening to music, removed his second earbud. "And why is that again? They've got great leaves and shit, right? That football team everyone hates?" he rolled his eyes. "Sounds like a goddamn paradise."

Abe's grip on the steering wheel tightened, his fingers whitening as the blood under his skin was displaced.

This isn't gonna be easy.

"Look, Simi, I know this is all infuriating and tough

for you to understand—"

Simi turned and glared at him. "Oh do you, Abe? You think you *know* what I'm feeling right now?" He yanked open the tiny cab window, behind their heads. For effect, he pointed his hand out the back and toward where they'd come from. "You know what I left behind there, right? How effed up that was that I had to call Mags, *without any warning*, and be all like, 'oh, hey, sorry to drop this on you, but I'm gonna be gone for… who knows how long, on a vacation, a thousand miles away with my dad.' You're telling me you *know* and you *understand* what's going through my brain right now?" He laughed, unsettlingly. "No, you definitely don't, *Abe*. And, you wanna know how I know? Because if you did and you *actually* loved me as much as you claim to, you never would have forced this."

An obnoxiously loud horn bleated from the left as a tractor-trailer blew past. It caught the both of them off-guard and Abe instinctively threw an arm across Simi's chest. In the seconds following, he sheepishly removed his hand, before attempting an explanation.

"Sorry, I… guess it caught me by surprise."

Simi, who'd been jarred fully upright, leaned forward to get a better look at the mack truck as it sped away. "Bastard. He almost clipped you right then." He turned to Abe who was still visibly shaken. "I am wearing a seat belt, you know."

Abe tilted his head and grimaced. "I know."

In a moment of uncomfortable silence, Simi fumbled with his phone and began to tap out a text. Abe could just make out who he was communicating with, which should not have come as a surprise.

"She mad at me?" he asked, casually.

Simi nodded and kept his eyes glued to the phone.

"Yep."

Abe shrugged. "Yeah, well. I'm okay with that. You know, sometimes you have to make difficult choices in life. It's part of the deal, is what I mean. And this one… my hope is it'll be a super temporary inconvenience. You guys should be back together in no time."

Simi ignored him and continued his tap-tap-tapping.

Without a response, Abe pressed on. "That said, even though this is a short-term kinda thing, I still want you to know how much I appreciate this sacrifice you're making. Hell, I hate to even call it that, but, well, you know what I mean. You're a kid. You just wanna be with your friends—"

"Not my friends. *Mags*," he looked up for an instant, before returning his eyes to their previous distraction. "Just Mags."

Abe threw one hand up in mock-apology. "Right. Of course. My bad." He took a deep breath, before continuing, ever worried about further widening the chasm between himself and his boy. "You just wanna be with *Mags*, and that's completely understandable. But, as painful as this feels, I want you to know that returning to this place, well, let's just say that it's the last thing I want to be doing too."

Simi stopped texting. "Then why are we?"

Abe squeezed the red leather covering on the steering wheel again, no doubt leaving a temporary indentation underneath his fingers. He opened his mouth to respond but struggled for the right words.

He needs some sort of an explanation, Abe. Something. Anything.

When he didn't, *couldn't*, immediately respond, Simi asked again. "No, seriously. Why? If you don't wanna do this, why not just turn the damn truck around now. Come on, just do it. You know I won't ask any questions." Simi was on the verge of smiling for some reason and Abe looked at him, unsure if his son's sudden playfulness was a turning point or a trap.

"Family."

Simi let his head drop and his shoulders sag. "Family?"

Abe sniffed. "Yeah. It's all about blood and, in Elma's case, I'm the only she's got left. Hence, there's no real alternative on my part."

Simi blew out some air from his lips and shook his head. "Gotta be honest, I still don't get it. You don't even really know her, right? I mean… what am I missing here?"

Abe reached out and turned the volume of the radio down a few notches. "You're right, I guess. I *don't* know her very well. Not now, at least. But, I did. A long time ago, in another lifetime, I did."

Simi picked at a bit of black nail polish. He appeared to be disinterested, but Abe could tell that the opposite was true. For the first time in a while, Simi was *listening*. Abe could see the gears working on his son's face, in his brain. He waited for him to ask the question; the question that Abe had never quite gotten around to answering before.

"Why'd you leave?"

Abe blinked and then, for good measure, blinked again. The road was still in front of him. He was heading north on I-95 and his son, Simeon Ward was beside him. Together they were barreling toward something the elder had been running from for most of his life.

"My family," he muttered, "is kind of… *complicated*."

"You're kidding," Simi deadpanned.

Abe guffawed. "I shit you not, you don't know the half of it. Let's just say, for now, that the Ward's never made things easy for me. It's why I left. The first chance I was able and had enough coin in my pocket, *bam*, I was off like a damn rocket. Never looked back. Never looked over my shoulder." His voice lowered and he seemed to lose track of himself and forget he was still speaking out loud. "Guess you could say I didn't want to know if anything was looking back at me."

"Huh?"

Abe snapped out of it. He shook the cobwebs off and smiled to soften the strange moment. "Ah, nothing. Nevermind. Look. What's important to know is that Elma Ward is the last of... *that* part of my life. The last of *those* Wards. It's up to me to come home and bury the past."

Simi squinted at him but seemed to be sitting up straighter. "Kind of a grotesque word choice, huh Abe? She's not even gone yet."

Abe gulped, only half-hearing what Simi was saying. He nodded but didn't offer a retraction. Elma had called on him to return so that they could discuss her final wishes. That much was certain. But he wasn't going to be playing any of her games. He'd left all of that behind him some thirty years ago and he sure as hell wasn't coming home to do her bidding.

I meant what I said. It's time to bury the past. No more fairy tales, Elma.

Five

Simi pretended to be fidgeting with something in the cab as Abe stood outside, filling up their truck. A few minutes earlier, they'd pulled into the Joe Biden Welcome Center reststop in Delaware. Simi'd been given a few minutes to use the facilities and, after poking around at some "I Heart The First State" magnets and the like, was already back in his seat. As his father stood with his eyes closed, whistling a tune inaudible to Simi with the windows all rolled up, he considered the red-flanneled, slightly gaunt figure, and wondered to himself how long ago it'd become an old man. As a kid, Simi thought his dad seemed so much younger than the parents of his friends—though, admittedly, that was likely due to Abe's extracurricular exploits and party-hardy exterior. The man was so often out of work—reveling with crowds and in scenes that his mother hadn't approved of—completely unaware of how to engage his own son as an adult, instead of the cool, older-brother persona that he'd seemed best able to convey.

But right then, as the tattooed scarecrow slouched against the gas terminal and the numbers on the display click-clicked up with the truck's intake of fuel, Abe looked—

Old.

Simi exhaled and let his head fall back against the headrest. His dad finished up outside and hopped in beside him. He started the engine and, as he slowly returned his car to the highway, Abe half-heartedly asked, "You ready?"

Simi sniffed. "For what, exactly?"

"To get back on the road. Just wanted to make sure you didn't need—"

"Naw, I'm ready. What other choice do I have? Let's just get this over with."

As their transport shuddered back onto I-95, Simi's cell phone lit up. He sat up straight and felt himself immediately brighten as he read the words on his screen. So simple and certainly not anything earth-shattering, but even the most inconsequential messages from her were comforting to him.

Especially as I'm moving further from you by the second.
Mags Downing: Hey

He considered his response with a surgeon's precision, as he always did.
Simi Ward: Hey
Mags Downing: How's the drive going?
Simi Ward: Sucks.
Mags Downing: ???
Simi Ward: ??? urself
Mags Downing: Wat sucks, Sim? Traffic?
Simi Ward: No, u kno
Mags Downing: …
Simi Ward: I just hate this. : (
Mags Downing: I told u this cud be a good thing. Did

u forget that already?
Simi Ward: Being away from u is never a good thing.
Mags Downing: Siiiiiim
Simi Ward: I kno.
Mags Downing: U will be fiiiine. I bet u aren't even gone very long.
Simi Ward: I guess
Mags Downing: I'm not going anywhere u kno.
Simi Ward: I kno : (
Mags Downing: ??? why sad?
Simi Ward: Just miss u.
Mags Downing: I miss u too. Now stop being a baby.
Simi Ward: k
Mags Downing: lemme know when u get there?
Simi Ward: k.
Mags Downing: k <3
Simi Ward: <3

As the phone dimmed, Simi placed it into the front pouch of his hoodie and started to crack a smile, but stopped when he noticed Abe smirking at him.

"I'm sorry, do you have a problem?"

Abe covered his grin, not wanting to upset Simi further. "Nope, no problem. It's just…"

"What? It's just, what?"

Abe chuckled. "It's just… kinda sweet." He saw Simi's nostrils flaring, his eyes widening, and quickly tried to cover. "You two, I mean. Such a cute couple—"

"Okay, well you can just go ahead and stop now."

Abe laughed again. "Alright, alright. I'm sorry. Guess I should just try and m—"

"Mind your own business."

Abe grimaced. "Took the words right outta my mouth. Roger that." He mocked saluted and, when Simi turned away from him, remained silent.

Simi kept his eyes focused on the tree-line flying past. He was starting to notice how, as they gradually moved further north, the foliage—

Is that what they call it?

—was starting change. Reds, oranges, yellows. The colors swarmed the tops of the canopy and welcomed him to the cooler temperatures as they galloped full steam ahead toward New England. For an instant, Simi wanted to savor it, to marvel at the natural beauty he'd never before witnessed, but he stopped himself. It was much easier for him to mope and to pine for Mags, and he didn't want to slip or appear, even for an instant, like he might be enjoying himself.

I don't want to be here. This isn't a vacation.

He closed his eyes and let himself slink further below the window, out of sight, hidden from the unfamiliar wonders reaching their gnarled limbs to greet him.

Six

The red-yellow sky was nearly finished burning away the straggling hours of the crisp fall afternoon, the sun nearing its final descent below the horizon, when the Ford crossed from Rhode Island into Massachusetts. Minutes later, they were sitting at a stoplight, and Abe caught himself white-knuckling the steering wheel as he waited for a green signal.

"Almost there."

Simi was only half-awake and mumbled a response, exerting enough effort to lift a single eyelid. "How close?"

Abe stared straight ahead, looking past the traffic lights. Not far up that span of road was their destination. No more turns. No more exits ramps or rest areas. No more refueling stops or pee breaks. Just one final stretch and—

"Abe?" Both of Simi's eyes were open and he was sitting up. "Yo, it's green. Are you gonna drive or—?"

"Yeah," Abe hit the gas and they lurched forward.

"Yeah, sorry. It's, ah, not far now. This road turns into Brown St. We'll cross the Foxborough line in a couple of minutes and then…" he trailed off. His eyes glazed over for a moment until some part of him forced a blink.

Simi was staring, annoyed, at the side of his father's head. "And then, *what?* Shit, Abe, can't you just finish your thought?"

Abe nodded, willing himself to continue speaking, to continue driving ahead and not stomp on the brakes right then and there.

There's still time. Not too late to turn this truck around and get your son out of here.

He looked, wide-eyed into the rearview mirror, as if to ensure no one was following him. Simi noticed and swiveled to look in the direction they'd come, out and over the vehicle's bed.

"Is someone—?"

"No," Abe stopped him. "No, I—I'm sorry. Just a little distracted. Being back here… it's so strange. Never thought I'd see this place again." He could sense Simi's gaze boring into the side of his face, though couldn't force himself to take his eyes off of the pavement ahead. "Her house is on this straightaway. I was just saying we'll be pulling up to it soon."

Soon after, they passed the "Entering Foxborough" sign. The sun was continuing its precipitous fall behind the treetops and, with the dips of the road, at times was already obscured entirely. Dusk was upon them, its arrival almost perfectly timed to Abe's homecoming. A sigh crawled from his trembling lips and in that same instant a black, winged shape darted across his windshield. He hit the brakes and, after a brief squeal of balding tires, they came to a stop just in front of a small embankment off to the side of the road.

"What the hell was that?" Simi rasped, leaning forward for a better look.

Abe hadn't released his death-grip on the helm. If he'd been any stronger, or if the steering wheel had been made of a weaker material, he wondered if he'd have crushed it under his grasp.

Still not too late, Abe.

"Bat," he said, shaking his head and himself awake. "I think that's what it was, at least." He let his foot off the brake and allowed the vehicle to move again. "You okay?"

Simi nodded. "Yeah. Helluva way to roll into town though, huh? What a welcome."

Abe faked a laugh. They crested a short rise in the road and, as they came down on the other side, he saw the spire and the familiar weathervane leering down from its precipice.

Waiting.

A single, unblinking, eye, its rusted lashes, and pupil mocked his expected return. The oculus swung lazily from the top of the blood-red steeple, its rouge matching the trim of the otherwise soulless black that swallowed the rest of the Victorian-Era homestead. As they descended the short hill, the rest of the property came into view.

Abe turned the truck into the driveway but stopped himself from pulling all the way around to the back. He parked just in front of a drunkenly-waving wrought iron gate, one side completely open and greeting their advent. Abe killed the engine and braced himself.

There's still time to—

"Wait here," he said and, before Simi could protest, threw open his creaking door and began his long-anticipated ascent back up the twisted, cobblestone walkway.

Seven

Simi did not wait.

Eff that.

He watched as his father paused before lifting the knocker and bringing it clanging down on the weathered mouth of the residence. Simi couldn't be sure from that distance, but he thought—at first glance—that the ornamental piece was shaped in the form of a screaming gargoyle or demon of some sort, its face twisted in visible agony. Abe had only just finished his second knock when the door swung open. Simi was unable to make out the figure standing in the unlit passage beyond the entryway, but his father stepped toward it and the door swung closed behind him before the spectacle could be scrutinized any further. The gargoyle—or whatever ghastly creature it was—stared down the walkway at him, its silently screaming jaws cautioning him of the hazards and horrors that surely awaited within the bowels of the old haunt.

Simi kicked open the passenger side door and stood up. He stretched his arms high over his head and allowed himself an audible yawn. Leaning against the pickup, he took in the sight before him. The architecture of the building was gorgeous—unlike anything Simi had ever seen down in Georgia— but he held his breath as it loomed, maliciously, over him. Carved into the ornamental trim, which seemed to border most of the structure's exposed edges (from the sharp fringe of the roof and spires to the decorative outline of the windows and stained glass above the main door) were hundreds—perhaps thousands— more of those screaming, infernal visages. Each was unique: some appeared to be faces of children, others elderly, withered, countenances. And yet, a good number of the immortalized masks could not have been described as human in *any* certain terms. Those petrified snarls were the most mesmerizing to Simi and, for a moment, he wondered if it were possibly their menace that was being reflected in the terror of the other howling expressions.

What is this place?

He looked at the front door of the house again, but it remained closed. Abe had told him to stay put, but there was still just enough late-day light peeking from behind the ample tree covering that he felt it couldn't hurt to take a quick look around. Besides, he'd been crammed in that un-air-conditioned space all day and needed to breathe.

Let's see what we're working with here.

The driveway angled down toward the backyard and curved around behind the building. Simi started following the pavement and quickly stopped himself. Fall in Massachusetts was nothing like he was used to, so he jogged back to the truck and pulled out his black hoodie. He zippered it all the way up, pulled the hood over his head, and shoved his hands in the front pouch. With the security of his cowl and stereotypical teenage armor, Simi felt emboldened. He bounded down the driveway in a few quick leaps.

At the bottom of the hill, the pavement turned into a small parking area behind the home. There were two cars currently stationed in the cramped space, once of which—an old Chevy Cavalier—looked like it hadn't been driven in many years. The other was a yellow VW Bug. Clearly someone a little closer to hip had also chosen that exact moment to pay Abe's old aunt a visit.

Simi hummed to himself and kicked a loose pebble out into the yard. The grass in the back was weedy and overgrown. A long absence of care had left a forgotten, lifeless, meadow. Without a doubt, it had been some time since any landscaping graced the property with its presence.

Great. I can already predict what he's gonna have me doing tomorrow. Just fan-flippin-tastic.

The overgrowth was high, but not high enough to obscure the multiple outbound buildings and sheds that littered the plot. There were at least three, brown, shed-like structures on the grounds and a fourth high up between two pine trees that could only have been a sort of ancient tree-house.

Behind the buildings, as far back as he could see, was swamp-land. Winding its way down the center of the picturesque landscape was a stream—a river, more accurately—and his eyes followed it all the way out to a large outcropping of white rocks. The river stretched from the back of the three sheds and ended at the base of the largest of the boulders.

Some sort of dam or—?

And then it hit him. As he walked toward the sheds to get a better view of the wetlands, a smell wafted past, filling his nostrils, causing him to gag. He coughed and bent over, placing his hands on his knees as if the air lower to the ground would somehow possibly be fresher. The stench didn't dissipate, but after the initial shock, he was able to breathe. He pulled his hoodie over his mouth and nose and took a few steps closer to the sheds.

Is this what New England smells like? 'Cause... damn.

But, it wasn't New England. And it wasn't the swamp. Simi's eyes searched the yard for the source and it didn't take him long to locate it. The closest shed to him was also the largest. Beside it, there was a shallow burrow, dug on one side. He could tell it'd been put there recently because the dirt and earth sprayed about was still dark. Still damp.

Simi approached the hole.

The smell became overpowering as he hung his face over it. Inside—in a neat, orderly arrangement—was a pile of bones, feathers, fur, and other assorted animal parts. Some of the scraps were still glistening. At first, Simi wondered what sort of animal would have left such a mess, but then he quickly corrected himself.

Not a mess. No, this is too...

He paused, arguing with himself.

Neat. Orderly. Almost as if...

He chuckled out loud.

Almost as if it's all been deliberately arranged this way.

He stared for a few more moments at the hole, before the bouquet became too much. He waved at the air in front of his face and turned his body away, toward the backside of the manor.

And there she was.

Standing at the highest window, on the third floor, was a macabre figure. Her long grey hair hung nearly to her waist and a tattered white gown hid what could only have been an emaciated, skeletal frame. Crooked toes lifted her into an unnatural posture and allowed the form to press itself against the glass, blocking all light from sneaking past her into the darkness behind. The being's mouth drooped wide, mimicking the hideous caterwauling grimace of her door-knocker.

Simi cried out and fell hard to the ground, slamming without an opportunity to brace himself, onto his own ass.

Eight

"D?"

At first, in the shadow of the poorly-lit foyer, Abe couldn't be certain who he was looking at. The woman standing before him was grayer and perhaps even smaller than he'd remembered, but, as his eyes adjusted to the light, he quickly realized she hadn't changed as much as nature would have had him believe. With her arms folded across her chest, leaning against a grandfather clock that likely hadn't chimed in decades, Daisy Peltzer smirked.

"Can't believe you came."

He started to take a step closer to her but stopped himself. "Yeah, well. Me neither."

Daisy was wearing a green flannel shirt, which hung down over a well-worn pair of jeans. Her knees were muddied as if she'd just come in front working in the garden. Immediately, she noticed his gaze.

"Elma has me cleaning out her flower beds. Not one

weed, not one stray leaf. Doesn't matter that nothing grows out there anymore or that the yard is an overgrown mess. So long as her flower beds are neat and tidy."

Abe looked around the main vestibule of the house. A tall spiral staircase loomed in front of the door, beckoning him to climb it once more. The walls surrounding him were the same lime green they'd always been, with the same white floral wallpaper dancing its way around the border of the space. Hanging heavy in the air was the stale odor of cigarettes.

Abe looked up the staircase. "How long have you been helping her? Never would have guessed this would be your thing."

Daisy laughed and stepped closer to him, though her arms remained folded, protectively. She was half a foot shorter than he was and, the closer she got, the more she had to arch her neck to make eye contact with him. "Not long. She started looking for help a few months back. I'd recently lost my job and needed the money. Plus, your aunt is a good woman. Everyone in town knows that. Who wouldn't want to help her, if they could?"

Abe arched an eyebrow in her direction. "Yeah. Who wouldn't?"

Daisy nodded toward the stairs. "And then, about a week ago, she fell. Things have been getting worse, each day since."

"Getting worse? What kind of things?"

Daisy sniffed. "She's deteriorating, Abe. Eating less. Sleeping more. Barely leaves that bed now. And she's been saying things. A lot that doesn't make sense to me. Her doctor says he's seeing signs of dementia."

Abe looked at her but didn't respond. She continued. "You know, forgetfulness, irritability, disorientation…

wandering."

Abe leaned back against the closed door. "Wandering?"

Daisy nodded. "Yeah. But, hey, we'll have plenty of time to discuss all of that. She's been waiting to see you."

He nodded. "Yeah. Yeah, I guess you're right." He took a step toward the staircase, but Daisy stopped him with a gentle touch to his elbow. He looked down at her. "D?"

"I just can't believe you're really here. It's been such a long time." For an instant, it looked as if she might embrace him, but she instead collected herself, took a deep breath, and gestured for Abe to follow her upstairs.

Elma's room was on the third floor and, as they ascended past the second, Abe noticed the state of disrepair her home was in. Deep water stains ran down the walls of the conical silo that encased the corkscrew. The blemishes had long since dried, but the trails and veins of leakage made the wallpaper almost appear to be bleeding around them.

"This place needs a lot of work. Guess I'm going to be pretty busy."

Daisy stopped and turned toward him. Their climb was steep and, though only a few steps ahead, she now towered over Abe. "Hey, I'm not going anywhere. Whatever you need. I'm happy to help."

"Thanks, D," he said. "It's good to see you too, by the way. I hate the way we left it—"

"It's fine," she interrupted, "That's ancient history, man. Come on, let's go."

A few steps later, they landed on the third floor. Abe remembered well that there was only one room on that level. It was Elma's. It'd always been Elma's.

Daisy approached the door and rapped gently. "Elma? You have a visitor."

There was no response from within. Abe looked at Daisy and she shrugged. "She doesn't always answer. Might be asleep."

"Elma? You decent?"

Gently, she turned the knob and peeked around the door.

"Elma?" Daisy started, "What're you—?"

Abe entered the room and gawked at the shriveled creature standing in front of the window overlooking the backyard. Her hands were pressed against the glass, her back to her guests. The first thing that Abe observed was how unrestrained the woman's hair was. He thought it possible it'd always been that long, that wispy, that *greasy*. But all of his memories of her were over thirty years old and back then she'd always had her hair up and out of the way as she toiled in the yard, repaired cars in her driveway, and wielded chainsaws on all those dead, soon-to-fall, trees. The skeleton standing on the other side of the bed from him looked nothing like the gristled Aunt Elma of Abe's childhood.

What Abe noticed next was the sound. Emanating from somewhere within or near his grandfather's sister.

Cooing.

"Is that—?" he began, before Daisy ran to Elma's side.

"Okay, honey, let's get you back into bed." She guided the old woman back down to the light blue comforter and, without a struggle, tucked her in again. "Look who's here to see you."

Abe stood by the bed awkwardly, waiting for Elma to turn and see him. After a moment, she did and squinted, comically, up at him. "Abel? Is that my Abel Ward?" she cackled, quietly to herself, musing on a private joke that no one else was in on. "Have you finally come home?"

Gently, Abe sat on the edge of her bed, afraid to sit too close. Afraid to *be* too close.

"I— yes, it's me, Elma. I heard you wanted to see me?"

Her eyes got wide and a smile etched its way across the petrified skin that stretched far too thin across her face. Abe winced at her grimace, its toothlessness, and the feeling that the edges of her mouth might soon crack open. "See meee."

Abe stammered. "Yes, yes. D—I mean, Daisy told me you wanted to see me."

Elma nodded and brought her hands together. Suddenly she was wildly clapping and bouncing up and down on her bed. Abe and Daisy each grabbed a shoulder in an effort to calm her down, but she would not stop. Something had come over Elma and she wanted nothing more than to share her excitement with the both of them.

"Yes!" she squealed, like a rusted bike chain over an even more-rusted chainring. "Yes! Siiii meeeee. He's here. Simi! And they brought him a gift!" She pointed an arthritic claw at the window she'd just been standing at.

Abe grunted, pulled himself back up, and stepped toward the window. Standing down below, dusting off the seat of his pants, was Simi.

He turned back toward the two women. "I told him to stay in the truck."

NINE

Simi couldn't hear what Abe was saying through the fingerprint-smeared window situated on the backside of the third-floor bedroom. The old lady had been dragged away moments before, and now his father, his bald head reflecting the day's final tease of fall sun, stood with hands spread wide, mouthing an exasperated question at his son. Simi couldn't hear him, but he didn't need to.

"Alright, alright. I'll wait back in the truck." And, when the man continued to stare down at him, his expression smeared with perturbation, Simi waved him off and added. "I'm fiiine. Jesus."

Abe eventually disappeared back into the black cavern behind him and Simi started moving up the driveway.

As if I'm never off on my own. We come to this place and now, all of sudden, he wants to chain me up? Hate to break it to ya' Abey, but I was taking care of myself long before you decided to dad again.

He was almost back up the top of the hill when he

heard the low rumble of hushed squabbling drift from somewhere in the woods on the opposite side of the house. At first, Simi hesitated. There was nothing in him at that moment that desired interaction with the locals. On the drive up, he'd read about the town and had this idea in his head that all they talked about was football and… well, *football*. Yet, something stopped him from reaching for the handle of the passenger door, burrowing himself inside, and waiting until Abe had finished doing *whatever it was* he was doing. Simi sighed, having a good idea of what he was about to encounter, and crossed the front yard to an embankment bordering yet another sprawling vista of woods and purple-sulfur-bacteria-scented swampland. He waited only a few seconds before hearing the voices again, bounding up at him from the bottom of the dimly lit ditch. Simi squinted down in the direction of the vocalizations and his eyes caught the familiar orange of a spark. The flick-flick-flicking was unmistakable to him and he absentmindedly patted the lighter in his own pocket.

"Quit hogging it dipshit," one of the voices hissed.

Even though the breeze was almost nonexistent, it carried the strong scent of weed up into Simi's face very quickly. Not that he needed to smell it to surmise what sort of shenanigans were happening down there in the bottoms of Elma's secluded property.

One of them (Simi still couldn't tell how many) started coughing.

"Quiet," another laughed. "Unless you want them to—"

Simi peered down into the gulley. He could just barely make out three shapes huddled around a makeshift fire pit. There was no fire burning, but the piles of charred logs and glints of crushed, strewn-about beers cans suggested this was not the first time the site had been occupied. The shapes stopped speaking suddenly and, he thought, looked up at him.

Shit.

Awkwardly, he started to turn himself around, but had only taken a couple of steps back toward the front of the house when an overconfident voice called up to him.

"Can we help you?"

Caught off guard, Simi pulled his hoodie closed a bit more and stammered, "I—I—was just—"

The teenager's voice cut him off. "Spying on us?"

Simi shook his head quickly and, as he did so, three figures broke through the underbrush and the overgrowth of the thicket surrounding his great-great-aunt's property.

Simi took a step back. There was nothing particularly alarming about the appearance of the three boys—Simi was easily the tallest of the bunch—but anytime a coterie of complete strangers emerges from the woods unannounced and ready to break into conversation, it is disquieting in its own right.

"Uh, no," Simi stumbled over his words. "Not spying, guys." He pointed back over his shoulder toward the driveway. "Was over there and heard some voices."

The first one up the hill, and closest to Simi, laughed, a joint still pinched and smoking between two of his fingertips. His chin was stubbled, though the rest of his face hadn't decided to play along just yet. He wore a Bruins jersey and a matching Bruins cap.

Okay, thought Simi. *So, maybe not just football.*

"Right," the joint-holder said, turning back to the other two. One was wearing an orange tank-top and cargo shorts (*an odd choice considering the time of year*) and the other was sporting a salmon-colored polo shirt and navy blue pants with lobsters all over them. They all laughed together as if their chortling had been planned in advance. Once the synchronized snickering died down a bit, Bruins Jersey spoke again. "And who are you?"

"Simi Ward," he answered. "I'm, ah, in town with my dad."

Lobster Pants sneered, "Your *dad?* Who's your dad?"

Simi pointed vaguely behind himself as if that'd be helpful in his explanation. "He grew up here."

"In Foxborough?" Tank Top drooled.

Simi shoved his hands back in his hoodie-pouch. The interrogation made him want to retreat. "No— I mean, *yes,* in Foxborough. But also, like, right *here.*" He nodded toward the house.

Bruins Jersey took a long toke, holding eye contact with Simi the entire time. After a few painfully long beats, he blew out the smoke, coughing slightly. "He grew up here? Wait… you said you're a *Ward?*"

Simi looked to one side, unsure if he should answer. "Um… yeah?"

There was a long, drawn-out pause as the three wordlessly communicated something to one another in a moment of apprehensive, oddly sophisticated, eye-contact. Eventually, the leader became cognizant of the silence and attempted an overconfident salvage of the conversation. "Ohhh, woah. Shit, man. Sorry. I guess we're smoking up on your gramma's property. Damn, this is super awkward now, isn't it?" Remorse of any kind was not evident in his smile.

Simi waved at him but also waved at the cloud hovering in front of his face. "She's not my grandma. She's my, um, great-great-aunt, or, something. Haven't actually met her yet."

The Jersey took another toke before carefully putting

out the burning end and placing the stub in his pocket for later. Simi noted that he didn't offer to share any with the new kid.

Nice guy.

"Cool story," Jersey said, indifferently. "I'm Jack Wils. This moron in the tank is my dumb little brother Harry and the loser who looks like he just got off his dad's yacht is Marv Barney."

Simi attempted to mute a laugh. "Your name is *Marv?*"

The kid scowled at him, his cheeks suddenly becoming the same shade as his awful shirt. "It's short for Marvin. Got a problem with that?" He took a step forward, but Simi didn't flinch because, well, *lobster-pants*.

"No, no problem at all man. Just curious. Hey, well, it's been nice, I guess, meeting you guys. But, I bet my dad's looking for me. Better go."

"Aw, why so soon?" mocked Harry. "Thought we made a new friend."

"Shut up, Harry," Jack glared. "He's gotta go. We don't wanna keep him."

Simi began to moonwalk away from the treeline. "Really, it was cool meeting you guys." He lifted a hand, insincerely, and turned around. Hoping that would be the end of his encounter, he tried to take a few quick steps, but almost immediately heard Jack speak again.

"Simi."

He stopped and forced himself to swivel on one foot. "What's up?"

Jack smiled. "Do us a solid and… don't mention we hang here. We, uh, like this spot. Most of the town is scared shitless of Ward House, which means they leave us be. Let us do our thing. You get me?"

Simi shrugged into his hoodie a bit more, as if it

might make him warmer. The air was getting chilly, but it wasn't just a result of the sun setting. He wanted to ask why the locals would be afraid of the place, but decided it was more important to end the visit.

"Okay, I guess. But, I mean, isn't this Elma's property?"

The smiles dropped from the faces of three boys. Jack pushed the brim of his cap up with one finger, showing his eyes more clearly. Simi immediately noticed that both were different colors. One brown, one grey. Harry adjusted one of his tank straps. Marv swiped some dirt off of his beloved crustacean slacks.

"Who gives a shit?"

Simi faltered. He looked back up at the monstrosity standing behind him and realized they were probably right.

Simi shook his head.

"Does that mean you won't say anything?"

Simi nodded. "Yeah, guys, it's cool. Don't worry."

He turned and heard the three cackling as they walked down the road. As they sauntered away, Lobster Pants muttered something that sounded an awful lot like "Gonna need to tell my dad," but, fairly quickly, they were out of earshot. Though Simi could still see them down the road when he looked over his shoulder, he decided it was finally safe to take a breath.

He approached his father's truck and leaned back against it, taking in the tiny, peculiar, suburban castle once more. It looked, to him, like something out of an Edgar Allan Poe story. A place that, without a doubt, had to have a pit, a pendulum, and an attic chock full of bats. Normally, that wouldn't have been such a bad thing, but, as the earth put itself to bed around him, he wanted nothing more than to hop back into the Ford and start driving far away. Back home. Down South. Away from Aunt Elma, her creepy window, the strange hole filled with bones, and those airheaded guys smoking in the swamp.

They're totally right, he thought, staring up at the creepy door-knocker. *Who gives a shit?*

Ten

"So, why I am here?" Abe asked, pulling up an old-fashioned red leather armchair with nailhead trim. He hesitated before fully planting his rear-end in the seat due to the person-shaped impression worn into the cushion. For some reason, it immediately made Abe wonder if someone had died in it. "And who are... *they*?"

Daisy had given them the room. She'd left after putting Elma back into bed, using the excuse to go get Abe a cup of coffee, though he was fairly certain she just wanted him to have a moment alone. There *was* a certain conversation he'd driven a thousand miles to have, after all.

Elma's eyes were already mostly closed (he was shocked how quickly that'd happened) but he could tell she'd still heard his question. Her head tilted to one side as if she were drowsily listening to him sing one of her favorite tunes. Her chapped-lip grin was also a clue.

"Elma?" he asked again.

She opened one eye a bit wider than the other, as if to remind herself who was speaking, and then closed it again. She started to laugh, but the moment of merriment quickly turned into a coughing fit. Abe reached for a glass of water beside the bedside and tried to hand it to her. Elma pushed his offer away. Her eyes still nearly shut, she cleared her throat.

"They smell the death on me."

Abe gripped both arms of the chair and bits of leather under his grasp flaked away as he did so. He brushed his hands together in annoyance and then folded them in his lap. "Elma, who's *they*?"

She clucked her tongue at him, chidingly. "Oh, Abe. Have you forgotten? Have you been gone so long that you can't remember this place? They're still here you know. They've been waiting for you. For this. For *now* and what is soon to become of me." Her smirk widened. "You know the rules."

Abe turned around to see if Daisy had returned, but the doorway remained empty. He listened, but couldn't hear her climbing the stairs. Presumably, she was still fixing his cup of coffee. Swinging back around, ready to deny any understanding of what she was referring to, he gasped.

Holy—

Elma was sitting straight up, alert, eyes wide, leaning toward him. Her breath or some other stench of the bedridden, leaked from her. Reactively, he leaned away and put an arm in front of his face. Elma didn't seem to notice—she appeared to become stronger, more energized, more alive—and pitched her aged frame over the edge of the bed. Abe marveled at how little of her body maintained contact with the mattress as she managed to balance with such ease on the edge of what should have been a terrifying precipice for someone in her condition.

"Elma, are you okay? Why don't you—"

"We used to sing it to you when you were a boy," she beamed. "You were such a cute little thing. Your parents and your grandparents loved you so, so much." She began to rock an invisible baby in her arms. "I always wondered if I did enough after they—"

"You did *plenty*." It was his turn to interject. "Best you could, considering what you had to work with. And, well, I'm grateful. You know that. At least, I think you do. But—" He stopped himself, unsure if she was paying attention. "We can talk about that some other time."

Elma shook her head. She *was* listening, still perched like a malnourished rooster on a fence. "There aren't many other times left, Abel."

He sighed, still confused by everything she was saying.

It's amazing she's gone this long without professional help.

"Elma, I—" he looked at her, waiting expectantly for what he was going to say next, a spot of drool pooling in one corner of her mouth. "—I'm sorry. I just don't know what you're talking about. I don't know who *they* are. I don't know what song—"

Elma flopped down, exasperatedly on the bed, like a kid just reminded by her parents that it was lights out. "*The* song! You know," she started to hum to herself, or at least that's what Abe thought she was doing. And then, she sang.

"From the depths of me 'art, to the pit of me soul, with ne'er a breath nor need for a hole,
O' Malevolent, Malevolent Nevers.
Here they wait for all our evers,
O' Malevolent, Malevolent Nevers.
Our demons to bear.
Our demons to share.

O' Malevolent, Malevolent Nevers.

Sometimes they be locked away, where no one can see 'em, outter sight.

Sometimes they be a droolin' face, starin' in through 'yer winder, in the dead of the night!

O' Malevolent, Malevolent, Malevolent, Malevolent, Malevolent, Malevolent NEVERS!"

And then, she turned to Abe, her great-nephew, and waited. Her hands were clasped and her eyes were closed. If she hadn't just been singing at the top of her lungs, Abe might have even thought her dead.

What is going on?

"Elma—" he started again and then recalibrated his approach. "That was—wow— that was some song alright." He swiped a hand over his head and then brought it back down to its partner. "Look, I get this means something to you, or at least you think it does…" He waited, but she remained silent, her head still facing him. "Have you seen anyone about this? I mean, like, a *doctor*?"

Elma slapped a hand to her head cartoonishly and Abe jumped. He leaned forward and put a palm on hers. "Don't do that, Elma. You'll just hurt yourself. I'm sorry, I didn't mean to upset you. It's just—"

"They want me, Abel," she whispered, pleading to him. "They have been waiting a long time. So, so long."

Abe stood up and paced over to the window. At first glance, it didn't appear Simi was out back any longer.

Kid finally listens to me.

On the opposite side of the bed, he turned around. Elma continued to face the chair as if he were still sitting there.

"Elma, I just don't understand. Can you help me to understand, please? Does this have something to do with me leaving? I know I should have come back much sooner. Life was, well, let's just say it was rough for me for a while." He moved back to the dead-man chair and begrudgingly sank back into it. "But, I'm doing a lot better. A *lot* better. A couple of years ago, I might not have even been able to make this trip. Things are changing though. I'm trying to be a father for really the first time ever... failing spectacularly, of course... but, at least I'm trying. It's not easy. It's never really been easy. But, I guess what I'm trying to say is... well, dammit, Elma. I'm sorry about all of that. I should have been here for you sooner, but I can't do anything about that. It's in the past. I'm here now and I just want to help you move beyond—whatever this is you're stuck on."

And then Elma cooed again. It was the same sound she'd made staring out the window at Simi. "Oh, Abel. I'm not mad at you. This has nothing to do with all of that. You're a good boy. You've always been my good boy."

He sighed. "Yeah, well, not *that* good."

Elma reached up and seemed to adjust an imaginary bonnet on her head. She tied an invisible ribbon around her chin and exhaled deeply. With nothing amiss, as far she was concerned, the old lady jumped right into her next point. "You must listen to me. All of this will happen whether you are willing to believe it or not."

Abe held his breath, unsure of what she'd say next.

"The ritual will happen. It *must*. For generations and generations, this is how it has been. When the time comes, you will do what needs to be done. There is no substitute for reality."

She was still lying down, with her eyes shut again, but the certainty and clarity with which she spoke was almost alarming. "Elma, I'm not—"

"Abel, you must! You are a Ward! If you do nothing,

if you prevent them from taking me—"

"Elma, what are you talking about?"

"—it would be disastrous for everyone. For the lovely people of this town, for you, for… *Simi*."

Again, Abel stood, but this time with more aggression. He crossed the room to her closet and stared into a small, circular, mirror hanging precariously on a rusted hook. "What do you want me to do? And… what's going to happen to Simi? What does he have to do with this?"

For a moment, all was silent. Elma did not flinch, nor was she even visibly breathing. Abe, having seen something similar a few minutes earlier, gave her a chance to collect herself and speak. Eventually, she did, but barely at a whisper. Abe had to bring himself closer to hear her. Elma's lips were moving, but the words were faint, due either to a lack of energy or because the message was too terrifying for her to speak aloud.

He leaned his ear toward her parchment-paper lips.

"—outside." He heard her say, mid-sentence. "Once I am gone. Leave my body on the edge of the marsh. They will find me there. But, please, Abel, you must *not* bury me."

Alrighty, time to find D.

Abel kept his face close to hers. "Elma, I'm sorry but, I'm not doing any of that."

Elma shot up, smashing her forehead into his. Abe stumbled backward grabbing at a spot just above his nose. He caught himself on the chair, and after regaining his balance, pulled his hand away. It was already damp with his blood.

"God, Elma, what the—"

She was sitting up straight in bed, wild-eyed, with red streaming down over her sunken orbital sockets and into her open and writhing mouth. "You must! Please, don't be such a fool. Listen to—"

Footsteps were pounding from somewhere behind. Daisy was on her way.

"Elma, I know these things are hard to hear. But, when the time comes, as you say, you'll be with all the other Wards. In our family burial ground down the road. You know as well as I do that for the past couple hundred years every goddamn-last one of us assholes has been stashed there in the end. And, as much as I love you, you're no different, Elma Ward."

Elma threw herself down on the bed and began to thrash about. If Abe had been around when Simi was a kid, maybe he would have had some experience dealing with an all-out tantrum. But, as he stood there, staring down at his post-centennial great-aunt, he just put his hands up. He didn't know what to do, or what to say next.

Daisy burst into the room. "What the hell is going on in here? Is she okay?"

Abe stammered and back away. "I—I'm not sure. Please, help her."

Daisy ran to Elma's bedside and immediately began combing a hand through her long grey locks and wiping at her face with a corner of a sheet. She sh-sh-shushed her until the woman began to calm. After a while, Daisy looked up at him. "Maybe you should go take a walk?"

"Huh? Oh, yeah. I'll do that."

"Welcome back," she teased. "Already up to your old tricks, I see."

Abe didn't have a response to her provocation. He shuffled toward the door in a daze, holding his head, and was halfway out into the hallway when Elma spoke again.

"No."

Abe paused to listen and could hear Daisy trying to

soothe her again. "There, there. No, what, honey?

She laughed weakly and then coughed again. "No, they're not." She looked up at Abe and held his petrified, bloodshot, stare. "They're not there, Abel. None of them. It's completely…" And then she seemed to begin drifting off to sleep. As her body sagged and dreamland embraced her, she muttered, with conviction. "Empty."

Eleven

There was a wrap-around porch with a swinging bench bedecking the front of the Ward House. Simi considered making his way up there, weighed making himself comfortable on the cushioned adornment, but instead stopped himself halfway up the front steps. Something prevented him from getting any closer. A whisper of a tingle, starting at the nape of Simi's neck, cascaded down his spine. He shuddered.

Creepy ass house.

Instead, he sat down on the second to last stair from the walkway and pulled out his phone. The stars were starting to appear on the night sky and Simi marveled at how much crisper the rapidly darkening display appeared in Foxborough than it ever had back home. Something flitted across the moon and, instinctively, he flinched. Tightening his hoodie further, his face illuminated by tinted-blue light, he began to type.

Simi Ward: U there?

There was no immediate response. Considering the time of day, Mags probably was eating dinner or doing homework. Or both. Usually, she was pretty quick to respond, but right then must not have had her phone nearby. After a few minutes of waiting, he lifted his device, flipped the camera setting to selfie-mode, and snapped a picture of himself in front of the gothic building looming behind. In the photo, he raised his eyebrows and opened his mouth wide as if he was being surprised by something sneaking up on him. He hit send.

A few cars drove by. Surprisingly, given how much wooded space fenced in the Ward property, the street got a decent amount of traffic. Even still, Simi easily pictured the home a hundred or so years earlier, before much else was built around it. Abe had told him on the drive down that Elma's place was one of the oldest in town and one of its few remaining relics. Venerable enough that—when it was first constructed—all else that existed in the vicinity was farmland, wetlands, and trees.

And whatever else lived on the farm, in the wetlands, and in the trees.

Simi wasn't sure where the thought came from and shrugged it off. He looked down at his phone again.

Still nothing. Where you at, Mags?

A commotion behind him, inside, caused Simi to turn around. A minute later, Abe slowly opened the door, shut it behind himself, and trudged down the stairs. He was holding a dishtowel up to his forehead and Simi immediately noticed the wine-colored stain leaking through.

"Um… are you okay?"

Abe jerked a shoulder in a half-shrug and plopped down next to his son. "I'm fine."

Simi turned to face him. Abe was a step or so higher

up than he was. "For some reason, I don't believe you. Like, at all. Maybe it's the bloody towel you're tough-guying, but who am I to say?"

Abe sighed. "Elma's not well. Not at all. And she—well, she accidentally did this. At least, I'm pretty sure it was an accident." He chuckled. "But see, this is why we're here, right? She's in a tough spot right now and she needs our help."

Simi reached for the rag, but Abe recoiled. "Maybe it's you who needs some help."

Abe pulled the ruined linen down and examined it. The wound seemed to be done with its bleeding. "Funny, Sim. You are a funny, funny guy." Abe furrowed his brows, remembering something he'd been meaning to say. "Hey, you know, I thought I told you to stay in the car."

Simi leaned back on his elbows, against the stairs. "I'm not a child, Abe. I'm seventeen years old. Pretty sure it's safe for me to walk around a quiet backyard in this Boresville."

Abe crumpled the rag in his hand. "I didn't say it wasn't safe. *Of course*, it's safe. I just—ah, never mind. You're right." He awkwardly tried to reach down and put an arm around Simi but was rebuffed. "Hey, anyway, you find anything interesting? This place is full of old treasures—"

Simi shook his head. "Not really. Though I think something is living out back by those sheds. Some kind of animal or... *something*. Left us a bunch of scraps."

Abe lifted an eyebrow. "Bones?"

Simi leaned forward and stuck his hand out in front of his face. It was dark out and he could barely make out the fresh coat of black he'd painted on before they'd left Georgia. "Yep. In a tiny pit by the shed. Pretty gnarly. Something ate something else."

Abe nodded. "Yeah, well, we are abutting an old conservation land here. All sorts of wildlife stick close to the river. I remember once we had a bobcat holed up somewhere back there. My parents wanted to hire a trapper to come and take it away, but Elma would have none of that. As I recall, she coaxed it out herself, somehow. 'Just a big kitty,' she said." Simi was looking at him sideways. "Hey, she's a character. You'll meet her tomorrow, probably."

"Tomorrow?"

Abe nodded. "Yeah, she's... sleeping now. I think."

Simi closed his eyes. "Whatever. That's fine. Think I'll be ready for an early night too. Today was balls."

Abe laughed. "Yeah, I guess it was. Long, long day."

Simi opened his eyes and sat up. "Hey, uh, probably something else you want to know about. Or, someone should know about, I guess."

Abe sat up straighter too. "Uh, okay. What?"

"They didn't want me to say anything, but I met some kids—my age, probably— out in the woods on the side of the house. Looks like they hang here, often by the sound of it."

Abe arched his other eyebrow. "Hang?"

"Jesus Abe, do I have to spell it out? Smoking. Drinking. The sorts of clowning around teenage delinquent-types do," he paused before adding, "You know all about that."

Abe cracked his neck. "Alright, alright. I get it."

They both sat in awkward silence for a few minutes. Again, something shot across the moon.

"That's like the second time I've seen that. Weird isn't it?"

Abe hadn't been looking up. His eyes were heavy, exhaustion pulling sleep all the closer. "Hmm? What?"

"I dunno. Something just—ah, forget it." He exhaled and watched his breath for a moment. "This place."

Abe nodded in agreement. "This place."

Though neither of them said anything, both were aware that the other's eyes were fixed on the skies. Waiting to see if any other scaries might skip across the twilight.

Nothing did.

"Hey," Abe said standing up. "Why don't you go grab your stuff? Let's get ourselves settled in before it gets too late."

Simi stretched and followed Abe to the truck. "Yeah, sure." He reached in and pulled out his duffel and they both slammed their doors. Smiling, he followed Abe up the stairs and onto the porch. "You afraid to be out here after dark?"

Abe froze, his hand on the doorknob. He looked at his son, and Simi couldn't help but see the worry in the creases bookending his hardened face.

"Welcome," he said, throwing open the heavy, groaning, oak door and blatantly avoiding his son's question. "To Ward House."

Twelve

Daisy was waiting, in the shadow of the spiral stairwell, as they entered. She hovered awkwardly until Abe realized what she was doing.

"Ohh, right. My bad. This," he pulled an arm around his son, "Is Simeon."

Daisy stuck out her hand. "Nice to meet ya', Simeon," and when Abe missed another cue, "I'm Daisy Peltzer."

"Simi," said the boy taking her grasp. "Just Simi."

She laughed, nodding. "I get that. To be honest, I'm usually just 'D' around these parts." She looked at Abe and their eyes locked on one another momentarily. "At least, the people I like best call me 'D.'"

Simi stared at them both, eventually grunting loudly enough that the two snapped out of their weird little trance.

Daisy blinked a couple of times, lifted a small canvas grocery bag onto her shoulder, and headed toward the door. "Well, it's been nice seeing you boys tonight. Glad you made it here safely. Though I'd love to stay and chat a bit longer, I need to do my own food shopping and get myself home. Got a cat waiting for her dinner and, if I'm not back soon, she's going to punish me by tearing up some toilet paper or my couch or... something even more expensive." Both men fidgeted and offered clumsy nods. "In any case, I'd rather not find out. I'm off. Elma's already asleep and, unless something strange happens, she should remain that way until I get back in the morning."

Strange?

Abe followed her to the door. "Should we expect anything unusual to happen?"

Daisy looked to him, then at Simi, and eventually up the winding staircase. She was clearly considering the question, her head lilting to one side as if she were listening to some silent debate, but— after a moment—just shook her head and smiled. "Naw. *No,*" she promised, convincing herself. "Definitely not. I wouldn't think so. You boys'll be good." She stepped out onto the porch. "*She'll* be good."

Abe let his frame fill the doorway. He shifted his bag further up onto his shoulder.

"Thanks for everything today, D. It's good to see you again."

She smiled, reaching back to adjust her ponytail, but didn't offer the same parting toast. "The pantry's stocked. You boys help yourself. Eat whatever you can find. I'll be back bright and early. Look forward to hearing all your ghost stories then."

Abe looked behind himself, at a rubbernecking Simi, and then back out through the front door. "Uhm, ghost stories?"

She sighed. "Relax, Abel. It was a joke."

She took a few steps down the walkway that led around

to her backyard parking spot. "Have a good night."

Simi joined Abe at the entrance and they both watched her disappear into the shadows.

"So, what's the story with you two—?" Simi started to ask, but Abe was already moving back inside.

Standing at the bottom of the staircase, Abe placed an elbow on the smooth sphere atop the post at the base of the handrail. Almost right away, he winced and lifted his arm into the air. Gingerly, he picked a splinter from the skin on his forearm. "Damn house is falling apart," he said. "Have some work ahead of us tomorrow. You in?"

Simi spread his arms wide. "Do I have a choice?"

"No," Abe grunted, his face stone.

"Well, okay then." Simi stood awkwardly at the bottom of the staircase, unsure of what to do next. "Since you completely avoided my question from a moment ago—"

"There is no story, Sim," Abe said. "Me and Daisy. It's…"

Simi shaped his lips into a straight line, his eyebrows raising, annoyed at the thought remaining unfinished. "Yes?"

Abe sighed and looked up the staircase. "It's ancient history. We're here for Elma anyway and nothing more."

Simi rolled his eyes. "If you say so." He looked around the space. "So, can you point me to a couch, or a bed, or a hammock or *something*? Anything. Not gonna be picky tonight. Just think I'm ready to hit the hay."

Abe roused himself. "Oh yeah, sure. Of course. Follow me."

As the two climbed the twirling innards of the Ward family homestead, the only audible sound was the groaning of the warped boards under their feet. Abe pictured the house crying out with each placement of human flesh and sinew on its own, brittle, bones.

On the second floor, they both paused and stared down a long stretch of corridor, carpeted with a long red runner. The strip of crimson rug was littered with the same screaming goblin faces that lined the outside extremities of the house.

Abe took a few steps into the depths of the musty passage, illuminated by a single candle perched on the center-most hole of a three-armed candelabra. The antique sat, patiently, on a decorative mahogany table, which greeted them at the otherwise unilluminated aperture.

"Candles?" Simi looked to his father. "Abe, what is this place? Aren't we living in the twenty-first century?"

Abe beckoned him to move further down the hallway. "Relax." He reached out and lifted a switch on the wall directly adjacent to where they were standing. An overhead fixture sprang to life. "Just like the rest of the house, these corridors are all electrified. Most of the rooms too. At least, they used to be. For some reason, Elma's always preferred the candles. Kind of nice touch, huh? 'Authentic', I think she'd say."

Simi shivered. "How 'bout 'sinister'? Or, 'freaking-impractical'?"

They moved a few paces further into the dimness until Abe stopped in front of the first door on the right. There were several peeling stickers scattered on the once-white paint. He absentmindedly flicked at one dangling almost completely off. A circus tent, or something that looked like one. The doorknob itself was a sardonic clown face, made completely from brass.

Simi froze. "You have got to be kidding me."

Abe cracked the door for him. "Not even slightly."

It was dark inside. A dark so deep both of the Wards held their breath, waiting to see if anything might jump out at them. When nothing did, Abe patted his son on the back.

"You'll be fine. Really. Have a great night. If you need me, I'll be only one door down." He stopped and smiled. "You know, this was my room. Used to have a bunch of Black Sabbath posters and my drum kit in there, but I took all of that away when I left. I bet she hasn't touched it in thirty years."

Simi lifted one corner of his mouth, disgusted. "Gross."

"Night, Sim."

"Yeah… thanks. Night."

Abe knew Simi was just standing in front of the bedroom door, steeling himself before entering. But, he didn't turn around.

Simi will be fine.

And Abe believed the reassuring voice. *Mostly*. He knew that anything birthed from the Ward family fairytales or the recesses of Elma's rotting mind, couldn't possibly be roosting in that room.

No.

Not there.

Of all places, not there.

He looked back over his shoulder as Simi still lingered just outside the dark fissure in the wall.

Not in the Clown Room.

Thirteen

Simi flicked on the light.

There was electricity in the room, but almost immediately he wished there wasn't.

Entering further, he threw the door open the rest of the way and winced as it came to a dull thud against the wall. Simi peered behind it, afraid he'd damaged something, and could immediately tell there'd been a leak at some point. From where the stains and mold originated, he couldn't tell, but the streaks climbing down the wallpaper were not new. Years—perhaps decades before—they'd dried and the drips and puckered bubbles looked crispy, as if they might crumble to the ground at any moment. Indeed, small flecks of plaster and peelings freshly littered the shag carpet as a result of his overly aggressive (if not warranted) entry into his father's old bedroom.

What the—

It wasn't the disintegrating wall that stifled the thought

from finishing. Simi's eyes took in the small enclosure, not much longer than the tiny bed at its middle. Festooning nearly every inch of the claustrophobic space were—

Clowns.

He took a deep breath and gagged on the dust, putting a hand in front of his mouth.

This is effed up.

Every knick-knack, wall-hanging, design element or frill, followed the disturbing theme. There were variations, of course; a circus scene playing out on aged curtains that Simi suspected were once bright blue, a carpet in the shape of an old-timey, red and white big-top tent. But otherwise, for the most part, everything Simi's eyes landed on was—

Clowns.

He placed his duffel beside the quilted, child's bed. Propped up against the pillows, sitting at its center—pleasantly grinning—was a massive, stuffed, monstrosity. On its head rested a hat—a beanie he thought it was called—complete with a propeller. Simi flicked the blades and a cloud of dust lifted off into the air. Instinctively, he coughed again and stepped back. In response, the deleterious imp slowly slipped off the pillow and flopped onto its side. In doing so, it somehow managed to keep its eyes locked on Simi's. Its lips stretched nearly from ear to ear, in a horrid, jack-o-lantern, sneer. Even worse, Simi thought that it looked like someone (a child presumably) had drawn on, in marker, two sharp, vampire-like incisors. On its shirt was a rectangular badge with a name stitched onto it.

"Barachiel," Simi read. "Well, that sounds terrifying."

He picked up the creature and pulled open the bottom drawer of the only dresser in the room. It was empty and Simi shoved the ghoulish thing inside.

"There," he said. "Much better."

He turned back toward the bed and regretted the too-hasty hyperbole. The room was still littered with the oddities of what he could only assume were Abel Ward's past. If what his father said was right, no one had lived in the space since he'd left thirty or so years before. By the look of things, Simi thought, it was believable no one had even *entered* the fool's den in the same span of time.

The wallpaper trim, and what once had been a long train of beaming, red-nosed, clown faces (bearing an unsettling resemblance to the plush character restrained only by the aged dresser) was now merely a wretched convoy of lunatic snarls and their pinkish, sun-faded, bulbous beaks. On top of the bureau was a smattering of disturbing baubles. Most notably, Simi spotted a dried-out snow-globe that housed a headless clown-torso. A painted, laughing (*screaming?*) face—long-since snapped off and lying beside it—was covered in the motes that'd been, decades earlier, dancing white flakes.

Beside the orb, Simi spotted a photo. It had a small piece of yellowed note-paper tucked into a front edge, where the glass met the withered wood frame.

Simi picked it up.

The image was an old Polaroid. Simi had never held one in his hands before, but he knew they were the sorts of photos you had to blow on and shake a bit before they fully developed. Or, at least that's what he'd heard.

In the picture was a boy; Simi guessed he was no more than ten years old.

Little Abe.

And there were four adults peering out of the image at him, as well. Based on other photos he'd seen, Simi recognized two of them as Abe's parents.

Delilah and Adam Ward. My grandparents.

On the opposite side of the child were two elderly individuals. One was a white-haired man, in suspenders and green corduroy slacks. He looked too-thin, fragile, as if he'd been propped up just long enough for the photo to be snapped. The other, a woman, was of similar age, but with a strength not visible in the man she stood beside. She gripped the back of a chair and her gaze pierced through the otherwise serene family image. Though he'd never before seen an image of either, Simi could only assume the pair were Amos Ward (his great-grandfather) and his sister, the infamous, and still-supposedly-breathing somewhere overhead—

Elma.

Simi pulled the folded document from the corner of the photo—careful not to tear it. Gently, he unfolded the artifact. Inside it read:

The last of the Wards. 1981.

He considered it—the importance and its relevance to himself—before quickly sticking the note back into the frame and returning the curio to the dresser-top.

Simi sighed and decided his further examination of the bizarre room, and its cache of weird, could wait until morning. He was beyond tired.

He pulled out his phone to check if there were any new messages from Mags. A notification greeted him and he was delighted to see she'd replied to his selfie. Her missive was simple, but a response was still a response.

Mags Downing: cute <3.
Mags Downing: U, not the house.

He tapped out a response. Just as succinct. To the point. Intentionally not overly needy or effusive.

Simi Ward: lol. <3. Night, Mags.

He found his charger in his bag and plugged the phone cord into the wall. Leaving the glowing device to re-energize on a small side table, he ambled over to the small octagon overlooking the backyard.

He'd only been peering through the darkness for a second or two when his eyes caught something just outside the window. On the ledge, just below the bottom of the dirty pane, were deep scratch marks.

Simi bent in for a closer examination.

The dagger-like, ragged, gouges ran the length of the sill, but that wasn't all that he noticed. Similar scores and blemishes stretched across the outside membrane of glass itself.

Simi took a step backward and then, after regaining his composure, returned to look out the injured porthole. He noted how far off the ground he was and how difficult it'd have been for any human, or creature with claws capable of doing that sort of damage, to have found their way up to that puny ledge.

It's almost as if—

Simi stopped himself, shook his head, and ran a shaking hand through his dark mane.

No, it's too high. Impossible.

He pulled the baby-blue circus curtain tightly shut and was unable to repress the thought again.

It's almost as if something was trying to get in.

Fourteen

"Abel!"

Abe sat straight up in the darkness. Eyes wide, he peered around the room, panting, at first unsure of where he even was. He caught his breath and tried to reintroduce himself to his surroundings. He was on an unfamiliar bed, in a room that he couldn't identify based on the shadows alone. His t-shirt was soaked and he was in his boxer shorts.

And then he remembered.

"You're at Elma's," he said aloud, sucking in air. "You were asleep. You're back at Elma's."

Reaching behind himself, he blindly swung his hand around before it found a lampshade, then the lamp, and then the light switch.

The room illuminated and he listened.

There was silence. No movement upstairs or in the next room over. The moon was still bright and the night remained sooty. He wasn't certain of the time, but no one should have been up at that hour.

I swear to God I just—

A wailing knifed through the quiet. Reactively, Abe jumped back against the massive oak headboard, hitting his head in the process.

"Dammit," he said aloud. "What the hell was that?"

The vocalizations—frenzied, pleading, lamentations—were unlike anything he'd ever heard, or at least unlike anything he'd ever heard coming from outside in the middle of the night. They were high-pitched and, with each repeating call, sounded increasingly desperate for his attention.

Like someone screaming. A small child, but... wrong.

He ran to the window and quickly opened it, releasing a waft of cool autumn air into the room. It was chilly and he folded his arms around himself, peering out into what would be impossible for him to see through.

The screeching sounded again. This dirge was longer-lasting, but gradually faded—as if the bereaved was being slowly strangled by another. Squinting, he tried to see if there was any movement, but all he could make out were a few splotches of moonlight that had found a way to besmirch the otherwise completely coal-black backyard. Having grown up on the property, Abe was acutely aware of the variety of large mammals that often visited the outskirts of the Ward estate, sipping at the banks from little trickles of river that leaked into and around the wetlands surrounding the home. Summer nights, with the windows thrown wide, were the most likely times of year to hear a coyote committing a violent act on a smaller animal. During the spring months, foxes had their own song to sing during mating season.

But this was different.

Abe listened patiently for the ululation once more.

Again, the cries came. This time, the call sounded like it was just under his window, near the back porch.

With complete disregard for his state of undress, Abe dashed out of the room. If he'd had time to rethink his action plan, he'd likely have grabbed his phone for its flashlight or even for the comfort of "911" should a beastie have chosen to leap from the cover of night and claw his face off.

Hindsight is 20/20 and all that…

Skipping every other step on his way down the uncoiled snake of a stairwell, Abe finally landed on the first floor. It'd been decades since he'd travailed beyond the main entryway, but he burst into the backside of the home with a familiarity that suggested he'd not forgotten what was where. The living room opened into a dining room, which opened into a small kitchen, which had a large sliding glass door spanning its far wall—one of very few modern improvements to the home. From his bank of childhood memories, Abe recalled French doors previously occupying the space. He flicked on the porch light, unlocked the slider, and threw it open.

The sickly yellow bulb cast just enough of its beam for him to see a few feet beyond the railing of the deck. Most animals, upon noticing a light suddenly turn on and after hearing the commotion made by one Abe's size, would hunker down or have been frightened off of the hunt.

But the screaming continued.

Abe stood there in his underwear, unafraid but perplexed. Whatever it was sounded no less than fifty yards or so away from him, in the murk of the marsh, but wasn't bothered by his sudden arrival at all.

Trying to make a bit more noise, Abe clapped his hands and stomped his bare feet on the coarse boards of the porch. The echo of his conduct bounded out and into the mystifying night. And yet, still, the yowling continued.

What is that—?

Something crashed out in the woods. By the sound of it, a huge limb had come plunging to the earth not far behind the closest of the sheds. Abe backed into the house and slid the door shut, sealing himself safely inside. After a brief vacillation, he threw down the lock and then, for good measure, jiggled the handle to make certain it was secure.

Sighing, he looked toward the green numbers floating over the stove.

4:00 am. Dammit. Not going back to sleep now.

He wouldn't have been able to if he tried. The cacophony outside persisted. A proper mauling was occurring feet from where he stood and where Simi and Elma were— presumably— sound asleep upstairs.

How are they unconscious through all of this?

Abe shook his head and made his way into the kitchen, spotting a coffeemaker. He grabbed the glass pot and held it under the cool water, keeping his eyes trained on the scene through the tiny window above the sink.

"Tomorrow—" he stopped himself, remembering the time. "*Today*, I'm giving this place a once over. I need a refresher on exactly what I'm dealing with here."

He chuckled quietly to himself, but noted that nothing stood out to him, in that moment, as being particularly funny. He poured the water into the top of the appliance and then returned the pot to its slot. As he began to scoop black grounds, he continued his musing, quietly— to himself— aware that it was still early and he didn't want to wake the other two.

What am I not remembering? In some ways, my recollection is so fresh, so vividly real. Like I was just here.

He pressed the blue button at the base of the machine. It lit up, signaling that the magic was about to happen. After a moment, the comforting gurgle of his brew followed.

And in other ways…

He stepped back in front of the window and listened as another blood-curdling cry made him grip the blue laminate countertop.

…I can't see past these shadows.

Fifteen

Simi stood at a bend in the spiral staircase, on the last turn before the final few steps to ground-level, and stared up at the painting that he'd somehow missed on his inaugural mounting of the twisting flight. The piece of art, which faced the main door to the house, was taller than he was. The center-most image was one of an ornate, gilded, gate, intertwined with glimmering vines and flowers. Slightly ajar, it appeared— to Simi—to be trying to force itself open. A luminous brilliance, in a spectrum of greens, seeped from its opening and the wrought-iron bars of the conduit. From unseen arms and persons, disembodied hands compelled the gate to remain closed. Joined by thick tree limbs, and an assortment of local flora, a battle was being waged to forestall the breach.

    Simi was mesmerized. Not just by the beauty of the artifact, but also at the dread and the fear pulsing out of it. The desperation with which those hands, of both human and natural origin, pressed back against what he could only assume was something—

Bad.

—suspended him right there, in the jello mold of his mind. Though he couldn't even come close to describing what he was seeing, he was congealed by a sudden, completely inexplicable, terror.

The popping of bacon, sizzling in grease, nudged him from his paralysis and he tore himself away from the canvas. Yawning, he hopped down into the foyer and followed the smell.

Abe didn't turn from his station at the frying pan when Simi entered the kitchen, but heard him coming.

"Mornin'."

"Morning, Abe. Up early I see."

Abe turned a few pieces of crisping pork. "8:00 am isn't that early, man. Especially when I've been up for four hours already."

Simi sat down at the table and began scrolling through his phone. "What, couldn't settle in on your first night? Bad dreams?"

Abe grunted. "Something like that." He turned and lifted an eyebrow at his son. "And how'd you sleep?"

Simi didn't take his eyes off of his screen. "Slept fine."

Twisting back to his cooking, Abe hid his confusion. "Fine, 'eh? You didn't hear that racket last night? Early this morning, you didn't hear—?"

"Naw," Simi said. "Slept like a baby."

Abe switched the stove off and dumped the slices onto a nearby plate. He walked the dish over to the table and placed it between himself and his son.

"Huh. Weird."

Ignoring the comment, Simi grabbed a piece of the

breakfast meat. "So, is this breakfast?"

Abe shoved a slice into his mouth, grease covering his fingertips. He put a thumb in between his lips to clean it off. "Hey, you're welcome to make something else. You heard the lady. Pantry's all ours."

Simi grabbed another couple of pieces. "Aren't you supposed to, I dunno, make sure I'm eating healthy?" he shook his head when his dad shrugged. "For shame. Mom would totally disapprove of your poor example."

Abe gobbled down more of the crumbly flesh. "Sucks for her."

They both snorted. Together.

Simi caught himself.

Alright there, Tiger. It's not that funny.

Straightening out his face, he wiped the back of his hand across his mouth. Abe noticed the quick change in expression and cleared his throat.

"Big day ahead of us."

Simi looked mockingly to one side and then back to the other. "It is? Really? What exactly do we even need to—?"

"Have you *seen* this place? Once we're both dressed, there's an awful lot of sprucing we need to do. While we're here, I don't see why we can't help Elma out." Simi's eyes rolled back, and Abe continued. "Lots falling into disrepair inside, sure, but the yard's a mess too. Used to be beautiful out there. Once was the most gorgeous property in town. I think that'd be a good place to start. Make ourselves useful, you know? Maybe Elma will get to see it lookin' good again before—" He stopped himself.

Simi sat waiting. Eventually, his father's head drooped. "You can say it. Before she dies. Right?"

Abe nodded.

"Okay."

Abe lifted an eyebrow. "Really?"

Simi reached for a napkin, deciding it was probably more useful than his bare arm. "Yeah, why not? You're right, we're here. And she's my…"

"You're great-great-aunt."

"Right."

Abe slapped his hands together and stood up from the table. He grabbed the now-empty plate and brought it to the sink. As he stood rinsing it, he looked back over his shoulder. "Thanks, Sim."

Simi waved at him and pushed his chair out. "Oh, calm down. It's not a big deal. At all." He glared at his father. "Let's please not make it one."

Abe turned back to the sink. "Sure thing."

Simi had one foot out of the kitchen and was just about to cross the dining room in the direction of the stairwell when Abe called out. "Hey, ah, and don't forget to keep checking on whatever online work your teachers are assigning you. This isn't a vacation. Got to stay on track best you can as long as we're away."

Simi groaned. "You know this wouldn't be a problem at all if we'd never left Georgia in the first place?"

"Simi—"

"I know, I know," he crossed the dining room. "Trust me. I know."

His head was down. He was grumbling about keeping up with his classes and needing to somehow manage to teach himself from thousands of miles away when he took the first stair.

Simi gasped.

The painting was still floating, just above the landing, but something had happened. The piece, over six feet in height, had— since he'd last seen it—been shifted. When he'd looked it over only moments earlier, it'd stood straight, no doubt fastened in the same position for an untold number of years.

How—?

He looked, frantically, up the staircase, pleading with his ears to hear some sort of sound to easily explain what he was witnessing.

No, no, no, no.

Now, the work was completely cock-eyed, violently listing at an angle. And, even more terrifying to him—

Elma?

—it was still wobbling.

Sixteen

"Oof."

Abe held a hand in front of his nose. He stood a few feet from the largest of the outbuildings, to the far left of the backyard boundary. He'd caught a whiff of the odor almost immediately upon stepping off the back of the porch, but hadn't been able to identify where it was originating from until he got a bit closer. Simi had mentioned there were bones out there, but this smelled worse than a few pieces of animal in a hole.

Smells like a massacre. A giant rotting pile of—

A flash of movement out of the corner of his eye caught his attention. Down at the very end of the meandering river, where the water split into two directions around a large, sun-bleached boulder, something had darted into the water.

Something big.

The ripples identifying the point of entry lingered,

confirming to Abe that some animal had been down there. He considered how large the creature must have been for him to have taken note at such a distance, but before long he shrugged it off.

Probably just a dumb turtle falling off a rock.

A screen door thwacked open and then slammed shut somewhere behind him. Tearing his eyes from the disturbance downstream, he turned toward the noise.

"Found your bones," he said.

Simi sniffed, reacquainting himself to the stench, and then stopped before he got too close. "Definitely not *mine*."

Abe beckoned him nearer, and Simi begrudgingly complied. He did, however, put his t-shirt up and over his mouth and nose.

"You see that river?" the elder Ward said, pointing in the direction of the giant rock and the unidentified disturbance. "That's Dead Rock River. We used to take our rowboat out there. After enough rain, of course. Couldn't just do it anytime. During the drier months, you'd easily get yourself stuck in the muck. And no one was coming all that way to drag you back in."

Simi squinted against the late morning sunlight and put a hand up to act as a visor. "What's down there?"

Abe looked back out over the marsh. "You mean, other than Dead Rock? Maybe some fish. Some big snappers that'd bite your finger off if you let 'em. Otherwise, not much."

Simi sidled up next to his father. "And, that's Dead Rock?"

Abe nodded.

"Why *Dead* Rock? I mean, how'd it get that name?"

Abe spread his hands wide, "Hell if I know. Probably named like two hundred years ago or something. I imagine there aren't many still around who do know why it's called that. Other than Elma." He scratched his chin and reconsidered. "Though, I'm not sure if I'd put a lot of stock into much of what she's saying these days."

Simi walked over to the hole and looked in. "God that reeks. Have you—hey, what a minute."

Abe joined him beside the shed. "What?"

Simi knelt and swatted at the flies barreling into his face as he did so. "I think," his voice quivered. "I think there are more bones in here than there were yesterday."

Abe took a closer look. The fragments were dirty, but white. Picked almost entirely clean. He could make out a few ribs, perhaps a jaw bone. Most of the other pieces were unidentifiable.

"You sure?" he asked.

Simi nodded. "Yeah. *Yes.* Definitely. This wasn't all here yesterday."

After a moment, Abe stood up and pulled Simi with him. "Alright, well, it doesn't change much. We know there's something out there, gnawing on something else. Coyote, maybe." He gripped Simi's shoulder. "But it's nothing to worry too much about. You see these kinds of things anytime you live near wildlife. You know, to be fair, they were here first. We're the ones encroaching on their territory. Animals, I mean. These things are getting pushed further and further out of their usual habitats. It makes sense we're starting to interact and see more of this kind of thing each year."

Simi was still looking into the hole. "Don't see much of this in Georgia."

"We live in the city, Sim. This is... *different.*"

Simi put his hands on his head and sighed. "You're damn right it is."

Not waiting for Simi to follow, Abe began walking

back toward the house.

"Hey, I need to go check in with Elma. She's probably awake by now and I have to ask her something."

Also, D's probably back by now too. Still a few things to talk to her about, as well.

He saw the exasperated look on Simi's face and tried to reassure him. "It'll be quick. I promise. Can you, ah— while you're waiting for me— would you mind grabbing my tool bag out of the back of the truck?"

Simi responded by letting his arms flop to his sides. Without a word, he started walking up the driveway.

"Fantastic. Big help, Pal. Once I'm back out, we'll get right to work. Already have a few projects for us in mind." He bounded onto the porch and, with his hand on the slider, turned back again. "Oh, and, feel free to do something about those bones. The smell is getting to me. Probably a shovel in one of the sheds if you look hard enough."

Simi grumbled a reply, though his eyes were already fixated on his phone as he stalked away.

"Thanks, Sim!" Abe called.

He turned to face the house once more.

"Alright, Elma," he said out loud, psyching himself up. "Let's talk."

Seventeen

The first shed, long enough to fit a couple of canoes end to end, was a more recent build. "More recent" was relative, of course, since most everything on the property was constructed pre-Grover Cleveland. Some things, the house included, were built even earlier. But the first outbuilding was newer and most of the articles inside indicated as much.

Simi stood in the opening of one of the two doorways. He'd expected to find piles of yard equipment, perhaps an old lawnmower or a barbecue grill. Instead, he was greeted by a hollowed-out tomb, the final resting place for nothing but a few spider webs, and something hidden in a far corner, under a large grey, canvas, tarp. There was a peek of a small tire poking out and he had a strong idea as to what was hidden underneath.

In a cloud of dust and unshelled acorns—

Chipmunks nesting in here.

—Simi threw off the cover.

Oh, hello there.

Leaning to one side, its kickstand rusted and crumbling flakes of red dust, was a—shockingly bright, electric-yellow— motorcycle. Simi ran a hand down the smooth, black leather seat. Remarkably, it hadn't been chewed through, which didn't make much sense. In fact, the entire treasure appeared to be completely preserved. Simi had a minor interest in motorcycles, starting at a young age after his mother once dragged him to a car show. Characteristically, he'd been left to his own devices and found himself, at no more than eight years old, wandering the rows of bikes and antique vehicles. Back then, he'd seen one that'd looked very much like the hog he stood in front of at that moment. He smiled.

"How'd you get in here? You've got to be—what—late 60's, early 70's era at the latest."

He wasn't sure if his analysis was correct, though he didn't care. On the gas tank, he noticed a large, black, "W".

"So, who'd you belong to? Presumably a Ward. Adam? Amos?" He looked behind himself, back in the direction of the house. "Elma?"

Simi sighed, thinking he'd like nothing more than to take a seat on the bike, but accepted that he had a job to do. He collected the tarp and dragged it back over the relic.

"I'll be back," he laughed. "And, if I'm lucky, maybe even with some keys."

He stepped out into the sunlight. Everywhere he looked, he found new and interesting surprises. His interest piqued, he turned to the next shed, a much smaller one. By the look of things— its paint completely peeled off, its shingles littered with debris from decades of storms— this second building was far older. Possibly, he speculated, even as old as Ward House itself.

He reached for the main sliding bolt and his hand froze.

Scratched onto the door, at chest level, was what appeared to be a child's drawing.

Simi stepped back.

The stick-figure illustration featured two distinct characters. The first sported a black bowler hat and, as far as Simi could tell, not much else. The figure next to it induced him to inhale sharply. It stood at relatively the same height as the individual in the hat. Otherwise, however, the form could not have appeared more different.

Its arms hung too low, straight down past where its knees would have been, and whereas the first illustration was drawn with straight lines, each "stick" of this image— its fingers, legs, neck— were all twisted and bent at unnatural angles. It seemed to be covered in either a dark sludge or shadow, but—due to the rudimentary ability of the artist—Simi couldn't discern which it was supposed to be. And the most ghastly feature was its face. The visage of the oddity was scratched out, as if whoever had drawn it couldn't bring themselves to fully manifest it, or—perhaps—because the creator wanted to prevent anyone else from seeing the thing's truest form.

Simi shivered.

I'm not sure I even want to know what this is all about.

He reached for the latch and yanked it open.

Moths fluttered out into his face and he waved at them. The space inside was tiny and he had to duck down a bit to avoid hitting his head on the decaying, slanting beams of the roof. After a moment, his eyes adjusted and, while he did locate a shovel just inside the doorway, the antiquities that hung on the opposing wall tempted him to peer closer.

Deeper.

Scattered across the inside of the enclosure, vestiges of another time and of an unidentifiable purpose, hung from bent nails. His quick count told him that there were upwards of fifty different tools.

Tools. Yes, that's what they are. At least, I think they are. And yet...

He reached for one. The first word that popped into his head as he pulled the item off of its hook was—

Sword. I'm holding a goddamn sword.

Except, it wasn't a sword. Not exactly. The blade—if that was an accurate description—was formed from a porous, black, stone. One of its sides was serrated, like a saw, and a dark, solidified layer of grime covered each of its teeth. The hilt also had a fanged edge, which—Simi noted—was coated in the same vile film. The tool appeared as if it would have made easy work of a piece of wood, an overgrown thicket, or maybe even—

Simi dropped the weapon to the ground.

Bone.

He stared at the sword, lying flat, harmless, on the dirt floor of the wooden crypt. It was clear the devilish tool was designed to be used for far more than protection. He'd never seen anything quite like it and decided not to even let himself wonder what its actual purpose might have once been.

He stepped back toward the doorway, taking in the rest of the medieval hardware displayed around the inside of the structure. A double-sided ax, with teeth chiseled into its blades. A spear, painted entirely in black and decorated with green, flowering, vines. A wooden bucket, with a carved, silently screaming baby-face at its center. All of it was grotesque. Bizarre. None of the items resembled anything he'd ever seen in textbooks or on any of his school trips to the history museum in Atlanta.

Shaking his head, he quickly grabbed the shovel and took one last look at the menagerie of grotesque, barbaric weaponry. It wasn't anything he'd have expected to find in a little shed, behind some kindly old lady's house in suburban Massachusetts, let alone anywhere else.

Slamming the door behind him, he quickly walked back to the bones-hole.

Abe's gonna need to explain this to me. That's some dark, dark shit in there.

He scooped all the unidentified remains on the first attempt and carried the shovel-full into the woods, down behind the out-buildings. He was nearing the edge of the property, where the water from the swamp and river began to slowly creep up the hill to meet the trees. Simi realized he could have easily buried the stinking odds and ends—that's what Abe would have preferred—but even that minimal level of exertion was more than he felt the moment warranted. Without much of an effort to get the animal remnants deep into the water, he half-heartedly tossed the bones.

Kerplunk. Plunk. Plop.

He listened as the white chunks came raining down and, once all was silent, turned back toward the yard.

Simi hadn't even taken a full step, his foot still hovering in the air, when he spotted something poking out of a pile of rotting leaves and bramble. With his shovel, he jabbed at the lump in the woods until a small brown object, no bigger than an apple or orange, rolled down toward him.

Reflexively, Simi jumped and held up the tool in front of himself.

Oh, shit.

Staring back up at him, its eyes wide and terrified, its mouth frozen in a death scream, was a furry, whiskered, head.

Eighteen

"Can I make you anything?"

Abe leaned against the entrance to the kitchen, his thumbs attempting to casually hang from the pockets of his worn blue jeans. "No, thanks," he said. "Sim and I already had a bite before we headed outside."

Daisy made a face. Her flannel, the same she'd been wearing the day before, rested loosely around her waist. A half-sleeve of tattoo, now visible, stopped just above her elbow. She gestured her head toward the pile of dirty dishes in the sink. "I thought so. Just bacon?"

Abe winced and stepped further into the space. "Something wrong with bacon?"

She still hadn't turned to look at him, intently focused on the omelet she was preparing. "No, nothing at all. It's more the *just bacon* aspect of your meal. Wouldn't exactly call it a well-balanced plate or—"

"Alright, D. I'll do better," he paused, considering his

words carefully before continuing. "You know, if you wanted to drop in a little earlier tomorrow, maybe you could even join us. I'd be happy to fix whatever healthy fare you might—"

Her jaw tightened. Even though she was silent, Abe could see enough in her face that told him to stop. He took a step back toward the door.

"Hey, what am I thinking? I'm sorry. This is your job. You don't want to come in early." He turned back in the direction of the stairwell. "Maybe some other time."

As he walked away, she cleared her throat. "Abe."

He stopped, quickly spinning around. "Ayuh?"

Daisy chewed on the side of her mouth and then exhaled slowly. "It's not a 'no' forever. I just… I still need a little bit of time. Being around you again… *seeing* you, I mean. It just going to take me a little while, I think." When he stood there without speaking, she added, flustered, "For god's sake it's been over thirty years, Abel." He thought he could see a little glint in her eyes, but she'd turned back toward her eggs. "You just *left*. Forever. At least, until now. We were only kids. I don't know you, not really." She put the spatula down and folded her arms across her chest. "And you definitely don't know me."

He hung his head. "D, I'm sorry, I just—"

She waved at him or—perhaps—was just trying to wave the sadness off of her own face. "Oh, stop, it's fine. I know you were just being nice. Shit, you were only offering breakfast." She laughed an unsteady laugh and sniffed. "Guess I'm still not even ready for breakfast, ya' know?"

Abe sighed and nodded. "I know."

Without another word, he made his way toward the base of the stairwell and began to climb.

Smooth, Abe. Super smooth. Should have figured she'd be

wanting to keep her distance.

He reached the third-floor landing, still lost in his own thoughts.

Back then, there was no social media. No email. Staying in touch wasn't so easy. But I can't blame her for still feeling stung and I can't blame myself for needing to do what I needed to do.

He tapped on Elma's door, absentmindedly.

Could anyone, anyone who knew what growing up here was like, really fault me?

"Abel?"

He jumped backward with such a force he smacked into a low-hanging picture frame on the opposite wall. He turned to fix it and recognized the image as a black and white photograph of Ward House. He guessed it was taken some time in the earlier half of the twentieth century. Before or after Elma came into the world, he couldn't be sure. Straightening the glass-encased picture, he moved back to the door. "Yes, Elma. Can I come in?"

He waited. There was no answer.

Gently, he wrapped his knuckles on the door again.

Silence. She did not seem to respond, and yet—

What is that sound?

He put his ear to the door and listened.

"Elma?" he called.

From inside the room emanated a hushed, husky, breathing. There was a whistle to it, like a bagpipe with a small hole poked in its side.

"Elma, are you okay?"

He slowly pushed open the door.

Elma was sitting up on the edge of her bed, facing the large window. Her palms were open wide, her little fingers wriggling like dried-up worms. Her head was flopped backward and, as Abe carefully walked around the edge of the mattress to examine the spectacle, he found her with her eyes closed and smiling widely. Her breathing was labored and she appeared to be soaking in an invisible radiance.

Abe looked at her and then out through the window. It was a rather nondescript morning. The sun was not particularly strong or warm and, in any case, wasn't shining into her room.

"Elma," he started, "Are you—?"

"Abel," she whispered. "Can you feeeeeel it?" She let her head flop forward so suddenly, Abe worried she'd hurt herself. And yet, she continued to grin. "Can you, my dear?"

Abe shook his head and sat beside her. "Feel what, Elma?"

She giggled. "It's been so long for them, you understand. Never before have they been forced to live through such a drought." She snorted again as if she'd made a private joke.

Abe was alarmed. He gently placed both of his hands on the sides of her face and pulled her gaze from the window. "What drought? Elma? Hey," he brushed a few grey strands from in front of her eyes. "Elma, talk to me."

A cloud moved from her vision and she blinked a couple of times. "Abel," she gasped, seeing him for the first time that morning. "Oh, I'm so glad you're still here."

Abe squinted his eyes and looked at her again. "Of course I am. You think I'd disappear after just one night?"

She smiled up at him. "I've just been so used to not having you around. For a moment, I wasn't sure if I'd actually seen you last night or if you were just a figment."

Helping her back under her covers, he chuckled. "Well, I'm sorry to disappoint, but I am no figment. Just old, Abel. In the flesh." He coughed "Good morning, by the way."

Elma rested her head back against one of the many sweat-stained pillows piled along her dark mahogany headboard. She lifted a gnarled hand and patted one of his cheeks. "Such a good boy."

Remaining seated, he tried to change the topic and move away from whatever he'd just witnessed. He'd come upstairs with a specific question for her, after all.

"Hey, Elma? There was a loud screeching sound outside last night. I was wondering if you had any idea what that might be. Did you hear any of it? Can't imagine anyone could have slept through that racket, though Simi seemed to—"

"They're calling to me," she said casually, almost bored at the thought.

Abe blinked. He looked again toward the window and in the direction of whatever nighttime rabble-rousing had occurred hours earlier. "Who's calling to you, Elma?"

Her veiny eyelids closed tightly, stopping her from seeing the fearful expression on her great-nephew's face. Inhaling slowly, she spoke again, confident. "They know it's not long."

"What's not long?" He placed his hands on Elma's shoulders. "Elma?"

It was clear almost immediately that she'd fallen back asleep. It seemed her limited strength afforded her only the briefest of moments and nothing more. Abe felt that her remaining days would mostly be occupied by her dreams, and her few waking moments would be inhabited with the foggy delirium that made one incapable of recognizing the difference between light and the light at the end.

That's all that was. Nothing more.

He pulled the down comforter up to her bony chin. "Get some rest."

Abe stood and made his way to the door, still without an answer. He'd hoped she'd be able to provide some sort of insight into what might be lurking beyond the rays of moonlight, on the outskirts of her property. Unfortunately, he'd discovered, that encyclopedia of everything Ward could no longer be considered a reliable source.

Abe reached for the doorknob. As he did so, a tittering started from somewhere behind him. He turned to find Elma, her eyes still shut, with her mouth cracked open. She was giggling, quietly to herself.

"Hee hee. Not long. Not looooooong." The last word came out in a breathless, sing-songy, rush.

Abe backed into the hallway and hastily shut the door before he could hear her say anything more.

Nineteen

Mags Downing: oh, hell no.

Simi had just texted her a picture of the fuzzy face with the caption, "look what you're missing." Even though it'd recently been removed from the rest of its body, he still imagined he could hear its final, shrill, wail. Something had taken the poor creature out behind the shed—literally— and dispensed the mortal wound.

Simi Ward: cute, huh?
Mags Downing: gross, no. what the F is that???
Simi Ward: my new friend.
Mags Downing: sim, srsly. ive never seen n e thing like that b4.
Simi Ward: me neither. gonna ask abe about it.
Mags Downing: k. hows everything goin with him btw?
Simi Ward: …

He didn't have a better response and, before he had time to elaborate, crunching footsteps from the direction of the driveway caused Simi to slide the phone back into his pocket.

"Watcha lookin' at?"

Simi stood up. "Dunno. But something's missin' a head."

Abe took his time walking down the length of paved path, having exited through the front of the house. As he got closer, Simi couldn't help but think he looked shaken. His eyes were red— they hadn't been when he'd last seen him— and his face was pale. Sweaty. Something inside had clearly rattled him.

What else is new? Guy probably needs to go smoke a butt.

Abe squatted, reluctantly, beside the grimacing object. He picked up a stick and rolled the grotesque, decapitated critter over.

"What the *hell* is that?"

Simi lifted his arms and let them fall. "Figured you would be able to tell me."

Abe leaned in closer. "Kind of a weasely lookin' thing, eh? Too big to be a weasel, though."

Simi was quickly losing interest. "I wouldn't know."

"Yeah. Sharp teeth. Sort of a pointed schnauzer. Think it might be a fisher."

Simi lifted one side of his mouth, showing mild disgust. "A what?"

Abe hopped up and chucked the stick deep into the woods. He wiped his hands on his pants—out of instinct, more than need. "A fisher cat. Nasty bastards. One of the bigger predators you'd find in this area. Especially right here, near the edge of the marsh. Pity the fool that accidentally stumbles onto one of those things." He raised both eyebrows and said, matter-of-factly, "One of those'd steal your cat right outta your lap. I remember 'em picking off the neighborhood kitties all over the place. One summer, in particular, was really bad. Balls of fur in peoples' yards and no other traces of Old Dinah, little Tigger, or Felix." He smirked, clearly aware he'd made his son uncomfortable. "Like I said, nasty bastards."

Simi pulled his hood on and tightened the drawstrings. "Well, if it's such a nasty bastard—as you say— shouldn't it be the king of this proverbial jungle?" Abe cocked a head at his son, confused. "I mean, what would kill a fisher cat?"

Abe scratched at an elbow scab he didn't even know he had. "It's a valid point. Not sure I have an answer. Got your phone?"

Simi already had it in his hands before Abe had finished the question. "Yeah, I'll look it up. Gimme a sec." He typed furiously. "What... kills... a fisher... cat?" He scrolled for a few seconds, having the result before Abe could ask again. "Huh," was all Simi said after a moment of reading.

"And?" Abe picked at his wound impatiently.

'And," Simi finished, "Not much."

Abe attempted to take the phone from him, but Simi was too fast. He pulled away and turned his back. "Not much, *what*, Simi?"

"I mean, not much could do that to a fisher cat, it seems. The only thing I see listed is maybe, *possibly,* a bobcat. But, even that doesn't seem likely."

Abe harrumphed, unsatisfied. "Well, what about a fox or coyote?"

Simi shook his head. "Doesn't mention coyotes, though it does specifically say a fox would lose a head-to-head battle versus one."

Abe slid his hands into his pockets. "Huh. Interesting. See, I might have guessed fox... they used to repurpose these sheds as a sort of den. *Underneath* the sheds, I mean. At least, I think those were fox dens—"

"Hey, you know what?" Simi interrupted. "As much fun as this is jawing back and forth over mysterious mammal skulls and carcasses, I have better—"

"I bet this was what we heard last night. I mean, what *I* heard at least. No one else seemed to." He hadn't noticed Simi's interjection. "I'll probably have to call animal control. Best to have some sort of idea what we're dealing with."

Simi was already halfway up the driveway. He'd started walking immediately after Abe'd spoken over him. His father often got lost in his thoughts and Simi's patience or ability to give the grown man any 'wait time' was nonexistent. "You do whatever you need to, man. I'm gonna be out front. I've had enough of this backyard BS for the time being."

Abe waved absentmindedly and yanked his own phone from a back pocket. Simi pulled his attention away and ambled up onto the front porch.

As always, Abe, I'll be somewhere else. Doing my own thing.

He tucked his itinerant bangs safely inside of his hood and collected himself, as he'd become accustomed to doing whenever his father's preoccupations clouded over everything else.

Don't worry about me. You just mess around with that dead animal. Do your thing. We're cool. I'm cool.

Simi heard Abe's voice move through the tall grass, over the gothic cupola of the house, spin by the aged weathervane— the one that looked like it might snap free during the next storm—and descend, like a monotone, confused, fog. Simi heard it, but quickly blocked out the conversation by inserting two earbuds. Immediately, he was overwhelmed by the familiar strum of his favorite bass player. Closing his eyes, he allowed himself to relax.

To melt.

To escape.
To forget.
Numbness took hold, as it so often did for the boy.
Yeah, Abe. I'm cool.

Twenty

"And what makes you so certain it's a fisher?"

Abe cracked his neck and sighed. He'd already described the grisly scene to the disinterested voice on the phone a couple of times and was hoping to not have to do so again.

"Like I said," Abe gritted his teeth, "I don't know for sure, but it looks like one to me."

There was some shuffling of paper on the other line and the man who'd yet to identify himself answered an unrelated question from someone else in his office. After a moment, he returned to the call. "I'm sorry about that, what were you saying?"

Exasperated, Abe closed his eyes and took a deep breath. "I said it looks like a fisher cat to me. I dunno man. What else can I tell ya? Can you come take a look or what?"

More shuffling of paper. "Yeah, yeah. Of course. You said you were down in the south end of Foxborough? I have another stop to make in that area." He paused. "Though, typically, we only deal with live animals."

Abe drummed his fingers over his bald head and then let them fall over his face. He pulled the phone away for a second so that he wouldn't say something he'd regret later. When he was sure his inside thoughts would remain inside, he returned the device to his ear. "Yessir. But, you see," he tried to will himself to not sound overly condescending. "Something *live* must be responsible for this. Understand?"

He could almost hear the man nodding on the other end of the line. "Sure, sure. Well, ah. Yeah," he slurped something. "Guess I could pop by in a bit. What's the address?"

Abe looked back at the house. Elma's window was empty, the shades drawn tight. A quick glance up the driveway suggested Simi was making himself scarce and hiding out of sight. "It's the old Ward place. You know it?"

Whatever beverage was in the process of being noisily dispatched down the animal control officer's throat suddenly caused the man to choke. He spluttered and gasped for a moment before repeating back what he'd just heard.

"The Ward place you say?" he gulped. "Over on Brown?"

Abe knew the man couldn't see him, but held his free arm wide as his agitation grew. He continued to try his best to radiate patience. "Ayuh. That's the one. You know it, right?" He'd assumed everyone did. It'd be impossible to have spent any real time in town and not know of the gothic mansion menacingly leering down on all passersby. There wasn't an immediate answer to his question. "Hello?"

The voice on the other line sniffed nervously. "Yes," it finally managed to say.

Abe stamped his foot and again held the phone away

as he silently screamed out in the direction of the swamp. He clenched his jaw and, once more, spoke as calmly as he could. "Yes? So you know it? Is there... I mean, is there some sort of problem?"

There was muffled whispering in the Animal Control Office. The person had placed a hand over the receiver. One voice was pleading with another. Abe waited.

The jittery voice returned. "Yes—I mean—*no*. There's no problem. I'll be there within the hour."

Abe, relieved, smiled. "Great. Meet me out back?"

There's was another long silence before the gentleman spoke again. "I, uh, actually, would prefer we, uh, just meet out in front. Of your house, I mean." He swallowed again. "I can't stay long, that is. Just faster this way."

Abe rubbed his eyes. "So, you don't want to inspect the area? The holes under the shed? You just want me to bring the head out in front of—"

"Yep, that's right," the man interrupted. "I'll pull up, take a gander, and then be on my way."

Abe was flabbergasted. "I, uh... well, okay I guess. And your name again?"

"Name's Mitchell." He didn't give a last name.

Or maybe that is his last name?

"Alright, Mitchell," Abe started, "Thanks. I'll see you—"

Click.

"Hello?"

The line was dead. Mitchell had already hung up. The conversation ended.

Abe stared at the phone for a moment, baffled. "That was weird." He stuck the device in his pocket and looked again toward the house. Elma was there now, palms flattened against the glass, smiling down at him. Her forehead was propped against the window.

She really shouldn't be up and walking around.

Eventually, Daisy came to lead the frail woman back to her bed. As Elma was pulled away, her head bobbed up and down, like the paw on one of those golden cats in Chinese restaurants. She resisted Daisy's grasp and kept her gaze fixed on the man with his flannelled arms crossed, brow furrowed, standing with the backdrop of sheds and swamp stretching out behind him. Just before disappearing into the shadows of her room, the old crone smiled and, for an instant, Abe swore he could hear her laughing.

"What the hell, Elma?" he said out loud, locking eyes with her. He raised his voice, slightly, hoping she might be able to make out what he was saying as she was pulled away. "What the ever-living *hell?*"

Twenty One

The swinging bench out front was gradually lulling Simi to sleep. He'd been sitting up texting with Mags, but when he heard Abe making his way around to the front of the house, he'd quickly allowed himself to lay down with his hood drawn over his eyes.

"Simi?" Abe had asked a few minutes earlier, but the teen didn't flinch.

If I'm not awake then he can't find something new to occupy my time with. If I'm sleeping, he can't talk to me. If I keep my eyes closed, I don't have to look at him or listen to him struggling to make me believe driving all the way up here was justified.

"Simi?" Abe spoke again, but this time more softly. "Got lunch whenever you're hungry."

Simi heard Abe sit down on the stairs nearby and thought he could make out the occasional chewing of what could only have been—acknowledging Abe's failings as a chef beyond the "bacon breakfast"—a peanut butter sandwich on white bread.

The phone in Simi's pocket vibrated, but he remained still. No need to disturb the ruse. He wanted his father to just leave him alone. He'd done enough already.

And Simi wasn't simply referring to their abscondence to Massachusetts. Abe's absence during the majority of his son's earliest years had left a stain on all the goodness and attempts at relationship rehabilitation that he seemed to feel obligated to bestow on his kid as of late. Simi knew it probably wasn't fair, but he couldn't help but frame everything the man did with a certain joylessness. He knew he was, in all likelihood, projecting his own doubt, but often found himself wondering whether Abel Ward would have preferred to be back with his buds and his suds. Simi knew the old crew still attempted to contact his father—he'd witnessed Abe staring blankly at his phone after an alert— but, thus far, it appeared they hadn't been able to steer him off course.

And yet…

Simi peeked an eye out from underneath his hoodie. Abe indeed was sitting, staring out at the road, chomping on a sad little sandwich. The blah meal reflected the man. As much as he desired to make up for everything he'd screwed Simi out of, it was blatantly obvious there was still something suffocating him, stifling whatever chance he had left.

Simi rolled over so that his back was facing the street and immediately regretted it. Black mold, that he'd somehow managed to miss entirely upon sitting down, slithered down the backside of the cushioned swing. Its webbed tentacles swarmed much of the pink-flowered pattern that'd once warmly welcomed visitors up Elma Ward's stairs. Without hesitation, Simi leapt up.

Immediately, Abe heard his alarm and turned around.

"Hey," Abe said, looking up onto the porch as Simi

brushed at his pants and the back of his hoodie. "You alright there?"

Simi unzipped his jacket and tossed it onto the ground. "I'm fine."

"You sure?" Abe squinted at him. When he got no response, he added, holding out a small tinfoil-wrapped package, "Lunch?"

Simi sat down, leaning his back against the doorway—intentionally, as to avoid looking up at the knocker that was undoubtedly judging him from overhead. "I'm good," was all he chose to give.

Abe opened his mouth to protest, half-chewed peanut butter and bread-bits sprinkling down his chin, when a brown Bronco with mustard yellow paneling and trim pulled up in front of them. Simi and Abe both looked at the driver, waiting for the man to emerge, but he did not. A yellow sticker on the side of the vehicle identified the visitor: Foxborough Animal Control.

A shadowed figure within leaned to roll down his passenger side window as Abe approached.

"Mitchell?" was all that Abe said.

The man shouted over his rather loud muffler, the engine still running. "Yessir. So, where's this head?"

Right to the point.

Abe walked back beside the staircase, bent over, and withdrew a small ball of tinfoil.

You have got to be sh—

"Got it for you right here." As he unwrapped it, Simi's jaw hung open at its father's peculiar decision.

Wrapping both our lunches and that dead thing at the same time, with the same stuff? Holy shit, Abe, even for you that's bold.

The man in the truck leaned forward and said something inaudible. Abe shook his head and pointed to his ears.

"You mind cutting the engine?"

The man looked back at him, hesitating for a moment, before obliging.

"Thank you," Abe said. "So, what were you saying?"

The man in the car removed his foam-domed hat and then returned it to his head. Simi could see the sweat mark banding around the temple. He was older than Abe, Simi thought, but not by much. A bushy orange beard and a matching ponytail, only ever-so-slightly flecked with grey, told very much the same story. Before speaking again, the man pulled a pack of cigarettes from his shirt pocket and popped one into his mouth, allowing it to hang lazily from between his lips. Casually, he flicked at a butane lighter until the stick glowed. Simi looked to Abe and wasn't surprised to see his dad's nostrils flare as the man with the trucker cap blew mouth-exhaust into his face. Abe didn't otherwise flinch.

"Well," the man finally spoke after a few long drags. "You definitely got a fisher right there."

Abe looked down at the beast grinning up from its bed of aluminum. "Without a doubt?"

The man, Mitchell, nodded. "Without a doubt."

Abe shifted and looked back apprehensively to Simi, before continuing the conversation. "And what, may I ask, could do this to a fisher?"

Mitchell half-laughed, half-coughed, half-wheezed. He smacked himself in the chest until the spasms, or whatever they were, calmed. "Bobcat could, I 'spose."

Abe nodded and smiled. "Yeah, yeah. A bobcat." He again looked to Simi's perch. "My son read pretty much the same thing. I guess it's just good to have some sort of answer and, well, now my biggest question would just be—"

"But that wasn't a bobcat that did that." Mitchell cut

him off and inhaled half the cigarette, right then, in one breath.

Abe froze and Simi immediately noticed his father was stuck. Coming to the rescue, he hopped down the staircase but still kept a healthy distance. The man in the truck was visibly uncomfortable being there and Simi recognized that too much of an inquisition might spook the guy. Keeping this in mind, the teen carefully considered his words. "And how would you know that? I mean, you just said that a bobcat could—"

Again, the animal control officer interrupted. He wanted the conversation to finish up. "Look, what I'm telling you both is that a bobcat *could* kill a fisher. But, what I'm also certain of, is that this little shit—" he wagged a hairy-knuckled finger at the petrified face, "wasn't so lucky."

Simi swallowed loudly and imagined he could hear Abe doing the same. "I'm sorry," he again beat his father to the punch. "But how can you say this guy was… *lucky*? Its head got ripped off."

Mitchell stuck his keys in the ignition. The engine sprang to life and he flicked his finished cigarette out onto the pavement. "I can tell you folks are nice enough and that you mean well. But," and again he adjusted his sweaty cap. "You're new around here. Believe me when I tell you, it wasn't a bobcat that done that."

He started to pull away, but Abe finally came back to life. He grabbed the open window, forcing Mitchell to delay his departure. "Wait a sec. I haven't exactly been around much in recent years, but I'm not new either. I grew up here. In this house. What exactly are you trying to tell me?"

Mitchell screwed up his eyes to look closer at Abe. "You're a Ward?"

Simi looked at his father and then looked back at the

man whose unease appeared to suddenly increase.

Abe nodded slowly, unsure if the correct answer would be helpful or not. "I am. Abel Ward."

Mitchell locked eyes with him for a moment. He was scrutinizing the man holding on to his car, though for what reason Simi couldn't fathom. Eventually, he let his foot off the brake and the vehicle, despite Abe's grip on it, began to roll away. "You wanna know what did that?" he asked as he started to pick up speed. "You go talk to Elma. No one, and I mean no one, can preach this gospel to you better than she can." His eyes got wide, terrified, even as the house appeared in his rearview mirror. "Please, be careful."

And then he stepped on the gas and his truck lurched away. Before either of them could respond, it disappeared down the road, into the early afternoon shadows, the animal control officer's warning hanging in the air behind him like the noxious cloud it was.

Twenty Two

Before pulling out of the driveway, Abe turned the radio on and jumped as he was immediately greeted by rasping, angry, static. He cursed and realized that he'd kept it off for nearly the entire second half of their trek up the coast. He'd last left the dial on *his* bluegrass station, which definitely wouldn't have had the frequency to reach itself up to New England. He spent a minute scanning the local waves until he found what he was hoping for. A college radio program, apparently based out of Salem, was entertaining its listeners with the stylings of a talented banjologist who—according to the jockey—was performing that night at some local dive. He let himself sink a bit into the torn leather seat and drown in the strumming and the picking of the young clawhammer.

    His hands gripped the steering wheel and he was suddenly reminded of why he'd jumped into his truck in the first place.

    You're gonna take a drive downtown. Talk to the sheriff.

He shifted out of park and let himself roll into the street.

That guy says it's not a bobcat. Well, okay then.

Abe waved at Simi, still sulking on the porch, as he moved down Brown Street. The brooding hoodie-wearer stared back at him, but did not acknowledge his father's departure. Abe ignored the awkward cold shoulder like he always did.

Must've been those dumb kids then. Shouldn't be drinking back there in the first place. Private property and all that. No doubt they found the poor thing and…

He didn't allow himself to finish the thought. Imagining kids torturing an animal, even a nasty critter like a fisher cat, made him cringe. With Ward House still looming large behind him, he passed a graveyard on his right. "Burial ground" would have actually been a more appropriate term for the hallowed area. The small plot of land raised up and off of the road, looked down its nose at him as he cruised by. Adorning the top of the rise was a low rock wall, which barricaded a garden of small, worn-down, and often completely halved, 18th century-era markers. Abe recalled wandering up there once, in his youth, and being particularly alarmed by the bevy of engraved grinning skulls and accompanying crossbones, little watching cherubs, and of the general stillness that met him on that day. In particular, he remembered stopping beside one tiny stone. Based on the etchings that were still legible, young Abe had deciphered that the deceased must have been a child, no older than he was at the time. And he'd never forgotten the stated cause of death.

"…by dog bite," had just barely been decodable.

As he turned left off of Brown and north onto North St. (surprise, surprise), heading toward the center of town,

Abe wondered if that grave marker had since crumbled. Had the relatively short span of time, thirty or so years since he'd last seen it, changed all that much? Without another instant of consideration, he decided that he didn't want to know. Didn't *need* to know. In any case, ghosts didn't age.

Do they?

Abe drove, the low twangings on the selected radio station his personal soundtrack. A few minutes later, he arrived at the town hall. The massive grey building looked just as old as it had to him as a kid. It served as a general, "everything" building, and was where the sheriff had his primary office. Abe pulled into a parking spot and lifted himself out of the vehicle.

He slammed the door shut and looked across the road. The shell of one of his favorite establishments, stood abandoned. Clay's Video Palace, now nothing more than a discarded carcass of kickass memories, was all boarded up. Remarkably, considering its location near the very center of town, nothing else had moved in or taken up residence there. He'd no idea when it'd officially closed but, by the look of things, it hadn't been anytime recently. The "a", "c", and "e" were even missing from "Palace" and the depressing landmark now simply read "Clay's Video Pal".

"Many a Friday night in there," Abe sighed. "Goddammit. Is nothing sacred?"

He turned and walked up to the massive front door of the town hall. One of the large oak doubles stood open wide and Abe recalled that was what typically happened, back in the day, anytime the heat was on too high. Considering the unseasonably warm October afternoon, he wondered if the building still played by those same rules.

He took a step inside and immediately realized he was correct.

A woman with an almost-pink perm fanned herself with a trashy romance novel; the shirtless man on its cover, his torso covered in library-laminate, reflected the abrasive, fluorescent, overhead lighting. Abe cleared his throat when she didn't immediately look up and welcome him.

"Yes?" was all she said.

"Ah, yes," Abe tried to sound as polite and composed as possible. Years experience of needing to constantly prove to people that you're not day-drunk or high will do that. "I was wondering if the sheriff is in today. I have to report, well, I have to report some kids hanging out on my property." He checked himself. "My *great-aunt's* property."

The pink-haired lady continued to wave the paperback at herself and the lenses of her tortoise-shell glasses collected Abe's reflection as well as her apathy.

"And who's your great-aunt?" she asked, the boredom painted across her overly rouged cheeks.

Abe cleared his throat. "Elma Ward."

The shirtless man on the book cover stopped waving. She placed her makeshift fan on the desk and immediately reached for the phone beside her. She pressed a red button and a voice on the other line picked up, annoyed at being interrupted. "Yes, Deborah?"

The woman's voice shook. "Will. Mind comin' out here? Gentleman here says he'd like to talk to you."

"Deb, I'm kind of in the middle of something import—"

"Says he's Elma Ward's nephew."

For a brief instant, Abe wondered if the man would even respond. Eventually, he did. "Be right out."

Abe didn't have a moment to scratch his head before a door behind the receptionist swung open. A man in a blue Hawaiian shirt and khaki short-shorts busted out. His hair, like the animal control officer's, was also bright orange. He stuck out his hand.

"Will Candler," he said. "And you're—"

"Abel Ward," Abe said. "Back after many years gone."

Candler put his hands on his hips. "Well, I'll be damned. Didn't realize there were any Wards still left— er, after Elma that is." He was smiling, but looked almost apoplectic. Beads of anxiety-induced sweat formed on his forehead, but he didn't seem to notice. "What, ah, what brings you back?"

Abe described to him what Simi had seen out behind the house, with the gaggle of teens drinking in the woods, and then, also, the discovery of the decapitated fisher cat. The sheriff looked at him like he wasn't making the connection.

"I think the kids might have done this, Sheriff."

Candler nodded. "Guess you could be right," he laughed nervously. "In any case, those boys shouldn't be hanging round there. No sirree, Bob."

"That's right," Abe said. "I mean, I don't want us to get sued if something, ya know, happened to them out there."

The sheriff slapped him hard on the back. "Well, of course. Who would want that? I completely agree and anyone in your shoes would certainly respond in kind," he said, unconvincingly. "And ya know, those kids should know better."

Abe looked at him sideways. "About the drinking?"

The man's face flushed bright red. "Well, yes. Of course, of course. The drinking," he again laughed way too loudly. "Those hooligans. I'll have to have a chat with them. Talk to their parents too. Make sure this never happens again."

Abe turned to face him. "You know who they might be? The culprits?"

The sheriff nodded, feigning the severity of it all. "Oh yes, I have a very, *very*, good idea who might be to blame for this. But, ah, don't you worry." He led Abe to the doorway and nearly pushed him out into the parking lot. "Sheriff Candler's on the case!"

Abe turned to try and finish the conversation. "Well, I just want to make sure—"

"You won't be bothered by them again, Mr. Ward. That I can promise. Thanks for stopping by and…" he lowered his voice and his upper lip trembled. "Take care."

Then the open door, despite the heat and apparent lack of air conditioning, was shut tightly behind him. Almost unbelievably, Abe heard an audible lock on the other side.

He stood in shock staring back up at the door, before turning toward his truck. The old video rental store stood opposite the town hall, nonchalantly admonishing him as he did his walk of shame across the blacktop.

"Oh, shut up Clay's Video Pal." He opened his truck door, which creaked to greet him. "Just shut your goddamn, goofy, mouth."

Twenty Three

From the porch, Simi looked across the road at the adjacent farm stand and wondered how long it had been abandoned. Wide-open fields behind it suggested that there once had been an active farm of some kind, but the former cropland was now nothing more than an untended pasture. Long grasses as tall as he was, swayed in a light breeze. When he squinted his eyes, Simi could just make out the grinning face of a forsaken scarecrow, left to fend for itself against the wild crows who'd perhaps years prior gotten past their fears of him and now pecked at his unseeing eye-holes; its ability to strike terror in the black-winged harbingers now as lifeless as he was.

The front door opened behind him. Daisy stepped outside, drying her hands on a salmon-colored towel. "Well, hey there," she said, surprised to find him and undoubtedly unsure of how to converse with the teen.

Simi removed his hood in an attempt to make himself

appear somewhat more approachable. "Hey, Ms. Peltzer."

She held up a hand, one eyebrow raising itself significantly higher than the other. "So, I'm gonna stop you right there. I've *never* been Ms. Peltzer. Let's not age me like that, okay?" She laughed. "Daisy or D is fine."

Simi craned his neck to see her better, but she was backlit by a dull yellow emanating from the foyer of the house. At first, he thought she was looking at him but soon realized her gaze was pointed down the road.

"He's gone to town, I guess." Simi filled in, surmising what she was wondering. "Not sure when he'll be back."

She stepped further out until her features were more visible in the light. There was a smudge on her cheek, a leftover from whatever she'd been cooking, and she caught him staring. "I miss something?" she asked, swiping at her face. "Honestly, I just caught a look at myself in the bathroom mirror. Gravy splattered everywhere. Thought I'd gotten it all."

Simi smiled back. "Just a little. You're fine though."

Daisy nodded, but, as she peered again down Brown Street, raised the towel to her cheek once more. She caught him staring at her staring. "Oh, well, not sure what he needs up that way. Probably should have talked to me first. Could have warned him."

Simi moved over to make room for her, and she lowered herself onto the ground beside him. She too avoided sitting on the moldy swing. "Warned him? About what, exactly?"

Daisy folded and unfolded her towel a few times. "That anyone he'd find at town hall is essentially useless. Not sure what he wants, but they sure as hell aren't gonna give it to him."

"So, like, normal small-town bureaucracy?"

She turned toward him, mouth agape, in mock astonishment. "And how would you, Simeon Ward, know anything of small-town bureaucracies? You, from the mean streets of Hotlanta?"

He scratched his nose, smirking, enjoying the positive attention from an adult other than Abel. "I mean, isn't that the way it always is? I read, watch a lot of movies. Every place like this has its ways and eccentricities. And any town that's given this creepy chateau safe-haven for hundreds of years has got to have its quirks. Its stories. It's *mysteries*."

She nudged him with an elbow and winked. "You're much cooler than your old man, you know that?" She snorted at some personal joke. "And you're also right. This place," She looked around at the trees rooted near the front of the property, the lampposts, the farm across the road, and the crows perched in the field. "This place certainly has its fair share of riddles."

Before Simi could ask for details, a laboring muffler made its presence known a distance down the road. They both turned toward the sound and neither was surprised to see the aging pickup chugging down the empty street.

"Riddles," Daisy said quietly to herself, watching the truck come to a stop. Abe hopped out and rested his forearms on the roof, staring quizzically at the pair sitting on the front deck.

"Good to see you two bonding," he said, though seemed unsure if his observation was accurate.

Daisy stood and draped her towel over a shoulder. "Is that what we were doing?" She looked to Simi who shrugged and then back to Abe. "I'm guessing whatever you went into town for remains unresolved?"

Abe walked around the front of the truck and approached the stairs. "Well, not exactly. I mean, I reported the teens drinking out back but..." he trailed off.

"You tell 'em who you are?"

Simi looked back and forth between the two of them. *Why wouldn't he tell them who he is?*

Abe cleared his throat. "Well, yah. And, that was... interesting. Couldn't have predicted the kind of reaction I got."

Daisy was unmoved, still staring down at him. "Oh, no? Really, Abe? I would have seen this coming a mile away if I were you. The first Ward in generations and you're surprised at their behavior? Goodness, I guess you really have been gone a long time."

Simi spoke up. "Daisy, why would they care that he is a Ward?"

Abe's jaw tightened. "Yeah, Daisy. Why *would* they care?" He asked the question, but Simi wondered if he already had the answer.

"Like I said, Simi. *Riddles*. This town's full of 'em." She turned and looked back in through the open doorway. "And none, I'd wager, is as big a puzzle as this house." She waved a hand to the sky. "And this land."

Abe put his hands into his pockets and hung his head. Simi watched, waiting for him to refute in some way, the strangeness of Daisy's comments. "Don't tell me Elma's still got this entire community under her spell? We're living in the twenty-first century for godsakes. Don't tell me we're still dealing with this madness, D."

She backed herself into the house. "Got some cooking still to do before I head out." She hesitated, perhaps considering if Abe would stop her, or try to continue the conversation, but he didn't. After a moment, she sighed and shut the door hard behind herself.

Simi looked at his father, whose head was pendulous

again, swinging toward the earth. "Abe, what was that all about?"

Abe climbed the stairs and sat down on the swing, oblivious to the mold. Simi opened his mouth to say something, but then snapped it shut. "What you have to understand is that this town is... ah, I don't know. They're a bit superstitious. When I was young, Elma fed into a lot of that. Told a lot of stories. I guess, when you've been around as long as she has, your tales tend to take on some life. They spread. People believe them." He locked eyes with Simi. "Just because the folks here in Foxborough tiptoe around her, doesn't mean we have to. You understand?"

Simi shook his head. "Um, no. No, I don't understand any of what you are saying."

Abe slapped Simi on the back. "'Sallright, Sim. Probably better that way. I left here wanting to be done with all of this, *hating* her for making me feel like I had to. With the small amount of time she's got left, I don't want to tarnish her for you."

Simi laid flat on his back, his legs hanging awkwardly down the stairs. "Abe, I haven't even met her yet. What does it matter if you both are going to keep her hidden upstairs?"

Abe looked across the street at the scarecrow. "Well, you *will* meet her. Soon enough. We got here late yesterday and today's been busy. But soon, when she's lucid, I'll formally introduce you."

Simi folded his hands behind his head and stared up at the underbelly of the wooden awning that hung over the porch. Scrawled on a tired piece of wood that quite likely hadn't seen sunlight or anything else in over a hundred years, were two words.

Welcome, Ward.

He stared at it. "Well, isn't that nice?"

Abe, misunderstanding the sentiment, continued. "Yeah, well I think it will be. She will want to meet you. It's important. And it's not every day you get to meet actual, *living,* history."

Simi sat up, already forgetting the inscription, eager to change the subject. "By the way, you reported those kids?"

Abe nodded.

"Great. That's just great. Probably gonna get my ass kicked now for ratting them all out."

"Well," Abe said, wrapping an arm around his son. "Fortunately, we got a ton of work to do. I don't know how you'll find time to get your ass kicked." He stood up and walked back into the house.

Simi sat briefly in silence, before turning and shouting in through the doorway.

"That supposed to make me feel better?"

He didn't get an answer and eventually lifted himself, fully intending to follow his father. Just as he began to turn, his eyes caught sight of something that'd changed on the landscape in front of him. For a moment, his breath caught in his throat, until he forced himself to choke it down. Raising a hand as a visor, shielding his eyes from the sun, Simi looked across the street.

Standing in the field, now swaying ever so gently, was the scarecrow. It waved to him, rocking from some unseen force, its head completely missing from its straw, sun-bleached, overall-wearing, torso.

Twenty Four

The top tread came up easily and Abe chucked it down to Simi. The boy stood at the bottom of the staircase and scowled—a sophisticated demonstration of teenage annoyance with being held hostage by his father's sudden urge to spruce up the place.

"Do you honestly need me for this?" Simi whined.

Abe ignored him and spoke through the nails clamped between his teeth. "Hey, pass me that other board, will ya?"

Simi did as he was told, but made no offer to take initiative or aide his father in any other way.

"That's not going to last, you know that?" Simi judged from below.

His father kept his head bowed, sweat beading on his nose until it dripped on the replacement stair top. Behind him, the enormous gate painting towered, framing Abe's resolve in between its floral draped bars. "It's a patch, man. Nothing more. I just don't want anyone's foot to go through this thing, that's all." He pounded a nail into the flimsy wood and then removed a second from his mouth. "We'll need to make a stop at the hardware store anyway, to get some supplies. Everything I find here is almost useless. Even the tools are really—"

"Ancient?"

Abe stopped, his hammer in mid-air. "Wait, you've seen some? Where? I can't find much of anyth—"

"In the shed. Bunch of weirdo tools, or… *something*. Probably right up your alley."

Abe thwacked another nail in and then placed the hammer down. "What'd you see in there? Anything functional?"

Simi sat down on the bottom stair and turned his back to his old man. "I don't know. Looked like a freaking torture chamber in there. Can't imagine what a person might use any of that for."

Abe descended to ground level and wiped a sleeve across his glistening head. "Show me."

Simi closed his eyes and let his head drop between his legs. "What, like now?"

Abe looked around. "Um, yeah now. You got something better to do? Somewhere else to be?"

Simi sighed, "I can think of so many places I'd prefer to be right now. Is that a joke?"

Abe grabbed him by both of his shoulders and half-lifted him into a standing position. "Alright, alright. Just lead the way. Haven't been out there myself since I was your age. Can't imagine what Elma might be storing in those things."

They cut through the kitchen and exited out the back of the house. Daisy was emptying the dishwasher when they walked past. She took a look at the two of them, but didn't ask what they were up to. Based on their previous interaction, Abe wasn't sure how much she'd even want to talk to him right then. There was something she wasn't saying and he could tell he was going to need to wait a while longer for her to get around to doing so.

Trudging across the still-unmown lawn, Abe let Simi lead. They came to a stop in front of the smallest, oldest looking of the out-buildings and Abe nearly choked on his own spit.

"What is this?" He pointed at the drawing on the building's door.

Simi folded his arms. "You expect me to know? Hello, Abe, I haven't been here before. Remember?"

Abe kept his mouth shut and turned back to the illustration. Something about it seemed familiar to him, but he couldn't recall what.

I've seen this before.

He brought his hand to the image and let his index finger trace around the small, hat-wearing figure, and then around the larger, more menacing one. Simi coughed and Abe shook himself free of his trance.

"Let's open her up."

He reached for the latch before Simi could and let the door swing open. There was scuttling inside, a rat perhaps ducking for cover. Abe let his eyes take a moment to adjust to the dim light.

Before stepping inside, he turned to find Simi had not joined him.

"You coming?" Abe called.

Simi shook his head. "Been there, done that."

Abe spun back to face the cadre of barbaric implements that hung before him. None were like anything he had ever used before or could identify by name.

And yet...

Something about the tools also stirred a memory burrowed away inside of him. He closed his eyes and an image formed of an older man holding the long, ragged one—the sword, Abe thought it was— out to him. Abe saw his own hands, smooth and absent of wrinkles, calluses, or the general wear of life, reach out and grasp the weapon. A voice, gravely and grave, intoned, "Always remember, Abel, what you are. What *we* are." He felt his chin grabbed and forced upward. "You must never forget."

Amos? What does this mean? I can't remember—

"Abe?"

He snapped himself around. Simi had entered the shed behind him after all. "You okay? Got a little quiet in here for a moment." He stared at Abe, who was cradling the cruel-looking tool. "Reconnecting with an old friend?"

Abe realized his mouth was hanging open. "Uh..." He paused, unable to express what he was feeling. "Something about this... I dunno. Stirring up something inside, I guess. Weird how memories can kind of percolate but not necessarily fully break through that fog. Ya know what I mean?"

Simi opened his eyes wide and pursed his lips. "No."

"Ah, well." Abe waved at him, distracted by what he was still holding on to. "Can't quite place this, but... think I've seen it before. A long, long time ago."

Simi stepped a bit closer and then flapped at a spider web that landed on his mouth. Sputtering he recovered. "Does that mean you know what it's used for?"

Abe returned the apparatus to its rusty hook. "Unfortunately, no. I mean, it sure looks like its main purpose is for....ah, *killing*. Doesn't it?" Simi didn't answer. "But, you got me. I don't know."

Simi walked deeper into the small place. "Killing? Killing, what, exactly? Do you mean, for like, *pest control?* Seems like a bit of stretch, doesn't it? And what about this other stuff? It's bizarre, right? Looks like it all came straight out of the dark ages or something."

Abe hefted a scythe-like device, the wooden handle of which had been sharpened to a point. "It does. These definitely aren't farming tools and are of no use to us with any of our repairs. And I can't imagine what sort of—*pests* these might control. Probably best to just leave this all right here." He turned to exit the shed. "Thanks for sharing your, ah, *find*. But, we better get back to work, Sim."

He stepped out into the sunlight and took a long, relieved breath.

Simi's footsteps crunched out behind him and Abe listened as the latch on the shed was fastened.

"Elma would know, though, right? She'd know what all of this is? Couldn't you just ask—?"

The concern on Abe's face as he looked up to the third level of the house, at the large window with its shades drawn, stopped Simi from finishing the question.

"Unfortunately, *yes*." He took a few steps toward the back porch and then turned to his son. "She would know. But I'm not sure we really want the answer."

Twenty Five

It was late.

Simi looked at the time on his phone as he waited for a response from Mags.

11:23.

Abe had long since called it a night, but Simi was up texting back and forth with his girlfriend. To avoid the unpleasant— and always watching— clown eyes that dominated his assigned bedroom, he'd decided to take the opportunity to explore. Alone. Two days into their little getaway, and there was so much of the house he still hadn't seen. No tour had ever been given and, similarly, no real restriction on where he could or could not venture to. Though his father had assured him that all of the indoor spaces were properly electrified, a few of the hallways still appeared completely void of any modern-day lighting and neither Abe nor Daisy had bothered to light candles in any of the corridors or off-shoots that veered off of the main arteries on each floor. There was a candelabra outside of his own bedroom, one beside Abe's door, and, based on the flickering light that danced at the top of the spiral staircase, another outside of what—he assumed—must have been Elma's quarters. Simi flicked on light switches as he came across him, but his quest that evening was still, generally speaking, a poorly lit one. Even so, the darkness didn't deter him. It usually didn't. Especially with the flashlight app on his phone, Simi felt himself without fear of the nooks and crannies and uncharted recesses of Ward House.

Simi looked upward—toward the source of the faint, coruscating, illumination—and began to climb the stairs.

Step by step he rose, without the squeaking of boards that were so familiar to and identifying of such old buildings. Simi noted the unusual quiet, and almost wished for the more predictable groanings and settlings from the night. Not that he was scared—Simi wasn't ever frightened by anything so simple as an appropriately aging house—but, he was susceptible to feeling sad when he was alone. Even though Mags was in the process of typing back to him, she was still in Georgia. So far away. Thousands of miles from where he currently lurked. Abe was asleep upstairs, stuck in the mire of his own confusion and—undoubtedly—restless and unforgiving dreams. For this reason, even an unexplained cracking or a whisper from within an unoccupied room would have been welcomed.

Or so Simi told himself.

Halfway up the stairwell, his screen lit up.

Mags Downing: have u even met her yet?

Simi typed a response within seconds.

Simi Ward: not yet. Haven't even stepped foot on the third floor yet. U think I should pay her a visit 2nite?

Mags Downing: be careful if you do. it's blood-sucking

time for vamps. bring yo garlic.
Simi Ward: lol. sorry, fresh out.
Mags Downing: don't be a creeper though, okay? Leave the ol' broad alone.
Simi Ward: I'm not spying if that's what you mean. just adventuring, Mags. If I happen by her room, then I happen by her room.

She answered by sending a laughing emoji with its tongue sticking sideways.

About to send a reply, Simi suddenly realized that, in his distraction, he'd made his way up to the third floor. He looked down the hallway, which stretched into an abyss of blackness in either direction. A few feet from the top stair, however, was a door left ajar.

Simi Ward: I'm here.

He waited for Mags' response and listened. At first, all he heard was his heartbeat pulsing out an accompanying, horror-movie, soundtrack. His allergies, after sleeping in his undusted bedroom, had left him completely congested. The effect was a strange echo in Simi's ears and the dull sound of blood pumping its way around inside of him.

Mags Downing: where?
Simi Ward: outside of Elma's room.
Mags Downing: you don't mess around huh? See anything?

And then he heard it. First, it was a placid whispering, like someone soothing a small child who'd awoken in the night. But the susurrant murmur soon melted into a giggling, which gradually became more frenetic.

Unbridled.

Mags was still typing, getting impatient that he hadn't responded to her, but Simi put the phone into his pocket. Carefully, with his hands now free, he placed both palms on the lacquered door and pressed his ear against the cool, musty-smelling, wood.

The tittering inside the bedroom continued. A voice, sapped of its strength, but not of its mirth, was exalting unresponsive subjects.

"Elma?" Simi tried to enunciate, but the words came out instead like a croak. The merriment and apotheosizing behind the door continued and he carefully pushed it open.

Simi gasped and nearly tripped over his trembling knees in acknowledgment of the tableau splayed out before him. Standing, silhouetted by the moon, on the roof ledge just outside her window, was a skeleton of a woman—her clothing, loose rags flittering in the crisp autumn air, mimicked the undulation of the skin under both of her arms as they reached toward the black night. Her cackling had reached its crescendo and Simi felt compelled to cover his ears. Her words, in their insanity, sounded tainted and he was afraid to listen.

"Take me!" she screamed toward the woods as a gust of wind howled past her. "I am ready and waiting! I descend now unto the earth so that you can finally reclaim what has been promised to you for so very long!" And then she tossed her head back and wailed. "Yeaaaahhhhhh!" She looked toward the ground and seemed to ready herself. The pitch of her cry forced Simi to keep one of his hands positioned at the side of his head, but he rushed to the window and grabbed at her, just before she leaned too far.

"Abe!" he yelled. "Abe, it's Elma! Come quick, I—"

The woman turned to him, her eyes bloodshot and enraged, tears streaking through the tributaries on her cheeks. "NO!" she cried. "It is MY time!" The tendons in her impossibly thin, parchment-paper-covered arms bulged and she clamped a hand around Simi's throat. Her voice deepened and transformed into a bestial growl that didn't seem to belong to her. "What must, *must*. What I become, so you shalllll. Together we fall, Simeon Ward!"

Elma began to drift out over the ledge, pulling Simi with her. At first, he believed he'd be able to overpower the woman and drag her back inside. Quickly, however, it became apparent that the sinewy arms of his great-great-aunt wielded a strength that belied the century they'd been marinating.

"Abe!" he shouted again. 'Help! I'm falling!"

Elma was hanging completely off the ledge and, with the hand not wrapped around Simi's throat, she clawed at him. At his face, his arms, his torso. Wherever she could connect. He felt the sting of her brittle talons, but somehow managed to brace himself against the frame of the window.

Oh, my god. I'm going to die. I'm going to fall and die and never see Mags again.

And just as he was about to topple out the window with Elma, a tattooed forearm reached out and engulfed them both.

Simi and Elma collapsed into the bedroom and landed on top of Abe.

Twenty Six

Elma's face was still damp and frozen in anguish as Abe pulled a blanket up to her chin. She did not speak, and her breathing was rapid and shallow. Her eyes were closed and she appeared to be asleep. Seconds prior, after moving the dried-up ragdoll off Simi, together father and son had managed to lift her into bed. Simi stood with his back to a closet door, massaging his neck, the impression of the old woman's fingers still lingering and indicating the placement of an all-but-certain bruise.

"Are you okay?" Abe asked, maintaining his position by the headboard.

Simi slumped down onto the floor. He grabbed a handful of his own hair and pulled it, absentmindedly, taught. "No. No, I'm not okay." His voice was hoarse and he continued to rub at his throat. "Not yet at least. I mean, I will be, but—*Jesus Christ*, Abe." He looked up at his dad. "Did you see that? What the hell was that? She tried to kill me!"

Abe looked back at the woman in the bed, her features slowly beginning to soften. Leaving her momentarily, he stepped to the window and quickly locked it. He pulled up on the frame to ensure it was secure. "I saw it." He rubbed the back of his head. "Just glad you're—well, I'm relieved that I got to you on time. She's a sick woman, Sim. That's what that was. Guess I gotta talk to D in the morning. We obviously need Elma to see a doctor."

Simi stood up and walked toward the door. "Yeah?" he smiled sarcastically. "Well, I'm *so* glad you're relieved. Your son nearly dies and you're—"

"Hey, that's not what I was—"

"She was calling for someone to 'take her', you know that? Said she was 'ready'. Any idea what that means?"

Abe crossed the room and attempted to hug his son, who allowed him to do so but also didn't reciprocate. Simi's arms hung, recalcitrant, at his sides. "I'm so, so sorry Sim."

Simi pushed him away. "I asked if you know what she was talking about? She nearly threw herself and me out the goddamn window. Something about 'reclaiming what was promised'. Is that—?"

"Just the rantings of a decaying mind. It's called *dementia*, Simi. Happens to some people when they get old. And she is very, *very* old." He looked back at Elma, making sure she was still quiet and resting. "Just find it remarkable this hasn't occurred sooner. Such a coincidence that you happened to be outside of her room, at the exact time she attempted this."

Simi grabbed the doorknob, his back to Abe. "Yeah, that was some introduction." He stepped out into the hallway. "Hey, I'm kind of exhausted now, but this is legit nuts and you should know I'm honestly not sure I'm gonna last here. It's getting to be way too much. For tonight, I guess I'm just gonna go lay down, but tomorrow we should probably talk." He shook his head. "Do you still need me at this moment or—?"

"No, I'm good." Abe walked back to the bed. "You get some sleep. And again, I'm sorry about this."

Simi grunted and disappeared, out of view of the doorway.

Abe turned to Elma and instinctively jumped back.

Her eyes were open wide and she was smiling up at him. "Abel," she rasped.

Getting over the shock of finding her suddenly awake again, he gingerly lowered himself to the ground, kneeling beside her. "Elma. Are you okay? You nearly killed my son. Hanging out that window like that—what were you even thinking?"

Her grin did not dissipate. She cooed at him. "Oh, I know you don't understand. You still don't remember the ritual. The rules we must follow. I know you've forgotten." She reached up and cupped his cheek with a wrinkled paw. Yes, yes, it's been *so* long." She gave his face a gentle tap. "I don't blame you."

"Elma, I told you I—"

"Oh, hush now," she waved at him weakly. "I know you told me. But that doesn't change a thing." She turned and looked back out the window. "You may have stopped this from happening tonight, but they *are* waiting." She inhaled deeply and held her breath for so long Abe wondered if her frail lungs might pop like a couple of over-inflated party balloons. "And I'm ready."

"Elma—"

"And it doesn't matter what you say. Regardless of anything you do or believe, soon enough—very soon— it will be time anyway. I've waited my whole life for this, Abel."

She closed her eyes, the smile fading slightly. "There is no stopping it. *Them.* My Malevolent Nevers. Their gate will be unlocked, once more, and I must walk through it." She gripped his elbow, suddenly, while continuing to keep her eyes shut. "You must not try and prevent this."

Abe brushed free a few strands of grey that'd fallen in front of her eyes. Her face was still damp from her earlier tears and he used the back of his hand to dry them. "Elma, I—" he was going to tell her again how he didn't understand any of what she was saying, but decided to hold his tongue. There was no rationalizing the twisted thoughts of the dying.

Better to just let her think what she wants. It'll all be over soon enough.

"Okay, Elma," he conceded. "Whatever you say."

Her head bobbed, gently—evidently satisfied with his promise. "Good," she whispered. "That's my good boy."

He stroked her hair a few more times, waiting to see if she would finally fall asleep. After a little while of sitting in silence, listening to her increasingly belabored breathing, he stood up from the bed. He'd taken only a few steps away from her when she spoke again, her words scraping up against the momentary calm that he'd somehow convinced himself to trust.

Elma's voice wobbled, sometimes too soft and sometimes too loud, as if she weren't in complete control of its modulation or volume. "Six days, Abel." She croaked. "Within six days it must…" she trailed off, her eyes fluttering.

He returned to the woman's bedside and touched her shoulder gently. "Elma?" Abe tried to rouse her. "What must happen within six days? What six days?"

"…after death." She continued, a piece of what she'd been trying to tell him lost to her inability to remain alert and awake. "After that…" she kept fading in and out of consciousness, her words interconnected and confusing to Abe's ears. "…would be too late. All lost."

Abe tapped her arm again. "Elma? Please, I'm not sure what you're trying to say—"

"Six days, Abel," she wheezed and began to sink into her pillow. "Six daaaaysss…"

"Elma?" Abe shook her, but she didn't respond. Her eyes no longer flittered and were instead squeezed tightly shut. "Elma?"

She didn't move. He watched her for a few more minutes, just to make certain she was still breathing. He could hear her wheeze with every inhalation and wondered if each gasp for air would be her last.

After a time, Abe picked himself up and sunk into the bedside chair. He folded his arms on top of his chest and watched the old lady sleep, on guard in case she decided, once more, to try and throw herself out of the third-story window above the waiting, godforsaken, swamp.

Twenty Seven

Barachiel the Clown was sitting up on Simi's bed, waiting for him, as he entered the room. The teen lurched to a stop, shuddering.

Nope.

After hesitating initially, Simi grabbed the monstrosity and tossed it and its grinning face back into the still-open dresser drawer. He stared back at the bed, over to the door, and then back at the stuffed freak's closed chamber.

Very funny, Abe. Real cute.

The thought went through his brain before he had a chance to discount it. Abe didn't play jokes. It just wasn't in his nature, never mind the fact that he was more than a bit distracted with the house and Elma.

Maybe Daisy stopped in to do some tidying?

He shrugged and stretched out on the bed to check his texts. There were fourteen missed messages from Mags wondering what was going on, half of which simply read,

"???". He scrolled down to her last note, which was sent nearly ten minutes earlier.

Mags Downing: well I hope ur ok… I'm heading to bed. Talk to u in the morning.

Simi didn't bother to respond. He knew she usually turned her ringer off at night and, besides, wouldn't have wanted to wake her. There'd be plenty of time to discuss that evening's ridiculousness the next day. Feeling like he just wanted to call it a night, he kicked off his chucks and slinked his feet under the matching sheets and comforter, which were decorated in an old-timey fortune-teller pattern. An image of a large purple crystal ball, with two spindly, long-nailed, hands hovering over it, shimmered in a repeating sequence, alternating with an image of yet another clown face. Simi endeavored once again to ignore the abnormalities that were plastered all around the space. He reached toward his bedside table and pulled the metal string on the lamp, the body of which was a clown torso. A red shade sat on the faceless jester's shoulders, obscuring what was hidden underneath.

Simi closed his eyes.

She's a sick woman, huh? He laughed out loud. *Seemed pretty damn strong to me.*

It wasn't long before sleep began to overtake him and Simi didn't attempt to fight it.

'We obviously need her to see a doctor.' Yeah, okay, Abe. What she really needs is a…

But he didn't finish the thought before slipping into a pleasant dream. He was with Mags, sitting outside their old movie theater again. *Glitter Zombies 2: Return of the Glitter*, was their date night flick and had surprised the two of them by being much better than the first. *Though that bar was set pretty freaking low.* Abe was late of course, which was fine with him.

All the more time for—

Simi sat up straight in bed.

Something had awoken him. A harrowing screech from outside. He held his breath and did not move, waiting for the sound to assail his ears once more.

Again, a primal wailing pierced the darkness of his cramped clown-covered enclosure.

It's coming from behind the house.

He threw his legs over the side of the bed and crept to the window. The moon was still bright, though somehow not as dazzling as it had been in cloaking Elma earlier that evening. And yet, he could still clearly see most of the backyard and the sheds. The marsh, itself, however, was pitch dark. The light seemed to somehow halt where the murk and the muck began, afraid to trespass onto or over the fetid, unhallowed, sludge.

The awful lament again caught Simi by surprise and he ducked his head, reflexively. He waited for another call and—when he didn't immediately hear one—cautiously unlatched the window and poked his face out. His cheeks were greeted by a surprisingly warm, tropical breeze, and his nostrils immediately caught a whiff of decay in the air. With the back of his hand, he covered his nose and peered into the gloom.

Something moved in the brush behind one of the sheds—or at least that's where he thought the sound came from, it was impossible to see beyond the reach of the moonlight— and, from the opposite side of the house, there was an audible scrambling up the trunk of a tree. Bits of bark and branches fell to the earth under the weight of whatever creature scaled the enormous pine and Simi couldn't instantly picture what animal native to New England—he envisioned it rather large, based on the noise— could climb with such speed and ease.

An object smacked into the backside of the house, just underneath his window. He flinched, but could see nothing in the shadows skirting the perimeter of the foundation.

And then he heard it.

Not another scream— at least not entirely. This outcry was still just as depraved, but he could almost swear—

No, it can't be.

He could almost swear that he heard—

That's impossible.

A name on the wind.

He froze, his arms holding the open window, ready to slam it shut if necessary. He waited, on edge, for what he hoped wouldn't repeat.

"Elmaaaaaaaaa."

The voice gurgled and sloshed on inhuman vocal cords, from the blackness. First, he heard it behind a shed and then—

"Elmaaaaaaaaa."

—from just under the ledge he was leaning out of. The skin on every inch of his body crawled. Simi threw the window shut and launched himself back into the room. In an instant, he was under his blankets, with only a fortune teller and a clown protecting him from whatever lurked in the woods…

…and from whatever called to him— or rather, to Elma— in the dead of that abhorrent night.

Twenty Eight

A door slammed closed somewhere below. Abe stirred, trying to readjust to a position more considerate of his aching lower back. By the sound of it, someone was humming and puttering around in the kitchen on the first floor. Even with his eyes closed, Abe could sense the warmth of the early morning sun. Daisy had surely just arrived to start her daily tasks. He wondered if finding him sitting—asleep—beside Elma's bed, might startle his old flame. It was too early to worry, though, and he didn't have the energy to immediately rouse himself.

He listened as Daisy climbed the stairs. She placed something in the lone bathroom, one door away, and he heard her exit into the hallway. The doorknob to the bedroom turned and he heard her hesitate as she stepped across the threshold. No doubt she hadn't expected to find him there.

Tiptoeing she approached the bed.

After a moment, she gasped.

Abe's eyes opened, just as she knelt to wake him. Her hand touched his shoulder and he let her think he'd been sleeping the whole time.

"Mornin', D. Betcha surprised to find me—"

"It's happened, Abe."

He sat up straight, at first struggling to understand what she meant. Peeking his shoulder over hers, he realized the only thing she could have possibly been referring to. Even still, he asked, just to be sure.

"What, D? Tell me."

Daisy swallowed. "Elma," she whispered, dampness now clearly visible in the corner of both eyes. "Elma's gone."

Abe looked toward the silent shape only feet away. He took in a deep breath, almost as if doing so one last time *for* her, and then nodded. He stood to face the spectacle, with Daisy hanging gingerly on one elbow.

"Take your time," she said mistaking the hesitation for him not wanting to approach the deceased. She thought he was staring at his aunt, when in fact his gaze was focused elsewhere.

If she'd looked closer, Daisy would have realized that Abe wasn't looking at Elma at all, but rather, past her. *Beyond.*

Out her window.

Into the bogs.

Toward the quagmire he feared now awaited him.

Twenty Nine

"How do you take it?"

Simi looked up at Daisy, who was fixing him a cup of coffee. He'd taken to drinking the stuff earlier that year, more out of convenience than anything else. At first, he didn't exactly enjoy the taste, but Abe almost always had a pot brewing. Even on nights when Simi came home well after midnight, he'd often find his father sitting alone at the table, under their depressingly-gaudy, Eighties-era chandelier, sipping from his "I Love Bluegrass" mug. Each and every time, Abe would offer him his own. Eventually, Simi got tired of saying no.

And now I can't quit it.

He shook his head at Daisy, politely. "Nothing, actually, I'm good. That's fine. Thanks."

"Nothing? A man after my own heart."

Simi again thanked her and took a sip. "It's good." He placed the mug on the table, but left his hands warming on its ceramic outside. "Hey, why don't you sit down. It's been a—"

"Pssh," she shrugged him off and continued to instead fixate on whatever was in the sink. The water ran and the rising steam caused a few loose strands of hair to stick to her sweaty forehead. She blew at them, but her bangs were plastered to the deep creases that became even more profound as she worked. "Better I keep busy. It's when I stop that I start thinking about things."

Simi took another sip and decided not to push her. He looked out through the sliding glass door at his father, who was in the midst of an animated phone call. With one hand, the man held his cell to his ear and with the other he waved at the heavens, repeatedly clenching a frustrated fist. Whoever he was talking to at the funeral home was not telling him what he wanted to hear. Abe stepped off the porch step, but then immediately changed course and bounded back up in the direction of the glass door, as if doing so might aid in his rebuttal to the individual on the other end of the line. He looked inside at his son and let his shoulders sag, an illustration of his exasperation.

Simi lifted his cup in support, though immediately wondered if it looked like he was toasting his father's anguish. He took another slurp of the hot, brown, beverage and his own phone buzzed. He glanced down at it.

Mags Downing: hey sim. So sorry I missed your texts. Really sorry to hear the news too. R u ok?

Simi sighed and braced himself for her reaction to what he was about to type.

Simi Ward: no worries. I'm fine, Mags. And hey, guess this means I might be coming back home sooner rather than later now. Right?

There was a long pause before Mags responded. Eventually, Simi could see that she'd started typing again.

Mags Downing: …I guess, Sim. But you should be prepared. These things can take a lot of time to sort out. Especially since you're her only real relatives, ya know? Might take longer than you think.
Simi Ward: I guess…
Mags Downing: do you need anything? I can have a package overnighted?

    Simi chuckled to himself, hopeful that Daisy wouldn't hear him over the running water and clanging pots.
Simi Ward: you know that we're up in Massachusetts right? It's… not exactly a third-world country here.
Mags Downing: k. well let me know. I'm worried about you.

    Simi took another glug.
Simi Ward: …
Mags Downing: what?
Simi Ward: why are you worried about me?
Mags Downing: c'mon Sim. This is the most time you've spent with Abe in 4 eva. Also, your aunt did just die. Death his hard. Even if you didn't really know her.
Simi Ward: she's not my aunt.
Mags Downing: whatever. You great-great-aunt. Did I get that right now?
Simi Ward: how the hell should I know? This is all so weird.
Mags Downing: I know it is. I miss u.
Simi Ward: miss u too.

    He placed the phone face down and swallowed the rest of his coffee. Abe was still pacing, but his free hand was now resting on a hip.

    Maybe the conversation is taking a turn for the better?

    He was about to stand and walk his mug to the sink when Abe suddenly kicked an empty planter into the yard and yelped as his toes realized how poor a decision that'd been. Daisy turned, acknowledging the noise, and dried her hands on a free towel. She took a few steps toward the door and then stopped, whirling to face Simi.

"You should go check on him, ya know? Be with the man. He's…" She looked outside, in the direction of another of Abe's yelps. "…he's having a rough day."

Simi rinsed his mug and then placed it into the dishwasher. "I don't exactly know how to *be there* for Abe. He wasn't the best model of that sort of thing for me. Like father like—"

"I'm sorry," she interrupted. "But, that's bullshit."

Simi froze, his hands halfway done drying on a paper towel. He crumpled it up and disposed of the trash. "Uh, what—"

"I said that's *bullshit*." She smirked at his mouth hanging open. "What, Simeon Ward, still too young to hear the bad words?" She sat down at the table and gestured for him to do the same. Slowly Simi obliged, positioning himself directly opposite Daisy. "That man," she pointed over her shoulder, "has spent a lifetime making excuses and running away from his problems. Don't use him as cover for yourself or attempt to ride those tragic coattails. Don't make his mistakes over again. He is trying to right this ship, best he can. You've got years and years to do it all better than he has. Best to start now."

"You don't understand—"

"No, I don't," she finished for Simi. "And I don't claim to. I didn't experience the last thirty years with him. All I can say is that I know who he was when he left and I can still see faint glimpses of that person now, for better or worse. Regardless of how inept he was in your earlier years, he's still your dad and it's clear—from what I've seen since you both arrived here—that he loves you. I'm not asking you to forgive all his sins for godsakes, but the man just lost his only living relative, other than yourself. He could use some help. That's all." She put her hands up in the air as if law enforcement had just instructed her to do so.

Simi exhaled. He hadn't realized he'd been holding his breath throughout her entire speech.

Where'd all that come from?

After a brief pause, he locked eyes with her. "I'll check on him, alright?"

A glimpse of a smile danced on one side of her lips, but Daisy quickly tried to hide it. "Okay then. But don't do it for me."

Simi stretched and found himself rising and then moving toward the glass door. He slid it open and stepped through, blinking—not because of the brightness of the morning sun, but as a result of the tongue lashing he'd just endured from the relative stranger.

What in the HELL was that all about?

Thirty

"Hello?"

Abe was becoming increasingly irked by the repetitive, long-lasting, pauses on the other end of the line. The director of Burton Barney and Sons Funeral Home—Burt Barney himself—seemed to be struggling to answer many of the questions posed to him. Inexplicably so. Abe smacked his lips together and for a brief instant, fantasized about how easy—and calming—it'd be for him to take a drink right then. How simple it'd be for him to hang up and make the short drive into town. *Just a quick one to take the edge off*, he thought, before suppressing the urge.

"Hello, Mr. Barney? Are you still—?"

"Oh, yes, yes. My apologies Mr. Ward. I'm *absolutely* still here. And, as I've already mentioned, please, please, do call me Burt."

Abe steeled himself to ask, once more, what he already had.

"Burt. Right. I guess I'm just having a hard time understanding what the problem here is. Should I be considering another funeral home? Perhaps from the next town over? Can you suggest another option in—I dunno—Mansfield, maybe? I just assumed, you coming so highly recommended and being a fixture here in Foxborough, that I—"

Burt Barney sputtered to life through the receiver. "Oh, don't be silly, Mr. Ward. Elma was such an important part of this community. An *institution*, really. Quite simply, there's no one else—other funeral homes, as you say— that could—I mean *should*— be responsible for fulfilling her final wishes. I apologize for giving you the wrong impression."

Then what am I missing?

Abe took a deep breath. "Alright then. So, you're able to accommodate the—ah—the burial in our old family plot? I mentioned the internment happening there, as it has for all of the Wards as far as I'm aware, but you seem to have some sort of an issue with that. Or maybe I was misreading the awkward silence on your end of this call?"

Abe expected an immediate explanation, a prompt reversal of tone and general flow of their conversation, but he was once more greeted with the same uncomfortable silence. This time, he could have sworn Barney was whispering to someone else in the room with him.

"Hello? Mr. Barney? Burt? I have to be honest, I'm at a complete loss—"

"Yes, I'm still here."

"Mr. Barney is there something—"

"Burt."

Abe pulled the phone from the side of his head and silently swore out in the direction of the swamp. He turned back to the porch to find Simi grinning and standing just outside the sliding glass door.

"You okay?" the teen mouthed to his dad.

Abe shook his head and gritted his teeth, forcing himself to smile, as if the man on the phone might somehow see him. "Burt. Yes. Of course. *Burt.* Is there something I should know? Anything at all you'd like to tell me? To get off your chest? Because I really feel like there's— like you are dancing around *something* here."

There was another brief bout of whispering—Burt Barney was arguing with a participant invisible to the conversation—and just as Abe was about to finally hang up, the man spoke once more.

"No. No, of course not," the funeral director collected himself and, though the pleasantry returned to his voice, the slightest tremble remained. "Of course, we can accommodate your—*Elma's*— wishes." The man paused. 'These are *her* wishes, correct?"

Abe had to stop himself from throwing his phone into the marsh. "I'm sorry. Why *wouldn't* these be Elma's wishes? Have you spoken to her?"

"Not recently, no. It's just that I'm well aware you only just arrived back in town and—"

"And how would you know that? I've told you nothing about myself."

"Just spoke to m'boy, Marv. Says he had a delightful chat were your son, ah, Simon was his name?"

"It's Simeon," Abe spat. "And I'd appreciate you not making any assumptions about who I am or what I want to do with Elma's burial simply based on the interactions of a few kids."

"The only thing, if I may, is that Marv seemed to observe—based on his meeting with your son—that you weren't fully aware of what—"

"Of what, Burt? Look, I'm about done with this—

whatever this is. Are you going to make this happen or not?"

Another hesitation and then Burt skipped cleanly past the query. "Mr. Ward. We will begin making arrangements immediately. Have a blessed day."

Click.

Abe stared at the phone.

His mouth hung open and he looked up to find Simi, arms folded, laughing.

"What?" Simi asked. "Lemme guess, the funeral dude is a weirdo?"

Abe nodded.

"And you're surprised because...?

Abe walked up onto the porch. "I dunno. The guy was just… I mean, if we weren't going to bury Elma in the old family plot, where else would we put her? I just don't understand what Burt's malfunction is."

"Burt?"

Abe shook a few loose stars off. "The funeral director. Seriously, there was something he wasn't saying. Makes me wonder if Elma was still sharing her wacky ideas with the people of this town." Abe considered, carefully, what he was about to say to Simi. "It's almost as if…"

Simi waited and, when Abe didn't continue his thought, prodded him along. "It's almost as if…?"

"It's like he was *scared*."

Simi sat up a little straighter and uncrossed his arms. "Scared? What of?"

Abe looked out over the bog, over Dead Rock River, all the way to the white boulder sitting at its terminus. A black crow flitted down and, momentarily, blemished the bleached stone surface.

"Dad?"

The devilish portend launched into the sky and Abe couldn't help but watch it fly away.

"No idea, Sim," he lied. "No idea."

Thirty One

Simi kicked a soda bottle down the street. Every few feet he'd discover it anew and then boot the plastic vial further. Mags—he conceded—for sure would've picked it up. Her mission, which she'd usually been successful in dragging Simi along with, was to protect the Earth at all costs. A lover of nature and all the gentle and not-so-gentle creatures that inhabited it, Simi couldn't help but be convinced to do her bidding.

I'll get it on the way back, Mags. I promise. It's keeping me entertained at the moment.

On cue, his phone buzzed. He picked it up to see an incoming call from his girlfriend. An image of her beautiful face, taken over the previous summer on one of their many movie dates, judged him. Her green-glittery eye shadow and matching green glasses looked up at him, questioning his delay in salvaging the recyclable.

Alright, alright. He joked to himself. *Holy cheeseballs.*

He was about to answer the call when he heard hushed laughter from up ahead. He pulled his eyes from the vibrating screen, and Mags' smile, to see three far-less welcoming sneers. No more than a few driveways ahead approached Jack and Harry Wils. Trailing them, by a few too-eager steps, was their dumb friend—old lobster-pants himself—Marv Barney.

Barney? Simi thought, making the connection. *Related to THE Burt Barney?*

As the three approached Simi, their smiles dissipated.

"Hey, shithead," Jack spat as he approached, dropping all pretense. "You call the police on us?"

Simi shook his head. "No, I—"

"Yeah, *ya did*," Jack said stepping closer, letting his overstretched nostrils hover inches from Simi's. "You called the cops on us, you snitch. For what, even? We weren't bothering nobody."

Simi backed up, creating space between himself and the thug's garbage breath. "Anybody."

Jack snorted. "What'd you say?"

Again, Simi took a backward step in the opposite direction, but still spoke confidently. The goons did not frighten him; he'd encountered far worse where he grew up. "It's *anybody*. As in 'we weren't bothering anybody.' Probably should pay more attention in school, big guy."

Jack looked like he was considering whether to throw a punch, and Simi was preparing to block his attack, when Harry suddenly—and without warning—snatched the phone from Simi's hand.

"Well lookee what we've got here," Harry squealed. Simi tried to take it back, but Jack stood in his way. The picture of Mags was still up on the screen. "Oh, she's *hot*. What's her name?"

"Come on man, just give it back."

"He asked you what her name is." Jack took a step closer. "Aren't you gonna answer my brother?"

Simi cracked his neck. "Look. Give me my goddamn phone, before I take it back."

The two brothers howled. Jack had his hands on his knees he was laughing so hard and the younger Wils was slamming him on the back. "Well, at least he's got a sense of humor." Jack took the phone from Harry. "This guy's a freaking comedian."

Simi took a step toward them both and then Marv chimed in. "Guys give him a break. My dad just told me that old lady finally kicked the bucket. He's in *mourning*." He could barely get "mourning" out of his mouth before he too burst into uncontrollable, hyena-like, chortling.

Jack wiped a real tear from his eye, brought on by his own hysterics. "He's in mourning? Oh, you don't say. Well, in that case—" and before he could finish, chucked Simi's phone down the embankment on the side of the road. They all listened as it rolled down the hill and finally came to a silent stop at its bottom. Through all the overgrowth and underbrush, it was hidden from their sight.

"Repayment for ratting us out." Jack grinned, a piece of something green sticking out of his bottom teeth. For an instant, Simi marveled at the idea that the bully had ever eaten anything healthy in his lifetime. "Why don't you go cry to the sheriff about it, mmm-kay?"

"What the hell did you need to that for?"

Marv stepped forward. "My dad says your shit for brains father needs to wake the hell up. We're all going to pay the price if he doesn't get his head outta his ass."

Simi blinked. "I don't even know what that means or what it has to do with my goddamn phone."

Marv and his lobster pants took a step closer, the smell of his sour body odor wafting into Simi's face. A leer crawled across his cracked lips and he whispered. "Why don't you go after it and find out?"

They pushed past him and Simi watched as their rejoicing and hollering carried them down the road, past the Ward place, and eventually around a corner. Out of sight.

Assholes.

Simi turned to the guardrail that warned him from what surely was shrouded on the other side of its boundary.

Guess I'm going in.

He stepped over the metal barricade—an impediment to any vehicle, but a mere hurdle for a reckless, foolhardy, youth.

The incline was steep and without much effort at all, Simi easily lumbered down the hill. In doing so, brambles pierced through the protective layer of denim around his shins. He lifted his pant legs and shrugged off the scratches and the small amount of blood beginning to bubble up. Otherwise, he'd been unharmed, and—once the initial sting subsided—immediately reminded himself of his purpose.

At first, his eyes struggled to adjust to the dimness. A thick canopy overhead blocked out much of the sun and gave his surroundings the appearance of it being much later on in the afternoon than it was. A small brook trickled past his sneakers and Simi wondered if, perhaps, a small tributary or stream had branched off of the much larger Dead Rock River.

And then he saw it.

His phone lay, seemingly unharmed—miraculously—inches away from the water. He picked it up and, though he expected it to no longer work, the device immediately lit up with his touch. He saw the "one missed call" notification and Mags' face still beaming up at him.

"Thank GOD," he exhaled. He kissed his girlfriend's smile and then realized how weird the gesture would've looked to anybody happening by.

You're alone in the woods, Simi. Chill.

He put the phone in his pocket, endeavoring to call her later—once he got back. His first order of business was to return to the road, pick up that damn water bottle, and then head home.

Not home. He corrected himself. *Definitely not home.*

As Simi began to ascend the slope, a stick cracked somewhere behind him. He spun around.

"Hello?"

He waited, expecting one of the three hooligans to suddenly poke a head out and fall on the ground, laughing at their own, imagined, comedic genius. None of them appeared.

"Hello?" he asked again. "If you guys are trying to freak me out or something… just, I dunno, grow up? This is getting old real fast."

Again, there was no response. He decided that maybe it wasn't any of them after all, likely just a normal, woodland, sound—a branch falling from a tree or a squirrel making a ruckus— and then, once more, turned himself toward the hill and the road. Almost immediately after spinning around, he heard another sound, this one far more alarming.

Breathing.

Heavy breathing.

Carefully, Simi looked over his shoulder. The hoarse inhalation ceased.

Time to go, Sim. On the count of three, just run. Don't stop. No more looking back.

He twisted his face back toward the embankment and

immediately the belabored panting commenced.

One... two... three!

Simi launched himself up the incline and, within seconds, thudded into the metal guardrail. Massaging his sore thigh, he swung both of his legs over the barrier and placed his feet firmly onto the safety of the pavement. Looking back down into the gulley, all was silent. Nothing had followed him out and into the light.

He wanted to stop and catch his breath, but decided against it.

You can breathe later.

Simi started jogging down the road, looking behind himself every few feet to make sure no beastie was trailing in his wake. As he passed it, he reached down and picked up the empty bottle he'd promised himself he wouldn't forget.

When he arrived back at the Ward place, gasping for air, Abe was standing out front talking with a man Simi didn't recognize.

Abe turned and beckoned Simi, not seeming to notice that his son had his hands on his knees, his chest heaving.

"Simi this is..."

But Simi didn't hear the man's name. All he caught, amid his own racing thoughts, was the title: Estate Attorney.

Simi waved and watched as the man shook hands with Abe, hopped into his car, and pulled away.

"He's an estate attorney, huh? So, what's that all about?" He gulped down a bit more oxygen and wondered if Abe would ever ask him if he was alright. "This guy gonna help us get everything in order so we can get outta here soon?"

Abe's head dropped and, with it, so did Simi's spirits. He turned to face his son.

"Well..." he appeared to wrestle for the right words. "Simi, we need to talk."

Thirty Two
Night One
October 26th

The sun escaped behind the tallest of the trees bordering the Ward property, mimicking the hasty departure of the estate attorney. Abe stood and stared at the confused face of his son, half of which was obscured by the swiftly approaching twilight.

"So, it appears that Elma left the house to… *me*. I don't have the deed yet, but the documentation is being worked on as we—"

Simi blinked up at him. "And?"

Abe swallowed. "And—well, now it's my responsibility." He noticed the color draining from Simi's already shadow-stained features and quickly tried to offer some reassurance. "But, it's not what you're thinking. Or, at least, I don't think it is."

Simi crossed his arms. "Well, what is it then, Abe? 'Cause, from where I'm standing, it sure sounds like—"

"Look, I have no intention of living here, if that's

what you're worried about. But, we do need to fix the place up before I can put it on the market and I…"

"What?"

Abe rubbed at his forehead and turned toward the house, either because he couldn't look Simi in the eyes or because he needed to more closely inspect what'd only just been dropped into his lap. "Look Sim. I just got this news myself and I'm still processing it all. My gut reaction—and mind you this could change once I've had time to think it all through— is that this might delay our departure." Simi threw his head back and Abe added. "Just a bit. Please don't be mad."

Simi walked over and got into Abe's face. "But *why*? You promised me this would be a short visit. I came up here with you, thinking I'd be back home in no time. That's what you told me. Remember?"

Abe scrunched his nose and rubbed at his temples. "I did. You're right. I definitely did."

"Well then," Simi's voice raised a few octaves. "Why can't we just leave and, I dunno, sell the place from back home? We don't need to physically *be* here, right? We did what you wanted. We came, you said your goodbyes and you were here for her. What more do we need to do?"

Abe, uncomfortable with how close Simi's nose was getting to his own, plopped down, dejectedly, onto the front stairs. "It's just not that simple, Sim."

Simi got even louder. "Yes, it is, Abe." He stepped forward, standing over his father. "You're goddamn right it's a simple as that. Let's go. I want to go home." He looked back down the road from the direction he'd just come. "This place. These people. I don't need this. *We* don't need this. Please."

Abe fiddled with the orange Velcro watch on his wrist

and then readjusted the noisy strap. "Elma didn't have any other real assets, Simi. All her worth is entombed in this house. There's no money to hire contractors. *None*. I will need to do this myself. I'm sorry."

Simi pulled his hood up. With the added shroud, and the sun nearly gone for the day, his face became almost completely masked. "How long?"

Abe considered. "We'll probably need to hang out at least a couple more weeks." Simi groaned. "If I completely dedicate myself to this, and do pretty much nothing else, I think in that amount of time I should be able to do *just enough* to list the place."

Simi didn't respond. For a second, Abe wondered if the kid might yell again. After an awkward silence that stretched on interminably, Simi instead stormed up the stairs and through the open doorway.

"Simi—"

The door slammed before he could get out another word.

Abe slunk further against the stairs. "Well, that's just great."

He sat there for a while longer, watching as dark completed its descent. After a moment of listening to the woods come alive for the evening, Abe picked himself up and followed his son inside.

The foyer was silent. No lights had yet been turned on. Simi was nowhere to be seen or heard. Not bothered by the fading light, Abe walked into the kitchen and flicked the first switch he came across. The room illuminated and he collapsed into one of the chairs surrounding the table. Resting on his elbows, he pressed his face hard into his waiting hands.

You can make it up to him. He'll get over this. Just like he's gotten over everything else.

Abe raised an eyebrow at his inner musings. *Had* Simi gotten over anything?

I mean, who could blame the kid? Shit.

And then he remembered. The estate attorney had handed him a folded sheet of paper. Much of what the evasive, twitchy little man had said at the time was foggy, but Abe remembered him saying that it was from Elma. A "will" of some sort.

Abe unfolded the document, sealed only with a single piece of scotch tape.

He blinked. It wasn't exactly a will, or not like any he'd ever seen before. Between his shaking fingertips, he held a handwritten note. The scrawl was messy, almost childlike, and accompanied by little illustrations in the margins. A flower here, a clown's face there. The doodlings, to Abe, made little sense and he immediately decided not to even attempt to decipher what they meant. The page contained a single, disorienting, sentence:

To my beloved great-nephew, Abel Ward, I leave the keys to the gate.

Abe scratched at the bridge of his nose.

"What gate, Elma? What keys?"

He took a deep breath and folded the document back up. Placing it into his pocket for another time, Abe rose and angled his body toward the refrigerator. It was possible Daisy had left something edible for them in there, but he hadn't thought to ask. Not that he would have been surprised if she'd completely forgotten, with the chaos of the day.

Daisy. D. Am I even going to see you now that Elma's gone?

He opened the fridge and pulled out an aluminum tray. As he was about to sniff at its contents, something screeched from outside. He threw the pan down and ran to the sliding glass door overlooking the backyard.

Abe waited. After a brief pause, there was another scream, closer to the house, he thought, and more guttural than the first.

He flicked on the porch light. Again a throaty yowl sounded, this one causing him to take a step away from the glass. After a brief minute to contemplate, he shrugged.

"Nothing I can do about that." He turned the outside light off. "No sir. Out of my element. Best to leave it alone."

As he fixed himself a plate, and as the eerie cries from outside continued, he wondered if he should bring dinner up to Simi. Eventually, he decided against it.

"Nope. Gotta let him be. Give him some space. Simi's—"

Another shrill whine echoed from nearby, as if the creature was standing on the porch. Abe peered outside but could see nothing through the shadows. Tempted to flip the switch again, he instead shook his head. He grabbed his dish and headed upstairs for the night.

"—out of my element."

Thirty Three

The graveside burial for Elma Ward was simple. Quiet. There were no tears and no stories to share. A few shuffling souls stood close to a priest, who offered a boilerplate little speech about the dead being in a better place and resting in the hearts of those present. Simi wondered if the man had just switched some other poor individual's name with Elma's—his sermon being one he'd delivered, languidly, many times over. Father Glass, wearing the most basic of what Simi could only label as "priest clothes"—the traditional black garments and the white-collar— sounded like he was "going through the motions" and might be ready, himself, for a nap later that afternoon. Upon hearing that a priest would be officiating the affair, Simi had asked Abe if Elma was religious. "No, not exactly," his dad had said, and—though the answer created even more questions—he decided not to follow up with another.

The maligned burial ground, sitting kitty-corner

across the road and visible from the front porch of the Ward House, was tiny. Simi counted less than twenty stone markers, a few even dating back as far as the late 1700s and early 1800s. There was no doubt the little plot had been there long before much of the town was built up; with the name "Ward" legible on the vast majority of the grey slabs, it also provided confirmation that his family was one of its earliest cornerstones. Directly behind the freshly-dug hole for Elma, were three moss-covered mounds: Delilah and Adam Ward (Simi's grandparents) and Adam Ward (his great-great-uncle).

Getting the whole family back together.

Simi shuddered at his joke and looked up at the other solemn faces standing around the recent excavation. Abe stood directly across from him, his head hung low, and his hands folded respectfully in front of himself. He was rocking, ever-so-slightly, and Daisy—who was standing to Abe's left—hooked an arm around his elbow to stabilize him. In addition to the three of them and the wooden priest, their group was rounded out by the massive, grey-suited frame of funeral director Burt Barney—who'd strangely rushed the internment, setting the wheels in motion to make it happen only the day after Elma's passing— and the town's sheriff, Will Candler.

Someone coughed, though even with the pitiful size of the crowd, Simi couldn't locate who or where the throat-clearing had come from. The priest, however, stumbled on his words, as if the sudden interruption awoke him from his monotonous, slumber-spiel.

After the brief stoppage, the man continued and—not long after—wrapped up what he'd come to do that day. Politely he began offering handshakes as if such a thing, especially from one so disinterested as he, could possibly have been comforting. Simi took the man's fish-hand, because he knew that's what he was expected to do, and then—before he could be drawn further into the banal, forced, murmurings of the adults as they peered down onto Elma's pine-box coffin—turned away.

Simi raised his arms over his head, finally able to stretch the stretch he'd been wanting throughout the entire ceremony, and—with his mouth fully open, a yawn escaping onto a dancing fall breeze—he froze.

On the edge of the woods, partially obscured behind the peeling skin of an old sycamore tree, stood an old man. He wore a green, fleece vest, under which sat a tan, checkered shirt. He held in his hands—respectfully, in front of a bulging gut—a tweed cap. His hair was thick, curly, and ghost white, like it'd only recently be sheared from a sheep and afterward placed directly onto his head. His cheeks were covered in spidery lines and his bulbous, purple, nose caught the light of a small bit of sun that'd somehow managed to peek its way through the thick overhang of dark pine coppice surrounding the site.

Simi dropped his hands and snapped his mouth shut.

"Uh, Abe. Who's—?"

The man saw Simi notice him. He gave a quick nod, placed his cap snugly back upon his wool-head, and then shambled away into the trees.

Abe was distracted by the priest's fake words of compassion, pretending himself to show gratitude, and didn't hear Simi's first attempt to get his attention.

"Abe," Simi repeated, with more urgency.

This time, he was heard. Abe pulled his hand away from the clergyman and offered another thanks and an apology. He stepped away, leaving Daisy to take her turn with the tedium of the father.

"What's up, Sim? You okay?"

Simi pointed toward the trees. "There was a man over there. A very old man. Just sort of standing around. Watching all of this."

Abe furrowed his brown and squinted toward the sycamore. "Where'd he go?"

Simi shook his head. "Just sort of faded away into the trees. Kinda weird, huh?"

Abe didn't seem bothered. "Oh, you know, probably just an old friend of Elma's. You'd expect she had to have at least a few. Lived quite a life, after all."

Simi kept looking in the direction the man had departed. "I guess. But, if that were the case, why wouldn't he have, like—I dunno—joined us?" He looked at Abe, who shrugged. "And, Elma was super old, right? How many friends of hers could possibly still be around?"

Abe was quickly losing interest, distracted by the few guests he still needed to attend to. "Yeah, well. I'm not too worried. Probably just didn't want to make a fuss is all. Not like we advertised this event to the public. The man just wanted to pay his respects and not intrude, is what I think. I'm fine with that."

Abe turned and walked back toward Daisy, perhaps to save her from the priest. Simi also spun, but in the direction the mysterious figure had vanished without a trace.

Without a "hello".

Without the snap of a dead, discarded, twig.

Just an old man, watching from the protection of the adumbral wood, at the Olde Ward Burial Ground.

Thirty Four
Night Two
October 27th

There was a stain on the ceiling.

Abe was flat on his back. Something had startled him awake, but he couldn't remember what. He'd flicked on the light, expecting to see Simi standing at the foot of his bed or something far worse, but the room was empty. Waiting to see if whatever had alerted him would do so again, he rested his head back down on his downy pillow and stared up at the peeling paint and the crumbling plaster that he'd found evidence of, sprinkled all over his comforter each morning of his stay. The blotch on the wall— a dark brown circle at its center, with yellowing concentric rings rippling away from the diseased bullseye— stared down at him. Though he'd only been sleeping in the room for a few nights, he could swear the blemish was growing.

Add that to the list. Another thing for me to deal with. Great.

Simi had gone to his room early, once again. This time, he'd at least brought dinner with him, but he still refused to listen to Abe's further attempts at an explanation or apology. All he wanted to hear was that they were leaving, which they *weren't*. Anything else was a non-starter for the time being.

But, at least he came to the funeral.

Everything about the morning had been curious to him. Simi's rather innocuous and respectful presence at the solemn affair, notwithstanding. From Burt Barney's rather unexpected phone call the day of the burial—with the pronouncement that he'd only be able to arrange for it to happen *that morning*— to the Sheriff's unforeseen attendance. Simi had also claimed to have observed some guy lingering just outside the boundary of the cemetery, but Abe had waved that off. So much he'd faced in the previous twenty-four hours had been beyond extraordinary, that he couldn't be bothered with a seemingly harmless—evidently elderly—sentinel.

You've got much bigger fish to fry, my friend.

Abe reached for the light, but before he could switch it off, a scream severed the false tranquility that'd tricked him into believing that evening might end up a more peaceful one.

"Damn animals. I can't take much more of this."

He leapt up out of bed and, hurried out into the hallway. Simi's door was still tightly shut and he couldn't hear movement from inside. With any luck, the horrible sounds coming from the yard hadn't woken him. Abe hustled his way down the squirming staircase and into the kitchen. Without any thought, he turned on the porch light.

For a moment, everything was silent.

"I wanna know what you are, you bastards." He pulled open the slider and stood in the threshold. A warm breeze—remarkably equatorial—smacked him in the face. Abe gagged. The stench was overpowering and reminded him of a chipmunk that once died in their heating ducts back home. He threw a forearm over his nose and took a small step outside.

Come on, let me hear 'ya.

Abe remained motionless. He wondered if the animal—whatever it was— could see him, standing there in his boxers, bathed only in the jaundiced light of the flickering bulb.

"Okay fellas," he slapped his hands together, hoping to scare whatever it was away. "Just want to inform you that things are gonna change around here. This is my house now, boys. Alright?" He clapped a few more times and stomped his bare feet on the rickety wood. "Please. Go. Away." He repeated the request a few times until he began to feel self-conscious. Not that he expected anyone to be awake at that hour or to be hanging out in the swamp, but he supposed it possible another resident of Brown Street might have been awoken by the commotion he was making. He listened for the familiar, comforting sound of a neighborly dog barking, but there was nothing. No noise. As he considered it right then, he'd never heard much in the way of anything outside at night, around the Ward House. No dogs barking. Not a single owl hoot-hooting. The cicadas were even quiet, though he'd recently heard on public radio how noisy they were supposed to have been that year— emerging from their seventeen years of stasis.

All he heard—all he *ever* heard— was the grisly shrieking, from whatever unidentified New England demons were on the prowl just behind the light of Elma's back deck.

Hey, Abe thought. *Like you said. It's your deck now. Elma's gone. Better get used to that.*

He cupped both hands around his mouth, deciding to give the critter another chance to show itself before he made his way back inside. "Hey, listen to me you sons-of-bit—"

Abe stopped. There was—suddenly audible to him—a low growl that came from only a few feet into the shadows. Something was watching his performance and, by the sound of it, not running off into the woods in fear.

Abe put a hand to his eyes to try and better see what was out there. He clapped his other free hand against his thigh and jumped up and down. "Hey, HEY," he shouted. "Time to leave, Bucko."

But the snarling didn't cease. In fact, with his stomping, it seemed to get louder.

Closer.

Deciding that he'd had enough fun for one night, Abe quickly backed himself inside and slammed the door shut. He waited to see if anything would appear on the porch, but nothing materialized. He sat down, with his arms folded on the table, waiting for something—anything— to show itself.

"Coward," he mumbled, but wasn't sure if he meant it for the phantom-growler or his own, hurried, retreat.

He tried to keep his focus on the backyard, but exhaustion would win out that night. Whether or not there'd been another howl or not, he didn't know. Before long, his eyelids—weighted by the peculiarity of the day—cascaded down over his orbital sockets, memories of his ordeal dimmed by the dark.

Thirty Five

"Up and at 'em," Abe said, kicking at a bare foot hanging off of Simi's bed.

Simi rolled over, pulled his leg in, and threw the blanket over his disorderly locks. "Go away."

This time, Abe tapped the bedframe with his boot. "That's a negative. Lots of work to do today, my friend."

Simi moaned, his voice muffled by a clown-covered pillow. "Please. I beg of you. Go away."

Abe yanked the fortune-teller sheets and comforter off of his son and tossed them onto the floor. Simi covered his eyes with an arm. "I get it, you're a kid. Kids like to sleep in—"

"Child Psychologist Abel Ward with his *genius* analysis of the adolescent mind."

"—but the sooner we get this done, the sooner we can go home."

Simi rubbed his eyes and sat up. "Fine. *Fine.* Just let

me get dressed. What are we starting with?"

Abe smiled. "Painting all the interior walls today."

"*All* of them?"

"All of them," Abe turned to leave the room. "You'd be surprised what a fresh coat of paint can do. Found a whole store of the stuff in a closet downstairs. Exactly the shade we need too. Must have been a fairly recent coat put on, but it still needs a bit of touching up. And I've already done most of our prep— drop cloths down, painters tape, you name it. Been up since the ass-crack of dawn, but coffee'll do wonders if you keep chugging it. All's left is to get started. Oh, and probably want to make sure you're wearing clothes you don't mind ruining."

Simi looked at him incredulously. "I don't have *any* clothes I'm okay with ruining."

Abe thought for a second. "You know, I probably have something you can throw on. You're close to my size."

Simi rolled his eyes and flopped back down on the bed. "Oh, yay," he said, the sarcasm dripping from his words. "It's always been my dream to strut around in flannel, smelling of decades-old cigarettes."

Abe was already halfway down the hallway, not fully hearing the last bit. He called from his room. "You'll like this. Black and white flannel. I barely wear it, but it sort of works with your, ah, look."

Abe entered the clown room again and tossed the shirt and a pair of ripped Levis onto the bed.

Simi glared at him. "What look?"

Abe leaned his head to one side and rubbed the back of his neck. "Ah, well, you're… ah. I mean, you do wear *a lot* of black."

Simi didn't blink. "Can you leave? I just want to get dressed in private, if you don't mind."

Abe put his hands up. "Oh sure, sure. See you downstairs in five."

"What about breakfast?" Simi called after him.

"We're gonna eat and work. The early bird and all that."

Simi stood up and cracked a shoulder. He checked his phone. The absence of any blinking lights or notifications told him Mags hadn't texted late last night or that morning. He blew air out from his lips and then got himself dressed.

"Gross," he said, sniffing the shirt. "Does the smell ever fade?"

He looked at himself in the cracked glass of the mirror, which was bordered with red and yellow balloons. "My God, this is awful." He twisted himself around and pulled at the excess fabric. The sleeves hung over his hands and the pants were baggy enough he could have safely parachuted into a warzone. "Jesus, Abe."

Simi walked downstairs—still muttering to himself about the injustice of Abe's Alec-Baldwin-in-*Beetlejuice*-shirt—and could hear his father already slopping away in the main foyer.

"Oh good, you're here. Grab a roller," he stopped to admire Simi's outfit. "Not bad, actually. Not bad at—"

"Nope, just stop."

Abe turned back to the area he'd been painting. "Okay, then. Well, what're you waiting for?"

Simi picked up the only other paint roller he saw. "Lime green? Don't you think you should change things up? Tad dated, I think."

Abe continued rolling. "This room's always been this color. No need to reinvent the wheel. I'm not interested in redesigning the place or starting over. The green rooms stay green. The beige stay beige. On and on. Just easier this way."

He looked around and up at the framed painting just at the top of the first landing. "Besides, this house has a story to tell. All these hipsters buying homes nowadays... they want that vintage look."

Simi lazily moved his roller up and down. "Why not just leave it completely *as-is*, then?"

Abe laughed. "Because *as-is*, when you're talking about a relic like this one, just isn't good enough. These millennials may want an old-looking house, but they certainly don't want to deal with the... *warts* of one."

Simi nodded, pretending to agree. "Oh yes, of course. Just leave the wart removal to the professionals."

Abe smacked him on the back. "Now you're getting it." He paused his painting. "Hey, that's actually not a bad business plan. 'Ward's Wart Removal'. Kinda dig the sound of that."

Simi sighed through his teeth and turned back toward the wall. "You would."

Abe chuckled again, but stopped when he realized Simi wasn't joining him. "Hey, you know what, why don't I go fix us something real quick? Just a breakfast sandwich or—I dunno. We can eat and paint?" He started jogging to the kitchen and turned around. "How do you want your eggs?"

"With Mags. Back home."

Abe pointed at him and continued walking backward. "Got it. Over-easy it is." He winked. "Be right back, Dude."

Abe was already puttering around in the kitchen when Simi lifted his head and whispered. "Dude? Why not Chief? Or Tiger? Sport works too. I'm *such* a Sport."

He could hear eggs cracking and the sizzle of the pan. Abe was humming to himself. Simi was focusing pretty intently on his task—making better progress without his father talking at him so much—when he noticed a weird fracture, a foot or so higher up on the wall in front of him.

Vintage my ass.

His first instinct was to just paint over the crack and not mention it to Abe. He reached up with the roller and applied a layer of green. The fissure did not fill in and was still quite visible. He tried again and experienced the same result.

"Oh, come on."

Soaking the painting implement again, he returned to the wall and attempted to administer a bit more pressure.

"Come on you dumb—"

The roller and his hand broke through the wall and were swallowed by the darkness behind it.

Simi yanked the tool back. "Aw, dammit." He looked toward the kitchen. "Abe's gonna be pissed."

The chasm in the wall gaped back at him. From his position on the floor, he couldn't see into it. No light seemed to penetrate the opening.

Simi searched around for something to stand on. An antique-looking chair stood guard by the main door and he grabbed it. The piece—more ornamental than anything else— wobbled a bit as he put all of his weight onto the upholstered seat.

"Woah, there," he said, bracing himself by grabbing at one ragged edge of the hole. He pulled his eyes up so that they were level. At first, all he could see were dust particles flying into the air, released after centuries of imprisonment. He coughed and waved in front of his face. Peering into the blackness, he saw some crumpled up newspaper and a stained scrap of flower-patterned fabric. He pulled a handful of the wall-stuffing out and let it drop to the floor. Slowly, he then placed his face back up into the breach.

"What the—"

Simi saw something—two somethings, actually —but couldn't force himself to immediately reach for either of the items.

"What'd you do?"

Simi jumped and nearly fell from the chair.

"Careful, that's probably worth something," Abe added, gesturing at the rickety piece of furniture. Each of his hands held a plate with an English muffin breakfast sandwich placed precariously at its center, steam still rising from the gooey eggs. "Ah, Sim. The wall—what happened?"

Simi waved the roller, splattering green paint on the floor tarp. "Pressed too hard I guess. But it probably was water damaged or something. Didn't take much."

Abe seemed to not know what to do with their food and fidgeted undecidedly with his occupied extremities. "It's okay," he offered generously. "I can fix that. I think. Why don't you hop on down."

Simi hesitated. "Uh, Abe."

"Simi, really it's okay. I'm not—"

"Abe, just shut up and… *look.*"

From the wall, he pulled two barbaric pieces of hardware and held them each in his fists, almost mirroring Abe's stance with his egg sandwiches.

"Is this some kind of joke?" Abe's jaw went slack.

Simi stepped down off of the chair and placed the two cruel-looking implements on the floor, hastily wiping his hands on his dad's loaned cigarette jeans.

On the left was a jagged dagger. The blade was stained in some sort of brown substance. At the base of its hilt was a skull, carved from a hard white material.

Bone. Simi labeled it almost immediately.

In the eye sockets of the skull, rested two green stones. Depending on where he stood and how he angled his body, they almost appeared to twinkle up at him.

On the right was a pair of iron shackles.

"More pest control?" the teen stammered.

"Simi," Abe began again. "I asked you if this was a—"

"It's *not* a joke." He took a step back and felt the saliva running for cover down his dry throat. "It's definitely not a joke."

Thirty Six
Night Three
October 28th

Counter-measures.

Abe dried his bald head with a towel. It was a futile exercise that he'd somehow never ceased, even after completely losing all his hair. On that night, however, with the chill of autumn seeping into his bones, he was grateful for a warm towel and the ability to wipe every last droplet off of himself. He'd exited the shower a few minutes earlier. Simi was already in his room for the night. They'd worked hard, with only a few breaks, and somehow managed to paint the entire main entryway, the walls wrapping the staircase, and the kitchen. It was a solid day's work and, with a couple of exceptions, everything went exactly as planned.

He finished with his towel, pulled on an orange t-shirt that said "Boo" in black lettering on its chest, and turned to stare at the two items perched on his nightstand.

A couple of exceptions.

The dagger and the shackles—he couldn't tell if they

were meant for wrists or ankles— sat harmlessly, out of reach. For some reason, he'd avoided touching either as much as possible. After Simi pulled the atrocities from the hole in the wall, Abe wrapped each in a rag and quickly rushed the items upstairs. The urge to get the crude-looking tools away from his son was strong, though he could not explain why that would be. Afterward, he'd given Simi some short, improvised, explanation—that Elma was a collector of the bizarre— and instructed him not to worry too much about it. Naturally, the excuse wasn't enough for Simi who was quick to point out the similarly barbaric sword and other archaic, primitive, looking weaponry he'd discovered hanging in the shed. Fortunately, the rest of the backbreaking labor they'd put in that day had distracted from the progression of the conversation and the kid hadn't brought it up again.

Not yet, at least.

And perhaps the most disconcerting piece of the puzzle, was a faded inscription Abe had noticed—in laying the oddities out on the nightstand— on the handle of the dagger. It read, rather simply, "Counter-measures." Someone had scratched the label onto the white—shaped obviously from bone— grip. Trying to decipher *why* anyone would have written that or *what* they might have required counter-measures against, was a path he didn't wish to tread and a hypothesis that he refused to let himself make.

Abe looked at his wristwatch.

"9:38 pm. The earliest I've been ready for bed in ages. Bring it on."

He yawned and climbed onto the lumpy mattress. Before he could even reach for the lamp, the now-familiar shrill caterwauling from the swamp began again. Having already experienced how ineffectual any effort to silence the beasts was, he decided instead to ignore it.

He switched the bedside light off.

Thwump.

Abe hadn't closed his eyes and so there was no need to open them when he heard the noise from above. Not from Elma's room, by the sound of it, but even higher—deep within the cerebrum of Ward House. Muffled by shingles and echoing through the empty crawl-space at the highest peak of the manor, Abe could tell instantly where the crash had come from.

"The roof. Godammit, something's on the roof now?"

He listened and it took him no time at all before he heard another collision, followed immediately by the raucous raining down of whatever material had just been torn from the canopy over his head.

Abe still refused to get up. "This has to stop." He placed his hands over his face. "I'm never going to get any rest."

The cacophony continued. One crash was accompanied by another and then another. And then —as if on cue—the snarling began, in what was quickly becoming a too-familiar refrain. One creature was fighting another—*or maybe playing?*—and, in doing so, causing quite a racket. Debris continued to sprinkle down, tinkling onto the sides of the house, past his room, and to the earth below.

Abe squeezed his eyes shut. "Nope, nope. I'm… going… to… sleep. I will not—"

Tap. Tap. Tap.

This time, Abe shot up and the hairs on his arms followed suit. Something was just outside the window. He could see a blurry silhouette. The moon was blocked. An indiscernible shape peered in at him. Whatever it was, knocked on the glass. It wanted to come in.

Abe turned on the light. Through the window, he could see the moon again. The mysterious shape was gone. He ran to the window and quickly scanned the area around the frame and the sill for any trace of the visitor.

"Where'd you go?" he banged on the wall, his desperation building. "Huh? Where are you, you little—"

And then, down in the middle of the backyard, he saw him.

Not a creature and certainly not the source of the noise he'd heard on the roof.

It was Simi.

His back to the house and his posture rigid—stuck in place like a petrified wooden tree—Simi was looking out over the swamp. Facing Dead Rock.

"Simi," Abe called, slapping the window. He threw it open and called again. "Simi—Simi, can you hear me?"

But Simi didn't react. He didn't spin in response to his father. He didn't call out in answer.

"Simi," Abe tried again, his voice beginning to shake. "Simi are you—?"

Fresh howling and cackling erupted and his attempt to reach his son was lost amidst the brutal discord. New guttural vocalizations burst forth from all directions and Abe could only watch, helplessly, as Simi took a sluggish step forward.

Out of the moonlight.

Into the shadow of the ugly, living, night.

Thirty Seven

Thou, there!
 Ward!
 Course ussss.
 Course ussss.
 Down, down, down.
 This way, this way.
 What is owed.
 Ay, yes.
What is owed, owed, owed. The blood of thy relations, hath been promised. Join now, join now. Owed, owed, owed. What is ours is ours is ours. We hast been patient. We hast been good. Abided by the covenant we hast.
 The covenant.
 The covenant.
 Be not afeard.
 This is the way.
 We hast obeyed.

'Tis thy turn.

Simi's eyes snapped open.

A chorus of hyena-like cackling surrounded him. It was dark, so much so that he could see no more than a few feet in front of his face. The moonlight was not a reliable enough guide, as its willingness to extend beyond the tree-line was minimal.

Ward!

The whispers were inside of his head. While he had no memory of leaving the house, he also knew that somehow he'd managed to get outside and that—without a shred of doubt—he'd been led by the voices. Simi clamped his hands over his ears in an effort to drown out the unwanted ensemble.

Ward! We attend thy arrival. Why doth thou hesitate, sirrah? Doth thou shun our bid?

The world around him was imploding. Screams beckoned him from behind trees, from beneath the fetid, decaying swampland, and from the now infringed confines of his own mind.

Sirrah? Sirrah? Thou canst not shun thy blood oath. Thy warrant. 'Twere written by the souls of thy ancestors. It canst not be undone.

Simi fell to one knee. The overlapping, discordant, bellowing was overwhelming and he cried out, the pain in both of his ears unbearable. He tried to force himself to stand again and a blur raced out from the darkness, passed by him in his haze, and slashed at an exposed shin. Unable to process or consider the ramifications of his actions, Simi removed the hands over his ears, bringing them to rest over the blood beginning to flow down over his bare foot.

Hark to us! Ward! Hark—

A strong, familiar, hand lunged at him through the

night and pulled him upright.

"Simi!"

"Huh? Abe?"

"Simi, what're you—?" Abe's words caught in his throat. "Jesus, your leg!"

Simi winced. "Why—? I don't know why I'm out here." His words were intelligible, but they sounded to him like they were uttered by another.

Abe removed his own shirt and wrapped it around his son's gaping wound. "What happened? I heard—howling. And now you're hurt. Did you see anything?"

The world was spinning and Simi felt as if he might black out. He sensed the bile slowly rising in his throat, but swallowed the quickly ascending acid and managed to force another disembodied imitation of himself. "I dunno. I was sleeping. Something—*someone*— called to me. The noise was so loud. Coming from everywhere. Could barely think. They wanted me to follow them, but I don't know where to. Once I realized what was happening, I tried to resist and then— then something attacked me. From the woods."

Abe tightened the bandage, using a small stick as a makeshift tourniquet. "Who's *they*, Simi? Who wanted you to follow?"

And then Simi, for the first time in many years, fell toward his father's chest. The tears began to flow and Simi sobbed. An arm found its way behind Abe's head and Simi squeezed. Abe, at first unsure how to react, eventually returned the gesture.

"I don't know, Abe. I don't know, I don't know, I don't—"

"Shhh, 'Sallright. You're okay now." Abe looked back toward the street. "But we do need to get you to a hospital. Definitely going to need stitches, I'm afraid to tell ya."

Simi sniffed and regained a bit of his composure. "Yeah. Okay. Help me?"

Abe obliged and pulled his son's arm over his shoulders. "Easy there. Let's take it slow."

Together they hobbled up the driveway and to the truck. As Abe loaded Simi in through the passenger side door, the boy couldn't help but look back toward the yard. The voices faded, slinking away into the night, but he couldn't help but remember the twisted tongues that'd only moments earlier beckoned him into their morass, and the rotten guarantee that he so hoped was not true.

'Tis thy turn.

Thirty Eight

Abe stood at the counter and gulped his steaming, bitter, black, coffee. His ball-point pen hovered over the sticky note as he contemplated how much to share with his son about his plan for the day. The previous night, he'd driven Simi to the Foxborough Emergency Room. Amazingly, they'd been quickly admitted. Twenty-one stitches and a rabies shot later, the Wards were sent back home. The ER doctor—Loomis, Abe thought his name was— refused, or was unable, to speculate on what sort of animal might have attacked Simi unprovoked. The rabies shot was a precaution in the absence of any other reasonable justification for the encounter and—much to Simi's dismay—they also were required to schedule three follow-up injections. Exhausted and grumbling, the two returned to Ward House. Simi had been sleeping ever since.

Abe took another sip of his beverage and twiddled the pen back and forth.

He, on the other hand, hadn't slept a wink. After pacing the back porch until the sun rose, waiting for anything that might decide to once again show itself, he'd figured out what next needed doing.

But how much do I say to Simi?

The pen began to move and he looked at what he'd written. He read it aloud to himself.

"Going into town to do some research. Be back later."

Satisfied, he stuck the note to the handle of the fridge door, certain Simi would see it once he got hungry enough to rouse himself from bed.

Still fully dressed, Abe grabbed his keys from the little hook inside the main foyer and, without another instant of hesitation, threw open the front door.

Enough is enough is enough. Time for some real answers.

And there was only one real place he thought he might be at all successful in finding any. The truck roared to life and rolled out into the street. A newfound sense of direction gave him life and he whistled as he passed the Olde Ward Burial Ground.

Probably some answers hidden away there too. But that's for another—

On his driver's side, a man was standing on his lawn, his hands folded compactly over the end of a rake. The neighbor lived a couple of houses down from Elma's and Abe didn't know who he was or anything about him. He sported a fishing hat, a simple white t-shirt, and poorly-fitting jeans. His unshaven face stared back at Abe, accusatorily, and he made no attempt to avert his gaze elsewhere—even after Abe waved back in an attempt to be friendly. The man did not lift his hand in reply, but his affixed eyeballing followed the truck all the way to the end of the road, where

Abe turned left onto North Street.

"What the hell was that?"

Abe ran a hand over his own stubbly chin. The morning hadn't been one in which a shower or shave made any sense to him. There were far too many, more pressing, issues to be dealt with. In particular—and this final, most recent incident was a prime example— he wanted to get to the bottom of the peculiar behaviors of the folks he'd met around town. Consistently, everyone he'd spoken with acted in a way that made Abe wonder if they all knew more about his home—and, in turn, Elma— than even he did. On top of it all, something was *wrong* with the swamp, with Dead Rock River, and with the woods that housed whatever wickedness had attacked Simi the previous night. After multiple days and attempts to figure out what the creatures were and why they were becoming increasingly agitated, he felt an explanation could wait no longer. The Ward House had a story that still needed to be told, and Abe was going to find out what that was.

One way or another.

He pressed his foot down on the gas pedal. His speed down North Street increased to a level beyond what was probably acceptable for the quiet—at points winding—school-lined road, littered with its blinking yellows and aghast signs that cautioned him to "SLOW DOWN". Abe ignored the admonishments of the small, leaf-covered, town and within minutes approached the rotary at the center of Foxborough. At the mouth of the roundabout, just before one would enter the "circle of doom"—a constant plague to out-of-towners unfamiliar with the traffic pattern—Abe parallel parked in front of the Town Archives Building. Resting above the stone building's massive, and intricately hand-carved, oaken door was a sign that itself looked preposterously modest. It read, quite simply, "Archives."

Having arrived at his predetermined destination, Abe let his driver's side door loudly croak open, hopped out, and then slammed it without consideration of how aggressive the action might have appeared to any local within earshot. With conviction, he jogged up the stone walkway, his fists clenching and unclenching, and pulled on the iron door-knocker. He let it slam into its worn groove and a few shards of rust flittered to the ground in response, admonishing his aggressive blow.

There was not initially an answer to his abrupt knock, but—just as Abe was about to repeat his action— a tired voice called to him from within.

"It's unlocked. Let yourself in."

Abe pulled on the handle, which itself was adorned with a twisting iron vine, and stepped through the antique portal. Inside, the lighting was incredibly dim and he'd only just begun to squint, to fully take in his surroundings, when the door crashed shut behind him. He jumped. In the poorly lit chamber, a voice chuckled, welcoming him.

"You are here," it said.

Abe peered into the small room. It was a circular space, its walls lined with the same rust-colored stones that formed the outside of the building, and the ceiling tapered up into a fine point. To his left were, perhaps, ten rows of book-lined shelves, the inhabitants of which were withering and dust-covered. So visibly aged were some that Abe wondered at the likelihood they would crumble if ever removed from their sanctuary. In front of each of the stacks was a small reading chair with an accompanying lamp and side table. The seating selection was eclectic and each piece of furniture appeared to be from a different era or generation.

To his right was a counter, covered with piles of books. A puff of smoke rose from behind the mountain of tomes, as did another chuckle.

"Yes," Abe said and then reconsidered, shaking his head. "I mean…" He didn't know what he meant. The greeting was odd and he wasn't even sure whether it'd been a question or a statement. "I'm here looking for answers," he said to the voice behind the books. "Are these—" he held his hand out toward the bookcases and realized the man couldn't possibly have seen him do so. "I'm wondering if I could do a little research. It's, uh, about my family, our home, and the little graveyard across the—"

The man's parched, slumberous voice, floated out toward Abe, stopping him mid-sentence. It hovered above his head for a moment before finding its way down to his ears. "You can," was all it said, without elaboration, though Abe was certain he detected a hint of amusement in the consent.

Despite the sensed derision, Abe reminded himself of his purpose and began pacing through the rows. He wasn't sure exactly what he was looking for. Anything on the history of the Ward House was a start. Beyond that, he didn't know what else.

On one shelf there was a pile of yellowed newspapers, but without any sort of system of organization that he could identify, Abe realized right away that searching endlessly through the documents would be too onerous and instead continued his investigation on another shelf. The next one was filled with row upon row of identical leather-bound books, all with the same golden, hand-tooled, lettering. Printed on the spine of each copy was "Town Officer", underneath which was affixed the year. The earliest edition that Abe could locate, in the top left-hand corner of the shelf, was from 1778— the year the community was incorporated. The latest volume was from 2020. At random, he pulled the texts off of the shelf. He flipped through each, seeking any mention of the Wards or Dead Rock River. With his cursory examination of each edition, Abe wasn't immediately finding anything useful. About to grab his fifth copy off of the shelf, the gentleman behind the counter again let out a hearty guffaw.

Abe poked his head out and walked back around into the main cavity of the building. After again locating the smoke cloud, he peered around the jumble of books. Sitting—waiting— for him in a small brown rocking chair, was a little man. His veiny hands cradled a large rawhide booklet or journal of some sort and he closed it at the moment Abe came fully into view. He had a long grey beard, braided into five brown-beaded points, and wore a black and white striped train conductor's cap, under which whisps of greyish-red hair shot out this way and that in an attempt to escape from their imprisonment. His shirt was a faded denim and matched, almost too closely, the color and material of his pants. His eyes were a bright, twinkling, blue and defied the aging process that'd taken hold of the rest of him. For a moment, the specter just stared at Abe. And then a smile bloomed, suddenly across his face, and the creases beside those sparkly eyes reached to join the corners of his mouth. His stubby legs dangled excitedly and his tiny feet just barely scraped the warped floorboards beneath him. From the pipe dangling from his lips, he took a long drag and puffed another cloud into the space above his head.

"This will not end like you think it will," the man said.

Caught off guard, Abe reacted by looking behind— back in the direction of the entryway. He forced himself to return the man's alarmingly entertained—almost eager— stare. "Come again?"

The man's laugh was like sandpaper. "Your property. Your family. It's all cursed. We all know it, but know wants to come out and say it. Well," he coughed. "I'm saying it." He squinted at Abe. "But you know that already, don't you? You know what you're supposed to do by now, right?"

Abe folded his arms protectively. "Look Mister, ah…"

"Shepherd. Lionel Shepherd. Town Archivist."

Abe pursed his lips. "Great. Mr. Shepherd. You see— what you just said there, I mean— well, that's just—"

"Insane? Crazy-talk? The blabbering of a madman?" Shepherd's eyes lit up again. "Perhaps."

Abe wasn't sure how to take that. "So, then that whole 'cursed' thing is—?"

"Son, you'll need to figure this out for yourself, it seems. Frankly, I'm surprised you haven't already."

Abe closed his eyes. He felt his breath refusing to leave his lungs and worried for a second that he might faint.

What is this guy talking about? My family is cursed? What does that even mean?

The man seemed to recognize that Abe was struggling to follow him. "Listen to me. The answers you seek will not be found in those old Town Officers," he waved half-heartedly at the book in Abe's hand. "Just the sad drivel of the hollowest of local politicians who want nothing more than to enshrine their pathetic accomplishments into pretty little collectibles that can sit on no one's shelf but these, waiting for some fool like you to be tricked into thinking you'll find something useful inside." He took another puff of his pipe. "*Drivel,*" he added again, for extra emphasis.

Abe stood up a little straighter. "You're the Town Archivist? Well, if these books are as useless as you say, maybe you can answer one of my questions then."

The elderly man raised his bushy, caterpillar, brows, but said nothing. Immediately after doing so, his entire body sagged a bit, as if even the small action of lifting the hair above his eyes was exhausting.

Abe cleared his throat. "What I'm wondering is…" he hesitated, embarrassed that he even had to ask what he was about to. Eventually, he spat it out. "Elma Ward—my great aunt—told me that no one is buried in our family plot. You know, the one over on Brown Street." He looked closely at the hobbit rocking in front of him. "Is that true?"

Lionel Shepherd tilted his head to one side in consideration. "Well," he began. "If it is, there's only one person I know of who was around for any of the others." He grinned again and Abe almost had to look away from the yellowed teeth and the multiple gaps in between them. "The death of a Ward, that is."

Abe shook his head. "What do you—I mean, what are you—?"

"Not many, besides your blood relatives, have ever been present for—" he stopped himself and restarted his thought. "Even your parents… you, their only child, weren't allowed to witness—"

"What do you know of *my* parents?" Abe shouted. The man across from him never broke stride in his rocking or his smiling. He simply looked up and waited for Abe to finish. After a few seconds, Abe collected himself and recovered. "If you're referring to my absence from my mother and father's funeral, well everyone thought I was too young at the time. They sent me away—Elma did, I mean." He shuffled his feet on the floor, finding himself thinking too much about the detail of that awful day. "I didn't return until it was all over with."

The man nodded at him, knowingly. "Yes, son. Exactly right." He tugged at his beard. "Think about that for a moment. If you weren't there, who else would possibly know the truth? The Wards are known to be notoriously private, with their, ah—*burials*, as you call them." He snickered and his rocking slowed, ever-so-slightly. "As far as I know, there's only one other—*non-Ward* —who's ever borne witness."

Abe gulped and rubbed at his forehead. None of what the archivist was saying made any sense to him.

Witness… witness to what? And how could only the Wards have ever been involved in their funerals? Surely the funeral director—

Abe froze, remembering Burt Barney's shock at being asked to bury Elma and his initial reluctance to host the service. There was something in Barney's reaction that'd not seemed quite right—a fear, almost— and conducting a simple graveside ceremony should have been routine for someone of his chosen profession.

But it wasn't.

Abe lifted his foot to take a step toward the aging archivist when something brushed against his leg, preventing him from completing the action. He looked down and a skinny black cat stared up at him, cautioning him from coming any closer to the counter.

Any closer to the piles of teetering books.

Any closer to the man whose eyes were laughing, entertained by Abe's lasting befuddlement.

Any closer to the *truth*.

It was as if Lionel Shepherd was watching the rusty gears turning in Abe's mind, awaiting the next question— one he knew would come—with glee.

"What *one person* are you talking about? Is it someone who can help me get some answers?"

The old fossil took the longest drag of his pipe yet and seemed to hold the smoke in for far too long. Eventually, he released it and reached a hand into the pocket of his denim shirt. Smirking wildly, he produced a small, folded, coffee-stained piece of paper and held it aloft.

"You probably should pay old Ulf Halden a visit."

He then slapped the document down on the counter, with enough force that Abe took a little hop backward. Shepherd slid the paper across the glass-top, his sweaty palm squeaking against the surface as he did so. With one final peek at his decaying gums, he grinned and lifted his hand into the air.

Abe hesitated, unsure if he should take the offering, but— after a brief moment of consideration—snatched it up. Unfolding the token, he found a nearly illegible scrawl. It was only an address. Nothing more, nothing less.

He looked back at the archivist. The fact that Abe hadn't seen him writing at all—and the idea that the address had been lying in wait in the man's pocket—was alarming, but amidst all the strange occurrences from the past few days, this one barely even registered.

Abe sniffed once, turned on his heel, and walked back out, into the safety of the sunlight, through the unforgiving, wooden, portal.

Thirty Nine

Ward!

Simi sat up in bed. The sun was high in the sky and, before long, it became evident that he'd slept most of the day away. Slumber had been only fitful for him, the echoes of the voices from the previous night having continued to reverberate off of the inside of his skull. At times, he couldn't tell whether he was merely dreaming or hearing the woodland whispers all over again. In any case, in sleeping so lightly, he'd been able to stay on guard and make certain he didn't take another enchanted jaunt outside.

His stomach growled and he made quick work of the spiral staircase as he hustled to the kitchen. The note from Abe he glanced at, but didn't touch. From inside the fridge, Simi located a package of deli turkey meat and shoved a few rolled-up slices into his mouth. Aside from a few other pantry staples—mustard, a jar of pickles, and an almost empty carton of eggs—there wasn't much else. Daisy, who'd been very willing to make sure they were eating at first, was no longer stopping by with any regularity. That he and his father were struggling to put together half-decent meals should have come as no surprise to anyone truly paying attention.

He chewed silently through the bland, processed, piece of poultry and was about to open a cabinet or two to see what else there was to satiate himself, when a loud *thwump* emanated from somewhere far over his head. Simi looked up to the ceiling and then toward the stairs.

"Abe?" he called, even though he knew for sure it wasn't him. He tiptoed to the bottom of the corkscrew and called up. "You home already?"

There was no answer. He grabbed the railing and forced himself up the few existing flights until he arrived on the third—and final— floor he could reach by that method alone. Just outside of Elma's old bedroom, he cleared his throat and attempted to summon his father once more. "Abe?" he asked, tepidly. "Is that you?"

Again, there wasn't a response. Simi was about to turn and walk back down to the kitchen when something caught his eye. Down in the shadowed recesses of the opposite end of the hallway, a small chain swung, silently, back and forth. Simi watched it and once more—even still shakier than his previous attempt—repeated his appeal. "Abe?"

The chain continued its dance. Something had moved it. A breeze—no doubt unlikely in a hallway without windows—couldn't possibly have been the real culprit. Cautiously, Simi tiptoed in the direction of the dangling metal and the attic door to which it was attached. He was only steps away when—

Ward!

—the voices returned. Simi froze, unsure if he was hearing the cries again or if it was all imagined—perhaps shell-shock stemming from the trauma of the previous evening. He stood, underneath the rectangle that presumably led to the attic, and stared directly up.

Ward!

Simi threw his hands over his ears and fell to the floor.

Ward, the invisible tormentors called to him again. *Doth thou detect an odor? From just above thy ignorant pate, it awaits.*

With his palms still protecting his ears, he carefully brought his eyes to look upon the rectangle in the ceiling again.

Answers thou seek.

The chorus continued and picked up in intensity.

Find 'em.

Find 'em.

Simi gulped.

Be not afeard. We shall not harm thou.

Simi stood, his body trembling, and reached for the chain.

Ward! Look fool upon thy past, ere it is too late.

He wrapped his fingers around the cool metallic serpent.

Find 'em, sirrah.

He took a deep breath, steeling himself for whatever beast was preparing to fall upon him.

Find 'em.

The door collapsed open. All was silent. The chanting ceased and Simi, after a moment, removed his hands from their positions by the sides of his head. Straining to hear, he listened. Nothing appeared to move or sound from within the dark, yawning, chamber. He pulled down the ladder and it clanged on the hallway floor and rug. Again, Simi waited to see if anything might react to the noise. And yet, still, he was met with a hush. Quiet. He took once last inhalation of the slightly mildewed air of Ward House's third floor and then bounded up the ladder.

His head popped up and into the opening. Letting his eyes adjust, he tried to take in his surroundings. It was indeed an attic or, at worst, a large crawl space. As in many a similar chamber, there were crates and footlockers and an old painting or two strewn about. In one corner, a seamstress dummy stood to greet him, one of its arms positioned as if to say "hello"—its other missing entirely. Simi shuddered and then pulled himself the rest of the way in.

If there's anything creepier than a creepy old Victorian manor, it's the creepy attic sitting atop the creepy old Victorian manor. In Ward House, this was, of course, no different. Simi did not know why he was there or what he was looking for. He recalled the sound and the swinging chain and immediately regretted that he had no readily available weapon or means with which to protect himself. Quickly, he searched the area nearest to him for anything that might be wieldable. With incredible fortune, he located a single croquet mallet, standing propped against a smeared—viciously smashed— vanity mirror. The once plaything would make for a suitable armament. He hefted the dusty implement, resting it on one shoulder, and progressed into the interior of the Ward attic.

Upon closer examination, he saw less and less of actual note. The first few trunks he managed to pry open were completely and anticlimactically empty. But then, in the fourth and final trunk— the one with the most intricate of nail-head borders and a giant greenish "W" painted on it its lid— Simi found something more interesting.

There was, in fact, only one item inside: a large photo album, covered with painted-on vines and yet another large green "W". Holding on to the mallet, he carefully pulled the scrapbook from its casket.

Answers—

He waved at the echo.

Answers thou seek.

Again he flapped a hand in front of his face, as if a fly were tickling the very tip of his nose.

Find 'em.

Simi gripped the front cover of the book—

Find 'em.

—and opened it wide.

Black and white photos from a long gone, long dead, time received him. Unidentifiable faces stared blankly back, mostly devoid of joy. Masks of apprehension, frozen in place, beckoned him to keep turning the cracking pages, even though each of the snapshots made him less certain he wanted to see the next. It took a few flips, but eventually, Simi found something that he recognized.

It's the backside of Ward House he thought. *Well over a hundred years ago.*

He identified the third story porthole of a window and the awful weathervane that'd outlived nearly every soul who'd slept beneath it. The ghastly, wide-staring, eye. It looked back at Simi, still unblinking, as did the faces of the two women who stood on either side of the fading picture.

Human bookends, he thought to himself.

Each donned a black, rather severe, dress that reached high up on the neck like a dark hand ready to choke the life out of its unsuspecting victim at any moment. Their sleeves were also long and covered all but the subjects' hands. And the dresses themselves touched the ground. Feet were invisible and—as far as Simi could ascertain—might as well not have existed at all.

The two women, he knew, weren't actually looking back at him. The reality—he realized— was that they could only have been staring out over the swamp. Waiting.

But for what?

Their austere, rigid, positioning reminded Simi of his own, the night before, on the precipice of the marshland. And then, he noticed something else. One the bottom right corner of the photo was a visible black blur. Though completely still, he couldn't help but feel that whatever caused it, was in the act of *rising* from the bog. At the precise instant the photographer enshrined the tableau for all eternity, something had entered the frame. Simi shivered and forced himself to believe it was more likely an issue with the development of the image, considering it had been taken—he guessed—during photography's earliest days. Without another thought, he turned the page—

—and gasped.

Up until that point, all of the images had been fairly run-of-the-mill. People standing. Posed groups of Wards. Nothing extraordinary. But this page, the final one in the album, told a completely different, altogether more spine-chilling, story.

It was no exaggeration at all to say that Simi wasn't sure what he was even looking at. The photos— themselves falling out and not even secured to the book in any real fashion or order— were all snapped out in the swamp. Simi immediately identified the setting for each as being the wetlands behind the Ward House, due to the large white boulder that found its way into nearly every image.

Dead Rock.

People gathered around, encircling Dead Rock. Torches held aloft and lining the river, all the way to Dead Rock. Shadowy figures in clothes from a bygone era, posed in grotesque dance, their flames leaving streaks on the night—all in close proximity to Dead Rock.

Dead Rock.

Dead Rock.

Simi sat up straight. There was only one characterization he could give to what he was seeing. Only one word that he felt could accurately define the imagery.

"It's... some sort of a *ritual*," he whispered.

And again, he noticed, in nearly every one of the photos, a blur leaking from a corner. Dark and foggy. Something was there, overseeing; a nefarious witness to a rite Simi wasn't supposed to know about.

Or am I?

Simi closed his eyes and tried not to let himself ponder or return to the previous night. Trembling, he slammed the album shut and tossed it back into its trunk. Its lid, too, he swatted down and ran toward the aperture in the floor.

Without hesitation, he plunged through the mouth of the attic, authorizing Ward House to swallow him—and his surging, unmitigated, dread—whole.

Forty
Night Four
October 29th

The moon was gone. Save for a handful of prancing fireflies and the sparkles of a few rebel stars, the night was dark. And Abe had left the porchlight off as well. He leaned back in the green and white lawn chair, listening at it squealed under his weight, and slapped the wooden baseball bat into his palm.

Come out, come out. Don't be shy.

His hope was that whatever had clawed Simi the previous night would show itself, without fear of the porchlight. And, if it dared to do so, he would be ready.

This time I'm not going anywhere without a good, long, look at 'ya.

The backyard was silent—

So far.

—but the swamp was alive, for once, with the song of the bullfrog and the hooting of omniscient owls monitoring all from high above. Abe craned his next to look up toward Simi's window. The light was still off and had been, as far as he could tell, all day. Simi hadn't come out of his room since Abe returned from his rendezvous with the archivist and, if it hadn't been for the crumpled sticky note sitting on top of the trash, he would've assumed his son hadn't woken that day at all.

Probably still shook up from last night. Or missing Mags. Or mad at me. Hell, it's probably all of the above. I'm not gonna bother him. Not tonight.

But was that what he was supposed to do? His inner, still-learning, parent wasn't so sure. He'd debated going up to check on the boy, but decided it better to let him be. Besides, Abe wasn't even sure he—himself—was up for any sort of real-talk right then. He stuck a hand inside his pants pocket and ran a thumb over the folded piece of paper that'd been resting exactly there ever since Lionel Shepherd handed it over to him. None of it made any sense, but it also didn't stop him from considering whether or not to pay this—

Ulf?

—a visit. In all likelihood, he figured, the old-timer might, at least, have some interesting tales to share about the Wards. A little bit of additional perspective certainly would not hurt and, at best, might shed some light on the occurrences at the house and the sensitivities of the townspeople he'd, thus far, run across.

And yet, you're hesitatin', Abe. Why? What're you afraid of? You think he's going to dig something up you'd rather not see? Something you're happy to remain ignorant of? You think—?

A single plank of wood toward the front of the porch leapt into the air, as if something was pushing up on it from underneath. It clattered back down into place and abandoned an echo that skipped out into the bog.

Abe remained still. Sitting. Waiting. He tightened his grip around the handle of the bat and a vein bulged under his tattooed forearm.

Thwack.

Another board on the opposite side of the porched jumped up and then crashed down. Abe tensed, but still kept his seat. Trying not to move, he tilted his head to the side and attempted to peek out over the far edge of the deck. There was a skittering— something crawling, crunching its way through the decaying leaves, in the dark space under the wood planks.

Thwack.

Another thump, directly in front of the sliding glass door and beside his chair. Cautiously and with purpose, Abe lifted the bat over his head.

At precisely the same instant, a faint green light emerged from the cracks between the wooden boards. It was weak at first, but as the seconds crept by and Abe remained positioned with his weapon held aloft, it grew to an overpowering, brilliantly fluorescent, blaze. Without dropping his bat, Abe tried to shield his eyes with an arm. Just as he was about to stand, a tremor rippled across the porch. Boards flew up and crashed back down, one after another. Like an earthquake, the rumbling grew and Abe was tossed out of his rickety seat and onto his face— the bat flying from his hands and caroming into the yard.

He tried, in vain, to regain his balance, but could get no further than his knees before being tossed down by the cruel, repeating, waves of undulating lumber. As the effulgence beneath continued to increase in its intensity, a murmur—craven, delirious, and hungry—erupted alongside it. The howling, though animalistic and void of intelligible language, was also full of derision. Whatever was below was taunting him.

Through his temporary blindness, Abe strained to hear over the bleating chorus of torment and ridicule.

Planks continue to slam into themselves and, at times, over him. Desperately, he tried to locate the baseball bat. With the complete absence of all, non-green, illumination, he couldn't see past the writhing of the deck. A single board smacked him hard in the face and he tumbled onto his back. Warmth ran through his fingertips as he clutched at his busted nose and he rolled toward the house. Just as he was about to attempt a grab for the handle of the sliding door, it was ripped open.

"Abe?" Simi screamed, immediately bending over to grab his father's arm. "What the—?"

"Get inside!" Abe choked as blood ran down his throat. He pushed and Simi pulled and before long both fell in through the opening. Abe climbed back to his knees and slammed the slider shut, smashing down the locking mechanism before anything seized the opportunity to sneak itself inside.

Abe's voice was still raised, in an effort to be heard over the heinous cacophony. "Sim! Get back. Get—".

All was silent. The rumbling ceased, the cries gone. The darkness was full once more, the ghoulish luminescence having slunk back into the earth. He held a finger to his lips and Simi nodded. Abe, cautiously, pulled back the white curtain in front of the door.

Smash.

Shards of glass sprayed out into their faces and a sickening, wet, blob smacked onto the laminate tiling of the kitchen floor. Abe and Simi both cowered, waiting for another barrage or intrusion, but nothing came.

Abe crawled to his son. "Are you okay?"

Simi wiped a few small pieces of slider out of his hair. He had a small gash under one eye. "Yeah, yeah. I guess so."

Together they both stood and turned their heads to confront the horror waiting for them.

"Abe—?" Simi began, but his father's hand on his arm quickly silenced him.

"I see it."

Splattered on the white tile was a mangled, hunk of shredded flesh and fur. It was impossible to tell what it was, how many critters' *parts* were knotted together, or if the grotesque glob was even just one species. Some poor creature had the complete misfortune to have stumbled across the predators living behind Ward House and—whether to intimidate or merely for the pleasure of it—the wicked nocturnal beasts had jettisoned their prey inside. A profane desecration, it lay—a pile of steaming death—at the terrified feet of the father and son.

Though neither could speak, both Abe and Simi recognized the horror for what it was: a vulgar warning to the last two—the only living—Wards.

For some inexplicable reason, Abe watched himself reach toward the gooey mass. As his fingertips grazed the glistening clump, he recoiled and—

Sunlight danced across his face, making it a struggle for him to fully open his eyes. Abe was sitting in the green lawn chair, with the baseball bat astride his splayed legs. He spun to the glass door to find it still intact. There was no gaping hole, no shards of broken glass, and no bloody mess desecrating the kitchen floor. The floorboards of the porch were similarly undisturbed.

A Canadian goose honked from somewhere not too far off, mocking the human's slow realization of what had occurred.

A nightmare is all, Abe promised himself. *Just a seriously messed up nightmare.*

Forty One

Sunlight, leaking in through a small window over the kitchen sink, roused Simi from his uncomfortable, turbulent, sleep. Earlier that morning, he'd come downstairs to find Abe snoring with his head flat on the table. Abe had awoken briefly and shared the details of some horrible dream he'd just had. At some point, they both must have passed back out, neither admitting the urge to avoid spending the remainder of the night alone. Though they easily could have found their way into the living room—and more reasonable nighttime accommodations— Abe had, surprisingly, insisted they keep watch right there, in front of the glass slider that appeared—to Simi—no worse for wear. The boy looked at his father and wondered if it truly was just a nightmare that had spooked him so. There was clearly much more Abe was not telling him—the menagerie of photographic horror that Simi himself had recently discovered supported that notion—and he wished the man would finally divulge what he knew. That he'd continued forging ahead, choosing instead to "go-it-alone" didn't surprise, Simi. Abe was as stubborn as they came, never adept at asking for help.

If he'd been better at it, Simi thought, *maybe he wouldn't have floundered in that rut of self-medication for as long as he did.*

Ready to start the day, and eager to avoid walking the path that train of thought might bring him, Simi knocked once on the hard tabletop. "Abe," he said. "Time to get up."

Abe groaned, but left his face smooshed where it was. His voice came out a bit muffled. "Time is it?"

Simi didn't bother to glance at his watch. "Time to leave. Last night—"

"Leave?" Abe sat up, rubbing the grog from his eyes. "We're not leaving."

"Abe," Simi chose his words carefully. "You're a wreck. And, I still have no idea *what* is going on. You're now having night terrors. I'm one rabies shot in. The people of this town are giving me the absolute creeps. We're finding bones in the freaking yard. What are we waiting for, huh? Look, I'm not mad. I know you felt you needed to come here. But, this has gone on far too long. I don't think we're safe here. I mean, we're obviously not. We need to split. Like *now*."

Abe shook his head. "No," he seemed to be responding to Simi and simultaneously his own conscience. "No. Soon, maybe. But, not yet."

Simi kicked himself and his chair out from the table. "But, *why*? What possible reason do we have to—?"

"I'm responsible for this place now. Until we sell it, it's all on me." He looked at Simi. "On *us*. We need to fix this thing up, put it on the market, and then—then we'll be in the clear." He nodded as if convincing himself. "Yeah, we're not going anywhere yet. Still too much to do."

Simi stood and began pacing the kitchen. "This is nuts. Look," he hunched down over the table, onto his elbows, bringing his face closer to Abe's. "I wasn't going to tell you this but, I found some super creepy stuff upstairs in the attic. There's something messed up going on here and—"

"What kind of stuff, Sim?" Abe interrupted, emotionlessly, his willingness to be persuaded ostensibly idle.

Simi rubbed a hand down over his forehead, frustrated at how much hand-holding his father needed. "Photos, Abe. Photos from like... over a hundred years ago, I think. Pictures of some sort of ritual. Out in the swamp. Torches and, and—"

"And, what, Sim?"

Simi gulped. "And there was something there. In the images. Like, a presence? Ah, shit, I dunno, man. There was this like dark blur in every single one of the photos." He sat back down at the table. "Really freaked me out. And then," he pointed outside, "And then you have this super intense, bizarre, dream last night. I mean, what the hell? What is all of this about? Seriously, *look* at me, Abe!" He slammed both of his fists onto the table.

Abe jumped a little and gawked at his son. "I'm looking, I'm looking."

"Well?"

"Well—?"

"For chrissake, Abe! I just asked you. What *is going on* here?"

Abe looked in the direction the bloody mess from his nightmare used to be and then blinked a few times. Eventually, he gathered himself and his waning, self-imposed, myopia up. "I'm not sure. Maybe Elma's death is starting to get to me. Feels like I'm starting to lose it, ya know? But, I hear you—you found some of our strange heritage up in the attic. Congratulations. Elma managed to hang on to a shit-ton of weird stuff. What else do you want me to say? And those bones? Hell, those kids that have been harassing you, putting thoughts in your head since we got here. Probably was them."

Simi flopped, facedown onto the table, and let out a deadened scream. "You've got to be joking."

"No, seriously," Abe continued. "Think about it for a second. It makes sense. They all know how gone Elma was. They probably were aware of her... ah, *affection*, for the local wildlife. Everyone was, I think. They were probably just making a mockery of that, right?"

Simi stared, unblinking, at him and shook his head side to side.

"Or maybe," Abe stood up, his finger wagging at the air. "And, I'm just spit-balling here. But, what if it *wasn't* a prank and, I dunno, maybe they've all sort of bought into this weird superstition of hers. If you ask me, I think that's it. *That's* what it is. This is some sick, sick, delusion—probably one that Elma shared openly with the locals— and they're all continuing to act out this mass hallucination, even with her now in the ground." He patted his stomach, satisfied with himself. "Yeah. That's got to be it, right?"

Simi pounded his forehead a few times onto the table. "Dammit, this is beyond lunacy. You do know how you sound, right? You are in complete and utter *denial*."

Abe ignored him and unplugged his phone from its charger. "You know what? I'm calling the sheriff. He needs to know about the mass hysteria that's got hold of this town, if he doesn't already. It's time he takes charge and makes this right. I'm reporting these damn trespassers. I've had enough."

Simi rolled his eyes. "I can already predict this will go absolutely nowhere."

Abe ignored him, dialed the sheriff's office, and turned the speaker function on so that Simi could listen along. After a few clicks, a bored voice droned on the other end. "Sheriff's Office, this is Deborah. How can I direct—"

"Hi, Deborah. I'd like to speak to Sheriff Candler."

"And who should I say is calling?"

"Abel Ward."

There was a long delay before she responded.

"I'm sorry, but he's—"

"Deborah, it's important. I know he's there. Put him on." When she didn't immediately reply, he added. "Trust me, it'll be better for us to talk over the phone than for me to come pay a visit, in person."

There was another elongated pause.

"Please hold," she finally said.

Smooth jazz filled the momentary silence. Abe sighed and snapped his fingers in the direction of Simi, whose hood had—at some point during the phone call—found its way over his head.

There was a click on the other end of the line. Abe dropped his hand and Simi sat up straighter. The music stopped and the Sheriff cleared his throat, preparing to put on his phony, aw-shucks-golly-gee-willickers-all's-well voice. "Sheriff Candler here. Now, what can I help you with Abel at this early hour? I only just got in myself and—"

"Sheriff," Abe stopped him. "There've been people on my property again. And, this time, I think it might be more than just a few dumb kids smoking reefer out back."

Candler continued to smile through the phone. "Well now, why don't you tell me exactly what happened?"

Abe swallowed and then told him everything that'd occurred since they'd arrived.

"And, it's getting worse. Every night, specifically since Elma passed, has gotten worse."

The Sheriff said nothing at first. He clearly was undecided on how to respond. He sniffed and his voice shook, audibly. "So, who do you s'pose—that is to say—what could have, do you think, possibly—?"

"Sheriff, I've told you what I know. I'm asking you to look into this for me. Please. Someone is harassing or, at least, trying to intimidate us for some reason. I don't know if they want us gone or if this is all part of Elma's—"

"Elma's what?" Sheriff Candler asked, his voice softening to a low growl, barely above a whisper.

Abe gulped and Simi's eyes widened. "Look, Sheriff. Elma wasn't well in the end. You know that, right?" There was no reply, so he continued. "What I mean to say is, I'm afraid her—uh—fantasy, became quite lifelike at the end. I think—well, no—I'm quite *certain* she must have shared it with others around town. And it's those *others* that I think are doing all of this. Putting us through this torture every night. And I need you to stop it. We can't sleep."

The Sheriff's voice remained in its lower register. Simi could almost hear him crack his neck from the other side of town and looked to see if his father had caught the report as well. "I'm not," Candler chuckled, though Abe was certain he wasn't laughing. The man sputtered for a moment and then his voice trembled to life again. "I'm not exactly sure what you'd like me to do about all of *this*."

The man's last word hung, like a moldy, wet, sock on a clothesline that hadn't been cleared off for weeks. Candler spat it out and Abe, again, choked down the small bit of saliva that'd managed to find its way into his parched throat.

"Well," he began. "Sheriff, I'd like to ask you to keep an eye on our place. You know, after dark. Make sure no one's up to anything. At minimum, a drive-by during your patrol. Would that—I mean—is that something you can do?"

Sheriff Candler snarled. "Well, I'm happy," he seemed to be struggling to hide his distaste for the request. "To take a ride past. Keep an eye out, as you say. But," and then his voice dropped to a depth that made the hair on Simi's arms stand on end. It was as if another, invisible, force was dragging the words from the man's gullet. Candler was panicking—evasive—almost like the thought of saying too much terrified him. "Not sure exactly how much good I can do or how much I can personally offer as a fix for what ails 'ya."

Simi looked at Abe who also lifted his ear from the phone. The man on the other end of the line didn't sound right, didn't sound—

In control.

"Uh, Sheriff, excuse me, but isn't it *your* job to—?"

"Like I said. *I* can't do much 'tall about this. But *you* Abel Ward," he stammered. "You, on the other hand…"

Abe pressed his mouth to the phone. "Me, *what?*"

The man let out a guttural, rasping, laugh that made Abe again pull the phone from his head. Simi also took a step back, though why exactly he reacted in such a way, he wasn't certain.

"You, friend, you could end this. Right quick," and then Candler added, his tone almost desperate. *"Please."*

Abe stammered. "I'm not sure I understand what—"

CLICK.

The phone went dead. The Sheriff, presumably, ending the call. Hanging up, without completing the puzzling conversation.

Abe placed the device down on the counter and looked at the ceiling.

Simi approached him and placed a hand on his father's shoulder. "*Now* can we go?"

Forty Two

Abe pulled the address out of his pants pocket. He stared at it, leaving his son still waiting for an answer.

"What is that?" asked Simi. "And did you hear me? Now can we—?"

"An address," he said, chewing on his bottom lip. "Got it from some guy downtown. Said this person might be able to help us."

Exasperated, Simi snatched the piece of paper. "There isn't even a name."

"It's Ulf something. At least I think that's—"

"Ulf?" Simi moaned, incredulously. "I mean, is this all real? *Some* guy downtown—"

"It was the Archivist."

"—Oh, right. Yes, *of course*, it was the Archivist. Gotcha. Okay, so this Archivist tells you... what, exactly?"

Abe took the address back, careful not to tear the paper. "I'd asked some questions, he didn't have the answers, and he thought this fellow might. That's it."

Simi scoffed, shaking his head. "What kind of questions?"

Abe grabbed his keys off a hook on the wall. "You know, about this house. This place. This— *whatever* it is we've been dealing with," he met his son's disapproving gaze. "Hey, I've got nothing else to go on. I'm not sure what more you want from me."

Simi's voice raised to a shrill octave. "I already told you! I want to go home!"

Abe began to walk toward the front of the house. "I get it, Sim. I know how you're feeling—"

"No, you don't."

"—but, I think we need to at least meet this guy. Maybe he really can help us." Simi groaned again. "Let's at least hear what he has to say, and then—then, we can make an informed decision."

Simi raced after him. "I don't believe this. This is ridiculous. You're—you're—"

"I'm heading over there now. No reason to wait. You're welcome to join me." He opened the front door and sighed as the warm sun soothed his tired cheeks. "Coming?"

"Fine, *fine*. Whatever."

They both hopped into the truck and Abe peeled out into the road. The address, Abe determined, was on the opposite side of town. With the GPS on Simi's phone, they made quick work of North Street and, within minutes, found themselves in a very secluded neighborhood. It wasn't far from the town common or any of the main thoroughfares, though the small, winding road— and the un-manicured limbs stretching across it —suggested they were somewhere remote. Homes were spread out from one another and there was more forest than friend between each.

They traveled the claustrophobic stretch of road—an artery filled with massive potholes, which Abe was careful to avoid— and the sun became veiled from view by the overhanging trees. As the pavement itself faded away into the natural shade, they passed a small brown sign that simply read, "Sunrise Pond". Sitting directly across from the small, sparkling, body of water was their destination.

Abe parked his truck on the opposite side of the road, wary of pulling directly into the stranger's driveway. The home, from the outside, appeared generally well-maintained. The design, complemented by a thick growth of ivy covering nearly half of the visible structure, looked like it'd come straight out of a children's storybook.

"Careful," Simi muttered. "Bet there's a witch in there that might try to throw you into her oven."

"Hah," Abe replied, but withheld a smile. "Fresh outta breadcrumbs too." He readied himself. "Welp. I, ah, guess we better check it out."

They'd taken only a few steps toward the front door, when a loud *thwunking* sound, emanating from somewhere behind the dwelling, caused them both to pause in their tracks.

Abe put a hand on Simi's chest to halt him, though it wasn't needed. Simi stopped on his own accord and scowled at his father. Abe removed his paw. "You hear that?"

Thwunk.

"Yeah, I hear it." Simi leaned to try and peer behind the home. "Think we should—?"

"Mhmm," Abe cut him off. "Follow me."

Together, they crept around back. As they turned the final corner, past a large holly bush, they discovered the source of the noise: an old man—his back to the both of them—was raising an ax, preparing to bring it down on top of another piece of wood. Just as he was about to do so, Abe cleared his throat. The man looked, casually over his shoulder, and then dropped the ax down hard. A log split into two pieces and tumbled to the ground. Keeping two hands tightly wrapped around the wooden shaft, he turned to face them.

Abe coughed, anxiously, again. "I, ah—excuse us, sir. We, ah—"

"I know who you are," the man spat. Removing one of his hands from his ax, he readjusted the tweed cap perched atop his wooly locks.

Simi's eyes widened. "Hey, aren't you the guy who was creeping around Elma's funeral?"

"Simi—" Abe tried to stop him.

"No, for real. Abe this is the guy I was telling you—"

The man swore and sunk his ax into a tree stump. He locked eyes with each of the Wards, in turn. "That *was* me, boy. You're right. 'Fraid, I can't be of much help to yas, though." He turned and began waddling toward a small door at the backside of the house. His knees didn't seem to bend entirely and the speed at which he covered the area was quite slow.

Abe easily caught up to him and deftly stepped in front of the arthritic gentleman before he'd an opportunity to reach for the door handle. "It's Ulf, right?" The man's rough, calloused hands clenched and a vein bulged in a sinewy forearm. One side of his upper lip lifted into a half snarl and the breathing through his massive nose was audibly belabored. He restrained an answer and Abe continued. "Ulf Halden? I was given your address and—"

"That bastahd Lionel Shepherd put you up to this, didn't he? Well, you tell him, from me, that he can go f—"

"Did you know Elma?" Simi, at some point, had

snuck up behind Halden and though his question stopped whatever curse the man had been about to spout, the senior citizen didn't appear at all startled.

Without turning to face Simi, he spoke, his eyes still locked onto Abe's. The strength in his gaze, undoubtedly, belied the truth of his real age and indicated he would still be able to hold his own in a scrap if necessary. "I did," was all the man said. He reached for his door, but Abe put a hand on it.

"Ulf," Abe pleaded. "I'm just asking for a moment of your time—"

"I *know* why you are here," he said. "Which is why I want none of this prattle. None of *you*. Please take your goddamn hand off my door before I do so myself."

"Please," Abe tried again. "All of this is so confusing to us. If you can offer—well, pretty much anything at this point—we'd be so grateful."

The man's eyes focused on Abe's face and a hint of sadness spread over his own, partially melting through whatever gristle and spit he'd elected to present with. "I was hoping youda just left this town by now."

Abe looked to Simi. "You're not the only one."

With resignation, Ulf sighed and pointed at a few rickety plastic lawn chairs, covered in grime and bird droppings. "Sit then. My legs won't let me stand for much longer." He shuffled to the nearest chair—his knees almost completely unbending—and plopped down into it, not bothering to wipe his seat down. He gestured again for the two Wards to join him. They both did and he inhaled deeply, as if attempting to suck in the wooded sentinels that towered over his home. "I'll tell you whatever I can, but then you'll hafta leave my property and never return. I've managed to stay outta this for the last eighty years or so and don't intend to turn over any new leaves today. Got it?"

Abe and Simi both nodded, though they also didn't have much of a choice. Ulf looked back at the two, waiting for someone to speak. "Well?" he said. "Someone gonna say somethin'?"

Abe leaned forward in his chair, folding his hands together. "Okay—for starters—how did you know Elma? You were at her funeral. Simi saw you. What was your, ah, *connection* to my great-aunt?"

Ulf folded his arms and something cracked. He grimaced and, as the words fell from his pale lips, each syllable sounded more painful than the next. "We were to be married."

Abe sat back and put his hands on his head. "Married?" he said. "You mean you—you and *Elma*— were engaged?"

Ulf sniffed. "For chrissakes man, didn't I just say that? Are you even listenin'? If I'm gonna hafta keep repeatin' myself—"

"No, no," Abe tried to salvage the start to his line of questioning. "I'm sorry. I was just taken aback. Elma never told me—well, she never told me. I hadn't realized there'd been anyone —anyone like you, that is—in her life. She raised me, for much of mine and—"

"Abel," Ulf interrupted, as if he were talking to someone he'd known for years. "It's not you that needs to do any educatin' today. I remember you as a boy. As vivid as if it were my last bowel movement. I know your story and of how much pain you caused that poor woman when you disappeared. I know because I saw it, from afar. I—*recognized* it, even. It was the same misery I'd dealt her when I abruptly ended our engagement, you see." He closed his eyes and turned his head up to face the heavens. "Not that it wasn't entirely her fault."

Simi, wanting to interject himself into the conversation, chimed in. "What wasn't her fault?"

Amused with the teen, Ulf almost broke into a smile. "Feelin' left out are ya, boy? Well, *don't*. Don't allow yourself to be dragged down into this mess." He looked at Abe. "You, either." He cocked his head to the side, reconsidering. "But then, I suppose, maybe it's too late for all that. Maybe you're already in too deep. It was, as I'd eventually find out, too late for *her*. For *us*."

"I don't—" Abe tried to interject, but Ulf kept going.

"Elma coulda left it too, ya know? At least, that's what a young, foolish, me thought those many years ago. I know now, of course, how wrong I was. Once I discovered the truth, I thought she should've abandoned this town to finally deal with the sin it'd allowed to fester and boil beneath its surface for so long. I wanted her to run and never look back, but she felt this inexplicable—*duty*, I'd guess you'd call it—to stay. Never told me why she had to be here. But, I *wanted* her to leave it all. To come away with me. Now, I understand how wrong I'd been. How impossible an ask that was of her. Still, I would've—" he swiped at an eye. "Aw, hell."

Abe and Simi looked at each other, unsure of how to comfort the unvarnished stranger. "What, exactly, did you want her to leave, Mr. Halden?"

The man sat up, sharply, his eyes on fire. "I wanted her to leave the devils behind. But that was never going to happen. *Never*. How could it have? She was—as I'd later learn—all that was keeping them at bay."

Abe inched his chair closer. "I'm sorry," he swallowed. "Devils? Look, Mr. Halden—"

"There's only so much, I know, Abel. I never seen exactly what plagued her with my own eyes— at least, not close up. Not with any real clarity."

A bird screamed from overhead. Abe and Simi flinched, but Ulf sat unmoved. Stone-faced.

"So, what," Abe began again, trying to steer the conversation. "*do* you know?"

Halden growled. "I'm tellin' ya, ain't I?" He wheezed and pounded himself on the chest. "Bloody hell." He cleared his throat and regained his composure before continuing. "As I said, we were to be married. In our early twenties, we both were, and—"

"Early twenties? Both of you?" Simi's mouth dropped. "That'd make you—"

"Nearin' my hunderd and fifth birthday. That's right. She was 'bout a year older'n me." He winked. "I always had a thing for older women."

Simi cringed and rubbed the back of his neck.

"So, what happened?" Abe jumped into the fray again.

The mirth faded off Ulf's face. He seemed annoyed at being pulled back to reality. The truth— the rest of it, at least—was evidently painful for him. The centenarian sighed. "Ah, yes. You wanna know why two so madly in love ended it. Called it quits. Right?" Abe and Simi nodded, uncertainly. "Well, it's a horrible thing. Monstrous even, if I'm bein' frank. Started with a death. Her father, suddenly. One day he was fine and then the next—gone. Kaput. Hello and how are ya to the sweet, long, goodnight."

He waited for a laugh of some kind from the Wards, but got no such reaction. "Anyways. He was deader'n shit is what's important. 'Bout a week or so before the wedding, if I'm rememberin' correctly, I get invited to—what I thought was— the poor man's funeral."

"But it wasn't a funeral," Abe whispered.

Ulf shuddered. "No. It weren't no funeral. For one thing—and this should have probably tipped me off—I was summoned to this *service* just after dusk. For one reason or t'other, I don't even question it. I show up at the small burial ground, expectin' to see everyone. But the place was empty. Completely. A ghost town." He chuckled at his joke. "No one was there. Fortunately—or unfortunately, depending on how you're viewin' m'story— the Ward House is just across the street, and I—I sees somethin' tru dem trees. Down in the swamp. Torches. Like little fireflies, flickerin' tru the woods. Showin' me the way. Maybe she wanted me to see them, maybe she figured I'd give up and just head home." He smiled. "Course, you know by now, I didn't just head home. Nossir. Not right away, at least."

"So, I cross that road. Still Brown Street, even way back then. I cross and look up at the 'ol Ward place and there ain't a single blasted light on inside. Darker'n the devil's arsehole. Everyone must be down there, I thinks to m'self. Standin' in the bog, I assume. And, as I comes into the back yard there, I hear voices." He lowered his own and spoke slowly, making sure the two heard every last one of his words. "Now, mind you, I can't get all the way out into the marsh and, for the life of me, I don't know how they did either. But, I needed a better view, so I climbed up on top of one of their sheds." He gulped and looked from Abe to Simi a few times. "And what I saw then—when I saw that, I knew—well—I didn't know what it was. But, I knew I had to convince Elma to come away with me."

Abe stood up and walked to the tree line behind Ulf's house. He held his folded hands on top of his polished head. "What did you see?"

Ulf wheezed again and Simi asked if he could get him some water. The old man waved him off. "I'm alright. Let me just—" he coughed again. "Let me just get this over with. I need this to be done."

Simi sat back down and, after a moment, so did Abe. "What did you see, Mr. Halden?" Abe asked again.

Ulf's eyes focused on something invisible, something cloaked in over eighty years of thick, impenetrable, denial. "I saw the Wards. All of 'em, at the time. Elma, her brother, and t'others. There were many more back then, still around. Still kickin'. Their torches lined the river, lightin' its path. The orange, *glowing*, trail led all the way up to Dead Rock and its big, fat, white face was grinnin' back at me. The Wards were surroundin' it, in some sort of circle. They were chanting and his body was…" he put his face in his hands. "His body was layin' there, splayed out. They sang and sang and then the shadows began to stretch." He licked his lips. "They started creepin' closer until—and this is the part that makes the least sense to me— the shadows started to call out. The shadows were movin'— and not because any clouds were driftin' past the moon or anythin'. No, no. They were movin' all on their own. And they were—"

"What?" Abe and Simi seemed to ask almost simultaneously.

"*Devouring*. Him. And, all the while, they sang. They sang and sang and I then—right then—did I finally run."

They all sat in silence. No one dared to move, at first. A tree limb crashed to earth somewhere behind them, but they weren't stirred. Eventually, after Ulf was induced into another phlegmy fit, Abe shifted in his uncomfortable bird-poop-covered seat. Ulf pointed at him. "You want to know what happened after that, right? Whatever came of Ulf and Elma? Elma and Ulf? Ah well, it may surprise you to hear it, but that night wasn't the end. No, that regrettable moment came a few days later. You see, I tried my best to get her to leave then. But she couldn't. She never was gonna. And, I—well, isn't it obvious? I couldn't ever be a part of—*what-*

ever that was. That vile, blasphemous, ritual. And, you know what's wild? See, I might never have realized what I was days away from marryin' into if that ol' fart hadn't kicked the bucket right then and there." He laughed an uncomfortable laugh, once again.

Abe seemed to wake up. "So, he wasn't buried in the—?"

"None of 'em are, Abel. Not a one."

Abe shook his head, furiously. "Their graves are all there. All the Wards are buried in that little, godforsaken—"

Ulf snarled. "No, they ain't, Son. Listen to me. They're all *empty*. There ain't nothin' there. Nothin', 'cept for Elma, now. Thanks to you. The rest are just markers. For show is all."

Abe stood up. "No way. This is fantasy. This is—c'mon, Simi. I think we've heard enough. Mr. Halden, I'm sincerely sorry for wasting so much of your time. Simi, let's—"

"Abe," Simi resisted his pull. "Maybe there's some kind of truth in this. I mean, the photos—"

'No, Simi," Abe stopped him. "We're leaving."

Ulf stood up and started walking himself back toward his door. As he ambled, he spoke and a slight tremor was audible in his aging voice. "Abel. Listen to me and listen to me good. If you know what's right for you—"

Abe was pulling Simi from his chair, trying to talk over Halden. "No. *No*. This is insanity, this is—" He caught himself and for an instant felt an overwhelming pity for the man. If it truly were dementia, he needed to be more considerate. Abe attempted an apology. "I'm sorry. I know you mean well. It's just that—"

"You came to me—remember, Son? If you know what's good for you, you'll do the same as they did. As they've *always* done."

Simi yanked his arm free again. Abe was already almost back around the side of the house. "Abe, maybe we should listen—"

"No," Abe said with finality. "No, I'm really sorry for bothering you, Mr. Halden." He lowered his voice and whispered to his son. "I'm not doing this. Simi, we're going."

As they both crossed the front yard of the ivy-covered home, Ulf's voice called to them once more, rasping its way to their ears. "You won't be able to refuse them for much longer, Abel!" he cackled. "What's today… tonight'll be the fifth right? The fifth night since Elma…"

The end of his sentence was cut off as an indistinct sedan barreled down the road. After it passed, Ulf's raving voice could still just barely be heard.

"…we're close to this all busting wide open, Ward!"

Abe had a grip on the door handle of his truck. Simi was climbing into the passenger side. Abe wanted nothing more than to hop in and drive as fast as he could from that spot, but Simi made one last attempt at getting an answer from Elma's ancient lover even as his father peeled away. "What does that mean, Mr. Halden? Please tell us!?"

Once more the man howled from his back stoop as he listened to the truck huffing down the crooked road. "If you don't do something soon," the wind whipped and with it, the man's voice smashed through the vulnerable serenity beside Sunrise Pond. "You'll find out!"

Forty Three
Night Five
October 30th

In many ways, night was the best time of day to be in the Clown Room. As far as Simi was concerned, at least, it was easily the most palatable. He'd never been one to sleep with any sort of nightlight or comforting illumination and the simple cloaking of the unsettling, painted grimaces and their accompanying red-noses was most welcome. Simi rolled to face his small dresser and tried not to think any further about the conversation he and Abe had finished up—only hours before—with Ulf Halden.

There's got to be some truth in this. Why would the man lie?

Abe was convinced that dementia, considering Ulf's advanced age, was the most likely culprit. Even though much of what Elma's former fling had said fit into and explained some of what they'd been experiencing, Abel hadn't been able to admit that any of it was even remotely plausible. He'd repeated, on their drive home, what—over the remaining hours of the day— had become almost a mantra; a belief that he couldn't shed for fear of what it would otherwise imply.

They're all there. They're all there. They're all there.

They, of course, being the dead Wards. *There*, without a doubt, could only have meant the ancestral burial ground. Simi was smart enough to realize that his father was repeating it for himself, mostly because he had to be convinced of what was now being brought seriously into question. Simi couldn't help but want his father's conviction—his maxim—to bare itself out. Everything else was just too terrifying to consider for more than a few twitches of his naked toes.

The darkness was the coldest it'd been since their arrival. Even with every last gaudy quilt and comforter he could find stashed in the room's lone closet piled on top of himself, he still shivered. A few minutes earlier—distracted by some cryptic texts from Mags—he'd felt a bit warmer. But, with the light from his phone completely dimmed, the trembling commenced. Mags seemed to not have time to chat. Her messages were brief and refused, for some reason, to provide any detail as to where she was or what she was up to that evening. Simi could tell there was something she didn't want to tell him, perhaps even something she was withholding. In an effort not to pry or come across as untrusting, he decided to let it be.

Probably just out with some friends. So, what's the big deal?

Simi rolled onto his back and, just as he was about to let his eyes shut fully for the first time that evening, froze with the musty comforter just inches from his flared nostrils. Something moved, to his left, just visible out of the corner of his eye.

A figure, completely shrouded in the pitch dark that Simi himself had induced unto the cramped space, stood upright at the open window overlooking the backyard. Simi held his breath and yet—somehow—still heard steady, rasping, inhalation. The shadow was breathing and Simi dared not move or call out.

Did I take that stupid clown back out of the drawer? Is that all that is? Why would it be sitting in the window now?

Again, he listened as the shape wheezed, heavily, and realized it could not possibly have been the demented, plush, doll. The humanoid form was devoid of all features—likely obscured by the night— except for two pulsing green orbs that sat embedded in its skull. Simi turned slowly, in an attempt to get a closer look. With each breath that the creature took, the hole where its mouth should have been widened, baring rows of razor-sharp, hooked, fangs. And then, quite abruptly, the being reached out to him.

Simi recoiled. At first, it seemed—with the creature's amorphous feet firmly planted on the outside sill—that it wouldn't possibly be able to touch him. More confidently, Simi sat up and faced the intruder. Though its arms remained outstretched, the demon would—for some, unknown, reason—still not enter. Stray bands of light glinted off of the taloned tips of its snakelike fingers, which writhed whimsically in an attempt to grasp at him. Simi stepped off the side of his bed closest to the dresser and slowly began to back himself toward the door.

"You're gonna have to try harder than that, asshole. What, you too afraid to step into this creepy—"

The shadowy limb suddenly started to stretch. Like the bough of a gnarled crab apple tree, backlit by wandering moonbeams, the rogue tentacle grew. *Unfurled.* The visitor's eyes grew brighter with the anticipation of a feast soon to be, and— just as the elongated demonic hooks crossed the threshold of Simi's bed— the youngest living Ward began to scream for his father.

Simi couldn't be sure exactly what words exploded from his mouth, but he knew he needed help. His muscles were—suddenly and without explanation— petrified to the point that he couldn't even turn away or tear his eyes from the horror that intended to pluck him into the darkness and from the confusing asylum that was the Clown Room.

He screamed and screamed. The blurry feelers of his would-be kidnapper encircled a wrist that could not flee. Simi felt himself lurch, unable to fight back against the glacial grip that tugged him forward. His shins thwacked against the wooden bed frame. He knew he was still shouting, but the terror that flooded into his ears was so loud that he heard nothing else. He was falling forward onto the bed—his arm pulled taught by the slowly retracting, serpentine clutch— when the door to his room burst open.

Abel entered swinging. Almost immediately, he connected with the offshoot of the shadow creature. It howled as Abel dropped a Louisville Slugger down with all of his strength onto the elastic appendage. Its grasp released and Simi flew backward into his bureau. Dresser drawers opened wildly, falling to the ground, and—as Abe continued to lunge with reckless abandon at the freakish trespasser that still hovered, unwaveringly, on its perch—the grinning clown doll, roughly the size of a very small child, tumbled out into the blackness of the room. Its face, startlingly white, was visible even though the rest of its features were mostly hidden. As it fell to the warped wooden floorboards, Barachiel tottered into a seated position, directly in the line of sight of the monster.

The demon shrieked once and threw itself out and into the night.

Abe chased the miscreation to the window and called out. "And don't come back, you bastard!" He turned to face his son. "Simi, are you okay? Are you hurt?"

Sore from making contact with the dresser, Simi stood up slowly. He held out his wrist and Abe flicked on the light. "*Okay*? Christ, are you serious? No, I'm not even close to okay. I haven't been okay since we got here." Abe continued to pant and stare at his son until Simi added, begrudgingly, "But, I'm not seriously injured, Abe, if that's what you're wondering. If you hadn't—I mean, thanks for—"

Abe shook his head, not sure what to say. "No, it's—I'm just glad I got here in time." He hefted the bat onto his shoulder, his confidence visibly growing alongside his adrenaline and the knowledge that he'd, moments earlier, saved his boy. "Fortunately, I found this in the shed and decided to keep it beside my bed. Came in handy, I guess."

Simi crossed the room and slammed the window shut, turning the lock tight. "What *was* that, anyway, Abe?"

Abe gulped. He sighed and shrugged. "I don't know, Sim. That can't be what—I mean, Elma's stories. Elma's song. They can't be real. They can't be—"

"What Abe? What can't they be? 'Cause that's about the realest shit I've seen in a long time. Take a look at my goddamn wrist!"

Abe's face softened and his eyes half-closed as he peered away into a long-repressed memory. "They just can't be real."

Simi stormed across the room and planted himself nose to nose with his father. "What, Abe? What are they, Abe? For godsakes, tell me!"

Abe sat down, gingerly, on the edge of the bed and looked as if he might cry. The clown doll stared up at him and he closed his eyes to avoid holding the ghoulish effigy's gaze for too long.

"Malevolent Nevers," he buried his face in his hands and let the baseball bat clatter to the ground. "That's what Elma called them, Sim. Malevolent Nevers."

Simi rubbed at his forehead. "Malevolent…" he lowered his voice until it registered only just above a whisper, his question escaping like an exhausted, autumn breeze struggling to move a single, pesky leaf. "Abe, what *are* they?"

In a trance, Abe began to sing. Simi heard only a couple of lines of the deranged dirge before deciding he could listen no more. Staring uneasily back at his father, simultaneously afraid of the evil beginning to percolate to the surface of the man's pupils and tired of his incessant obfuscation, Simi hung his head and stepped through the open door and into the hallway.

"I'm leaving in the morning, Abe. With or without you. You can sit here and continue to ignore what's happening, but I'm out. You may still have demons you need to face, but to hell with dragging me along for the ride."

Abe's tormented voice followed him like a sad, just-awakened, ghost into the dark recesses of the Ward House.

"*…Here they wait for all our evers,*
O' Malevolent, Malevolent Nevers."

Forty Four

Abe stared at the phone cradled in his hands. The message he'd texted Daisy, almost an hour before, gawked back at him, unanswered.
Abel Ward: Are you around? I'm struggling here.

He wasn't sure exactly why he'd reached out to her, other than that he just really wanted someone to talk to. Abe was under no illusion that she would have any answers for him, though he secretly hoped she might. There was no one else who'd spent as much time with Elma in recent years as she had and even a small amount of insight into the pandemonium of the preceding few days, he figured, could be very valuable. Besides that, he also wanted something to tell Simi beyond the regurgitated fairy tale Elma had lived by until her dying day. The boy hadn't spoken a word to him since running from his room that night, since he declared he'd be leaving in the morning, and Abe had decided he wouldn't be able to change his mind. Simi wanted answers and Abe refused to fault him for that. The problem was that even Abe couldn't bring himself to believe the only explanation he'd come remotely close to providing.

He slumped back into the dusty folds of the sunken couch cushions. The earliest of the morning's light was finding its way in through the stained glass arch above the main doorway of the house, and its rainbow-colored refraction lit up the floor just beyond his outstretched, splayed, legs. His feet were still bare, just as they'd been when he'd dashed from his room and into Simi's, and the yellowing of a soon-to-be bruise was forming around his right ankle. He'd no memory of injuring himself, though assumed it could only have happened during his flight or, perhaps, the ensuing, brief, confrontation.

Come on, D. Are you still sleeping? Just answer the text. I thought you were an early bird these days.

He ran a hand at the stubble beginning to form on his unshaven scalp. Typically he never missed a day, but, admittedly, had been a bit more distracted than usual. He'd just about decided to head to the bathroom for a shower and a fresh razor to his dome when there was a quick tap-tap-tapping at the front door. Someone—or some*thing*—had just brought the knocker down rapidly, in three consecutive thumps.

Abe only hesitated for a moment, before rising to his feet. He crept along the cold, stained wood of the foyer and grasped the door handle. Wishing that Elma had invested in a peep-hole, he steeled himself.

Alright, you son-of-a—

He pulled the door open and—

"Huh?"

A beaming face smiled up at him. Her dreads, tied off in a variety of rainbow colors, hung loosely, and bounced as she hopped, spritely, up onto the last step.

"Mags?"

"Heya, Abe," she smiled, adjusting her green horn-rimmed frames. "Surprise! What's doin'?"

He fumbled for the right words. Her presence, he immediately realized, was the bitterest of sweet. "Uh, hi. Jesus, Mags. Why—I mean, what are you doing here?"

She tilted a single, pierced, eyebrow, clearly unsure what to make of his welcome. "I wanted to surprise Simi. Seems like he's been having a tough time—uh—being so far from home. Thought I might be able to cheer him up. He hasn't run away yet, right?"

Abe still hadn't moved out of her way. "Do your parents know you're here?"

Mags laughed. "Of course. And they're cool with it, I promise. Paid for my bus ticket, even. I've traveled alone to my aunt and uncle's place in the Berkshires many times before. In the fall, to watch the leaves change over. They've got this cute little place at the foot of the mountain in Adams and—"

Abe blinked, still stunned. She stopped talking as he pinched at the migraine forming between his eyes. "I just wish you'd—look, Mags, I get what you're doing. This is a super sweet idea. But, you see, there's just a lot going on right now. A lot that—well—maybe right now just isn't the best time for—"

"Mags?"

A tired voice squeaked from behind him on the staircase. Abe twirled to meet it and Mags finally stepped past him into the house.

"Hey, Sim! Surprise!"

Simi had his duffle in one hand, but tossed it over the railing. The two rushed to embrace and fell in a giggly mess onto the couch. "God," Simi gushed. "I'm just so glad you're here. But, why…"

Abe lost the rest of their conversation as he quietly shut the door. Their happiness and joy at being reunited should have been uplifting, a time for celebration, but he couldn't help but feel an even heavier weight upon himself than he had only minutes prior. Leaning forward, he placed a hand on each of his knees as the room started to spin ever so slightly.

Forty Five

"Oh, *hell* no."

Mags had only taken a couple of steps into Simi's room before halting. Her eyes nearly popped out of her skull as they toured the whimsical sleeping chamber.

"Nice, huh?" Simi laughed.

Mags poked at the doll teetering on the edge of the bed. "Yeah, if you're Stephen King. And, you actually *sleep* here?"

"Mhmm."

"Like... *alone*? All night?"

He picked up the clown and tossed it in front of the closet. "Well, I try. But there's hasn't exactly been much in the way of rest here. Not yet, at least." He pursed his lips. "Hey, listen, Mags, there's a lot you should know—"

"Well," she interjected. "We've got plenty of time. So you're aware, my parents said I could hang here for as long as I want. Or, at least until your dad kicks me out. I told them he wouldn't, though, of course. I mean—duh—it's me." She winked at him. "Ooh, and my teachers are gonna be forwarding my work so I don't have to stress about falling behind at all."

Simi sat down on the bed and gestured for her to do the same. "It's more complicated than that, Mags. Like, *way* more complicated. To be honest, before you arrived today, I was planning on leaving. This place is..." he stopped, unable to find the right words.

"What, Sim?"

"I swear to God, you're not gonna believe any of it. I'm talkin', like, even less plausible than glitter on a mother-effing zombie."

She rolled her large, dark brown eyes at him. He hung his head and his messy hair covered up his consternation. Mags reached over and pulled Simi's bangs back. He looked up at her and the shock on her face told him that she understood how serious he was being.

"Tell me," she pleaded. "I promise to listen and take it all in stride." He tilted his head to the left and she pulled it back to face her once more. "I mean it. Tell me *everything*."

And so, he did. The best he possibly could, at least. It wasn't exactly like he could *explain* much of it, or label his experiences, but he relayed what had been happening since they'd arrived—point by point—and bravely displayed his battle wounds. Throughout his story, Mags listened and barely broke eye contact with him. She nodded and didn't overreact to anything, as if Simi were merely describing his dismay that a pizza had been delivered late or that he'd earned a C+ on a History exam. When he finished, she sat up straight and then immediately proceeded to flop onto her back.

"It's crazy, right?"

She stared up at the popcorn ceiling. "I mean..." she closed one eye, focusing on something he couldn't see. "It's not *not* crazy," she smirked and punched him in the leg.

Simi flopped down next to her. "But, isn't it? Shadow gremlins terrorizing us at night? If Abe weren't seeing 'em too, I'd be seriously concerned for my own well-being."

Mags rolled to her side, facing him, and propped herself up on one elbow. "But Abe *is* seeing them, right? So they must be *some*thing. We just need to figure out what, exactly." She furrowed both brows. "You know what I think?"

He shook his head. "No."

"I think it's probably just those kids you told me about. Or some other weirdos in this town. I bet someone is, like, obsessed, with your—your—"

"My great-great-aunt."

She pointed at him. "Exactly. It makes sense. She lived here for like a thousand years. And they, I dunno, maybe they, like, worshipped her."

"Worshipped her?" Simi cocked his head.

"Okay, okay. I'm exaggerating, Sim. Obviously. But, you get what I mean." Mags stood up and began to pace around the room. "She dies, after all this time. These people who… idolized her, or whatever, can't deal with her being gone. And so, they act out her fantasy as a sort of… way to commemorate her. Who knows, maybe they're even responsible for making her believe all of this in the first place? Maybe they've—the people of Foxborough, I mean— maybe they've been terrorizing her, and your family, all of these years. This could just be a continuation of that. There are certainly weirder things that happen in small towns."

Simi sat up. "I dunno, Mags. This is sort of similar to what Abe's been trying to convince himself of—but, I'm still not sure. It sounds… kind of *cultish*. Doesn't it? And, what about that thing that attacked me? Your explanation conveniently leaves that event out. I mean, I have a hard time believing—"

"You have a hard time believing… what? That some bog demons are paying you nightly visits? That some swamp sprites are dancing at your door? That these hobgoblins from the Hell-Marsh are… *hell*-bent on menacing the Wards?

"Had to try real hard to fit that extra 'hell' in there, didn't 'ya?"

She folded her arms and glowered at him. "All I'm sayin' is, is it so much weirder to think that the locals are a tad wacky around here? Cults are a real thing, you know. Like, they *actually* exist, Sim. I don't know about you, but I have a much easier time accepting that than, well… the *alternative*."

Simi was quiet for a moment, before standing to wrap his arms around his longtime girlfriend. He knew the atrocity standing in his window couldn't possibly have been human—he'd felt it's dead, glutinous, grasp on his wrist for godsakes— but was too sapped to argue. "Maybe you're right. Maybe it really is just some weird, secret—"

"*Cult*," she finished for him.

"Right. In any case, thanks for talking this out." He pulled her in and gently kissed her on the mouth. "Still am processing that you're here with me. In this creepy-ass room."

Mags looked around at it. "Yeah, well. This room is a whole other… *thang*." She raised herself on tiptoes to kiss him on the nose. "Hey, by the way. Happy Halloween."

Simi stepped back and clapped a hand to his forehead. "Holy shit, that's tonight? I completely forgot."

She turned and walked toward her duffle. "Yeah, well, you've sort of been going through a lot. But, it's a big part of why I picked to today to get my ass up here."

"Yeah, but… damn. Halloween, huh? Our favorite night of the year. So wish we were back in Hotlanta. Would have been fun to catch the midnight showing of *Rocky Horror* again. Get all dressed up."

Mags bent over her bag and turned to wink at him. Slowly, she rose back up, holding something behind her back. "Well, just 'cause we're stuck here, in this eerie town, doesn't mean we can't still have a bit of fun. Right?"

"Well, I dunno, Mags, it's not exactly—"

Before he could finish the thought, she revealed two old-timey, plastic Halloween masks. One a bright green Frankenstein's monster and the other an orange, grinning Jack-O-Lantern. Thin white elastic bands hung from the back of both.

"Woah. Straight outta the Eighties," Simi nodded, approvingly.

Mags shrugged. "Probably even older than that."

Simi took the masks from her, but his delight was short-lived. "Mags, I don't think you realize how serious this all is. I'm for real worried these creatures are going to keep coming back. Last night was like something out of a horror movie. And I don't know how I would manage if anything happened to you. Do you fully understand—?"

"Simeon Ward," she lowered her voice and folded her arms in an attempt to sound like an overbearing parent. She couldn't keep up the act for long, though, and eventually relaxed, giggling. "I already told you, I believe you. Buuut…"

He sagged. "But, what?"

"But, I think you need something to take your mind off of all of this. Even just for a couple of hours."

"Mags—"

"Just a couple of hours, I said."

Simi closed his eyes and then opened them again. "Okay," he said. "Fine. Just a couple of hours and then—then, we'll leave." He snatched the Frankenstein mask from her. "But I get to be Frankie."

She kissed him. "Deal."

Simi walked toward the door. "So, what exactly did you have in mind? Shenanigans?"

Mags smiled. "*Of course*, shenanigans." She pulled on the pumpkin mask and snapped the band to the back of her head. "So, what'll it be my good man? Tricks or treats?"

Forty Six

Abe locked the door behind himself. He knew the kids were both still inside and likely would be able to fend for themselves— especially in the remaining hour or so of daylight— but turned the deadbolt anyways.

Until I know exactly what we're dealing with here, a little added deterrent won't hurt anything.

He spun toward the street and jumped back as Daisy waved at him from the end of the walkway.

"Shit, D. You scared me."

She frowned. "Got your text."

He walked past her and reached for the door handle on his truck. "Yeah? How come you didn't respond?" The creak of hinges squealed as he pulled the driver's side open.

Daisy raised her shoulders and let them drop. She pulled her puffy, blue-fleece-lined, jacket closed and yanked up on the zipper. The air was finally reaching a normal-for-fall-in-New-England feel. "Figured this conversation was better to have in person."

Abe stopped. "Conversation? How do you even know what I wanted to ask you?"

She pursed her lips and turned her gaze down the street. A light wind moved the stray strands of light brown hair from in front of her face and she closed her eyes. "Because Elma's been dead for six days, Abe, and—"

"*And?* And what the hell does that even mean, D? Huh?" He left the car door hanging open and took a step closer to her. "I'm getting just about sick of all this cryptic hinting that everyone single asshole and their grandma seems to be doing in this town. Mind enlightening me?"

Daisy kept her eyes shut and didn't face him. "Abe, anyone who's heard the stories—anyone who's spent even five minutes with Elma would know about—"

"About, what D? *Malevolent Nevers?* That fairytale horseshit she was selling since I was a kid? Is that what you mean?" he gulped. "Of all people, I figured you would know better than to believe—"

"What? Say it."

"It's a stupid nursery rhyme, D. That's it."

"No, it's not."

"Oh, come on, D. You can't be serious—"

"Jesus, Abe," she cut him off and finally opened her eyes. "What's it gonna take for you to believe what's happening around you? Now, I've never seen with my own eyes what's out there," she pointed toward the swamp behind the house. "But I don't think I need to. We've all grown up with the stories. We all have a general knowledge of what she was doing out here. And… then, I came to work for her. Not just because she needed my help, but, because we all *knew*, Abe. Every last person in this town. We all *know*. Someone had to help her."

Abe put his hands in his pockets and look at the ground. "Help her... with *what*, D?"

She folded her arms. "I'm not sure I ever fully realized what it was I was doing. I mean, I knew she fed them. That much was just something everyone in this town—I dunno—*knows*. She put food out there, by those sheds. Always has. Not that I think anyone, other than her, understood exactly what they were. *Are*. But we've all heard the song. How could we not?"

"Fed?"

She swallowed. "I put out scraps of whatever we'd had for dinner each night and that seemed to be enough. But she—and I'm not sure I ever grasped what she meant and probably still don't entirely—but, she told me that soon—soon, it wouldn't be enough. It was an appeasement, she would say. Just something to hold them off for as long she..."

Abe stared at her. "As long as she what, D?"

Daisy looked up into his eyes and again the cool breeze lifted her bangs and dropped them gently over her forehead. "As long as she was still alive."

Abe turned away from her and opened the truck again. He sat down in the driver's seat and looked up at her. "Great. Fan-*flipping*-tastic. So, what am I supposed to do now? That's what I need to know."

Daisy shivered and again looked down the road, this time in the direction of the old burial ground. "I don't know for sure, Abe. Or, maybe I do, but I'm just too afraid to say it."

He hit his head against the headrest. "Dammit. Dammit. Dammit." He nodded to himself. "Okay. Fine. Get in."

She hesitated. "Where are we—?"

"Back to Ulf's. I'm ready to listen. If he'll still talk to me, that is."

Daisy ran around to the side of the truck and hopped in. Abe started the engine and pulled out. They sat in silence as he took the left onto North St. and headed for the center of town. Eventually, Abe realized that Daisy was staring at the side of his head.

"Yeah?"

She put a hand on his shoulder. "I appreciate you taking me with you, *this time*."

Abe didn't take his eyes from the road. He pretended to fiddle with the visor, even though the sun wasn't in his eyes. "Oh," he said. "I mean—uh, what?"

She chuckled to herself. "It's okay, we don't have to talk about this now. More important things to deal with. I just thought—oh, I'm not sure what I thought. But, it's good to be with you again. To be near you. Sharing the same space. Even considering the circumstances. Hadn't been ready to say that until now. With everything going on with Elma, it just felt like a bit too much to manage. She was dying and you were rolling back in after such a long absence. Can you blame me?"

Abe winced and tightened his grip on the steering wheel. He felt his mouth drying and tried to swallow. "Daisy, I—"

"Really, Abe, it's okay—"

"No," he said as they pulled around the rotary and the town common. They passed the library and a white church. Someone was in the cross-walk and Abe stopped. The woman, a mother pushing a baby carriage, waved a thanks at him. He waved back. "No," he said again. "I'm sorry, Daisy. About—well, all of that. Leaving you. I know it was a long time ago and—"

"We were just kids," she finished for him.

"Right," he agreed. "We were so young. And, I had

my own demons to deal with back then. One day, I just had to get out. And I'm sorry I never—"

"It's okay," she whispered as he pressed his foot on the gas pedal again and they lurched around the remaining portion of the roundabout. "It's okay." There were tears in her eyes and her "okays" didn't appear to be convincing even herself. "Teenage love isn't necessarily—"

"Right," Abe nodded again. "But, I still regret not talking to you. And— shit, D, maybe—who knows—maybe, if I could do it all over again—maybe I'd have taken you with me. Or have stayed." He sniffed. "Maybe I would've stayed."

Daisy inhaled deeply. "Oh, Abe. You never would have stayed here. In fact," she looked over to him. "I can't believe you ever came back. Still in shock about it, actually."

"Yeah well," he cracked a smile. "I'm here. And, for what it's worth, I'm sorry. My life didn't turn out so hot, aside from having Simi. I guess that's the silver lining to my screw-up, huh?"

Daisy wiped something from her eye. "Absolutely, Abel. And that's one helluva silver lining."

They sat in silence the rest of the ride. As they drove by Sunrise Pond and braked in front of Ulf's Hansel and Gretel house, Abe pulled on a canvas jacket from his back seat. "Care to join me?"

Daisy stepped outside. "Been a while since I've seen old Mr. Halden. Still old?"

Abe couldn't help but laugh. "Yes," his smile was wide. "Still so, fricking, old."

He wanted to offer his hand to her, but something told him they were still far away from such pleasantries. Almost as a confirmation, Daisy quickly inserted hers into her jeans pockets.

"After you," was all she said.

Abe looked both ways, which was silly—considering how untraveled it was—on that particular stretch of road and side of town. He jogged across the silent street. "Quiet, tonight," he said absentmindedly. Daisy didn't respond.

There wasn't a light on inside of Ulf's home. Abe approached the door and hurriedly knocked. He waited a minute, without an answer, before raising his fist to knock again. Before he was able to bring his knuckles down, there was a rustling from within.

Abe stepped back as the door was unlocked. A white mop and two bloodshot eyes peered out from the crack.

"Mr. Halden—" Abe began.

"Go away," the man behind the door spat. "Before you bring this blasphemy down onto my old head. Already told you everything there's to know. Tried to warn your ass, but you know better'n I, dontcha?" He tried to shut the door, but Abe grabbed at it with both hands. The elderly gentleman was strong for his age, but Abe was more than capable of overpowering him.

"Just tell me whatever it is I need to do, Mr. Halden. Please, I'm begging you—"

Halden continued to try to force the door shut from the inside. "You goddamn fool. If you only listened the first time, I'd be safe downstairs in my bunker by now, enjoying a good smoke—"

"I'll let you shut this thing and smoke your face off once you tell me what I want to know."

The man groaned from inside. "Ya dumb bastahd. Leaving your kid at home on a night like this. What's even going through your skull right now is beyond me. You know what you need to do."

"No, I don't. Would you just tell me?"

Halden finally stopped struggling. The chain was still bolted, but he spoke through it. "They want her."

Abe stepped back and felt Daisy's hands on his lower back, almost as if she were propping him up.

Or preventing me from running.

"Who?" Abe shivered. "Elma?"

Halden nodded. "Give her to them, or else..." He tried to shut the door again and Abe stuck his foot in the way.

"Or else, what, Mr. Halden?"

The sadness returned to the man's aging eyes. He looked up into Abel's. "Or else you'll never have an opportunity to do anything. Ever again. None of us here, in this town, ever will. That is, if you don't give her to them. *Now.*" He stuck a fat, gnarled, finger through the crack in the door and poked Abe in the chest. "We're outta time, Son. Better get a move on." And with that, he slammed the door in Abe and Daisy's faces. They could hear the locking mechanisms slamming, one after the other.

"So, what now?" Daisy sniffed as Abe turned back toward the car. The temperature was dropping rapidly, and her cheeks were turning into blooming roses. He began to walk and she jogged after him. "Abe?"

"First we get home to the kids. Then—*Christ*, I can't believe I'm even thinking this, D."

Daisy said nothing and followed him into the truck. They sped off across town, around the rotary, and back down North Street. As they rolled by the Town Hall, they saw the Sheriff hustling to his jeep.

He had a large shovel in one hand.

"Kind of early for Sheriff Candler to be closing up shop for the day," Abe said, not removing his eyes from the man.

Daisy gulped. "Yeah, very early."

Abe rolled down his window and half-heartedly waved. He wasn't sure what sort of reaction he was hoping for, but realized part-way through the act that the neighborly gesture felt inopportune and awkward. The sheriff looked back at him and, after a delayed realization of who was passing by, began to shout. Over the din of the rumbling, aging, truck engine, Abe could only make out bits and pieces of what the guy was yelling.

"...brought this on Mr. Ward! ...not too late to fix! ...all suffer the consequences!"

Neither Abe nor Daisy said anything to the other. In the rearview mirror, the sheriff stood in the middle of the road, waving his shovel. Otherwise, North Street—and the town of Foxborough—was oddly silent. No other cars were on the road. No lights blinked on or off in living room windows. Basketballs and skateboards sat untouched in the community park. The barking of man's best friend was, once and for all, silent.

Evil has a way of signaling those who are willing.
Willing to hear it.
Willing to smell it.
Willing to *absorb* it.
Something *was* about to happen.
An entire town braced itself.
And Abel Ward and Daisy Peltzer rumbled on back home to Ward House.

Forty Seven
Night Six
Halloween Night

Simi hovered in the foyer. Mags was staring up at the painting of the gate as it leered down at the both of them. She twisted her head to one side, perhaps trying to see the peculiar depiction from a slightly different angle. Like many things, art presents in new ways with even a slightly altered perspective. Simi knew that—*believed* it, even—but couldn't tell if Mags was consciously attempting to shift her viewpoint of the piece or just lost in her own, unrelated, thoughts. She *hmmphed*, apparently satisfied, and turned to him.

"So, are we going out? Staying in and watching some scary movies? Waddaya think?"

Simi bent down to straighten a small corner of the hallway rug that'd gotten rolled up. "I dunno, Mags. I think sticking around, even for a little while longer, is a mistake. I'd rather be outta be here before dark."

She groaned. "What, Dude? I thought we discussed this."

He sighed and stood back up. "We did. I just have a really bad feeling about tonight."

Mags glided over to him and placed her hands on both of his shoulders, forcing him to face her. "Look, I don't want you to stress. How 'bout we make a deal?" She waited for him to nod before continuing. "What if we just go out for a little while? The sun," she looked out through the stained glass above the front door, "The sun is only just setting now. Maybe we do like a half-hour—an hour tops—of walking around and seeing what's hopping in this burb. Then we come back, get ourselves an Uber to some nearby motel, and settle in for a nice, scary movie or two. See what Michael, Jason, and Freddie are up to. Cool?"

He shook his head. "Mags, I'm serious—"

"Sim, I'm serious too. Please? How often am I gonna get an opportunity to do Halloween up here in New England? This *is* where all the best spooky shit happens, right? Salem and all that?"

He cracked a smile, evidently caving. "But we're not even in Salem. That's like forty-five minutes from here or something."

Mags led him toward the door and he let her pull him. "Whatever. Close enough. Probably close as I'll ever be, in fact. Can we do this, please? For me? Super quick, I promise." She put on her fake, puppy-dog, eyes and pouted her lips.

"Alright, alright," he conceded. "But, really quick. I still don't feel great about tonight. Truthfully, I feel the opposite of great."

They both exited the house and Mags leapt down the front stairs. "You just need to chill. Tonight's our night. Let's have fun."

They stopped at the end of the walkway. "If you say so," Simi said. "Which way we going?"

Mags looked down one end of Brown Street. "Well, I was going to say that way, but there aren't any lights on... like, at all."

Simi pointed in the opposite direction. "Nada that way either. Not a single jack-o-lantern. Weird, isn't it?"

Both of them were silent. Listening. Waiting. Nothing stirred down either route. Not a car engine or muffled laugh from an early rabble-rouser underneath a vinyl mask. There were no surprise "trick or treats" or—really—anything audible at all.

"You think there'd be more people out tonight," Mags mumbled, herself sounding concerned.

Simi's face twitched. "You'd think."

From somewhere behind them, on the opposite side of the house, there was suddenly a quiet, garbled, humming. Like a song from a sick—but merry—child, with a throat full of gooey phlegm.

"Hmmmmm, hmmmmm, hmmmmm."

The playful melody floated out alongside the encroaching shadow of twilight, over the spired roof and mad-eye weathervane of Ward House, and tickled past the shivering ears of the young lovers.

Both Simi and Mags spun around and lifted the plastic masks they'd only just pulled down over their faces.

"You hear that, right?" Simi gulped.

Mags nodded, slowly. "Unfortunately, yes."

Simi reached out and grabbed Mags' hand. His feet began walking in the direction of the persisting lullaby, but hers stuck and he jerked back after a few steps.

"Mags?" he said.

She shook her head. "I don't wanna go."

"I don't either, but we need to see what it is."

"Simi—" she begged once more, but he kept moving forward, and eventually, so did she.

Together they crept around the right side of the house. The humming, as they got closer, got louder and, somehow, increasingly less-human.

"Hmmmm, hmmmmm, hmmmmm."

The sing-songy quality gradually developed into a more mocking, sneering, tone and what originally seemed to emanate from the vocal cords of a small girl, sounded more like it was being belched from the lips of a dead bullfrog. The humming—or whatever it was metamorphosing into—lingered in the air like septic fumes, and—just before Simi and Mags were about to turn around the corner—he put out an arm and stopped them both.

"Hello?" he whispered. "Who's out there?"

The humming continued, blissfully unaware of his arrival or unwilling to cease. After a moment, Simi stepped forward with Mags' hand tightly gripped around his own.

They walked into the backyard.

And the humming stopped.

A cricket chirped and the teens stared, wide-eyed, into the open space.

"Hello?" Simi asked again, his voice a little less timid.

Mags tried to speak. "Maybe it was—maybe—"

Simi straightened. "This doesn't feel right. I think we should head back in."

This time Mags didn't fight him. "Is the porch door locked? Or do we—?"

"We need to go back around," he confirmed. "To the front. My key only opens that one."

Mags hooked her arm a little deeper, more tightly, around his. "Okay. Let's go. Fast."

They took a few rearward steps, afraid to fully turn their backs on the swamp, and then spun and began to sprint.

As they entered the front yard, headlights caught them both in a blinding beam.

A door squealed and relief flooded into Simi's brain as he recognized the voice. "Simi? Mags?" Abe shouted.

"Yeah," Simi said, holding a hand to his face and squinting. "Where have you been?"

Abe turned the truck lights off and was about to answer when a chorus of primal, ravenous, screaming and chattering erupted from the wetlands.

Daisy jumped out of the truck and approached the kids. "Abe—"

He quickly joined the three of them. "I think we need to get inside," he said. "Now."

Forty Eight

What is owed.

Ay, yes.

Abe shook his head. He was standing inside Ward House. Simi was just out of reach, in front of Mags, blocking her from the door.

"Abe!"

He turned to the voice.

"Abe!" Daisy screamed. She was struggling to turn the deadbolt and hold the door shut. "Help! Something is pushing from outside."

He ran to her and, with his added weight, they were both able to force the heavy oaken slab shut tight. He turned the lock and they backed toward the kids and their position in front of the stairwell.

The front door shook and rattled as an alarmingly vigorous force smashed into it. There was a scratching sound, a crawling, as something on the opposite side reached for any sort of handhold or leverage to pry the entryway back open. The howling continued, seemingly coming from all directions around the house, the desperation of the cries intensifying with each passing second.

Mags sat down on the stairs with her hands over her ears. "What *is* that?"

Abe kept his focus on the front door even as Simi lowered himself to the ground next to Mags. "It's them. They've finally come."

The sound of glass tinkling, somewhere in the direction of the kitchen, caused them all to turn their heads. Mags stood upright quickly.

"Abe," Daisy said, the calm leaving her voice. "Where—?"

'The basement," he answered, before she could even ask the question. "Move."

Abe led the way, the kids following immediately behind him, and Daisy took up the rear. The basement door was nearby, in the main hallway off of the foyer. Abe ripped it open, flicked on the light switch, and listened for any warning, any sign that descending into the musty hole would be a mistake. He heard nothing.

"Let's go," he said, pulling the others behind him. As one, they clambered down the groaning steps and Daisy yanked the door closed.

"Get against the front wall," Abe ordered. "We're underground in this cellar, but we still need to stay away from those windows." There were two tiny apertures, on the opposite side of the staircase. "We should be safe here." He said it, but didn't believe it.

There was tumbling overhead and they all looked up. Little feet were scampering, scraping at Elma's finished floors, no doubt disturbing the perfectly straightened throw rugs. More glass was broken and furniture—by the sound of it— was being knocked to the ground.

Something ran past the cellar door and Abe approached the stairwell, placing a hand on the rickety railing. "Find something you can use as a weapon and then—" the room around him started to spin and he gripped the banister more tightly.

"Abe?" he heard Daisy say as the room got darker. "Hey, talk to me—"

He fell to his knees and tried to block out the lightlessness that was eclipsing all else. Voices, jeering him, leaked into his brain, and—as they began to bombard him—he pressed both hands to his ears. He could see nothing—in that moment he was completely blind— but the tormented chanting bled into his skull and created agonizing pressure from behind his closed eyes. The devils left in his charge called to him.

The covenant.
The covenant.
Abe screamed.
Be not afeard.
This is the way.
We hast obeyed.

The ancient tormentors giggled past his consciousness and Abe threw his head between his knees. "Stop!"

'Tis thy turn.

More hysterical giggling. Abe tried to stand, but fell backward onto the wooden planks. "Please, aggh—"

Hark!
Why doth thou cower, sirrah.
We hast waited patiently.

He shook his head as if trying to throw the taunts away.

Daisy tried to break in, "Abe!"

Ward!

What is thy delay?

Grant us the flesh of thy blood.

"I can't!"

'Tis thy warrant.

Thy oath.

The covenant.

The covenant.

We command thou to allow us—

"Please!"

—To bathe 'i what hath been promised.

"No!"

To feast.

On the blood.

On her blood.

The covenant.

The coven—

"Abe!"

He opened his eyes.

"Abe!" both Simi and Daisy seemed to be calling. Abe pulled himself onto his feet. Glass was showering out and into the room. Eyes of pulsing, radiating, green filled the murkiest recesses of the chamber with an unnatural glow. Dark, slithering arms crept inside the newly formed openings and pulled larger, ill-defined forms behind. One by one they toppled in, scrambling over each other, squealing in delight at having breached. And then, the malignant sprites noticed the four cowering in the back corner. One lifted its head and howled, summoning its brethren. The flood of shadowy figures scattered around the room, cornering their prey. Aside from their eyes and the faint glint of saliva dripping from sharp fangs, the monstrosities were completely featureless. Roughly the size of small children, they waved excitedly at the exposed, vulnerable, humans and then—

"Find something to swing!" Abe screamed.

—the little beasts charged.

Abe heard Mags cry out and then, himself, was overwhelmed, drowning in a sea of writhing, foul-smelling, scrawny bodies. Despite their diminutive size, the creatures were strong and knocked the man—who was nearing six feet—to the ground with little, if any, effort. Abe reached for anything he could grab and, almost instantly, felt his fingertips touch hard, cool, plastic. Whatever it was lifted easily in his hands and he began to take aim at the demons, swatting them off of himself. The few he made contact with shrieked as he smashed them into the surrounding cement walls. Each made little green splat stains as they flopped down, lifelessly, to the dirt floor.

It was then that Abe realized what weapon he'd chosen. He held it up to the minimal amount of illumination that'd somehow found its way to him. Directly in front of his eyes, he brandished a large manikin leg, freshly covered in swamp goblin blood.

"That'll do," he barely had time to say as he ran toward the others. Daisy had a golf putter in hand and was connecting with each of the creatures that dared approach her. Mags was standing in front of Simi, wielding a can of bug spray.

There was a temporary lull in the action and, as Abe tried to catch his breath, he nodded toward her. "Bug spray?"

She shrugged. "Deep woods."

Before he had a chance to laugh, the entire room started trembling. The four tried to keep their balance and a deafening *crrraccckk* gave them all reason to look toward the ground.

"Oh, shit," Daisy breathlessly whispered.

A huge fissure opened in the middle of the cellar floor and they all leapt to the staircase. Green bile bubbled up from the growing crevice and dark limbs began to reach and grab at them from within its depths.

"This isn't gonna work anymore!" Abe tried to yell over the cacophony, but he wasn't sure they could make sense of what he was saying.

"Where do we go?" screamed Daisy. "We need to get out of here!"

Simi fell to the ground and Mags pulled him back up.

"I think I know where to go!" Simi hollered, his hands cupping his mouth.

Abe put a hand to his ear. "Huh? Where, Sim?"

Simi began to run up the shaking cellar stairs, pulling Mags behind him. "This way!"

"Sim!" Abe called. "Where are we going?"

The rumbling was getting even more violent. A few of the monsters were just about out of the opening in the ground. There were few options left.

"Just trust me! We're heading to—"

The entire basement seemed to lurch and Abe lost what his son was trying to say. Debris fell on top of them—years of loose tools and other items Elma had hung on the inclined wall—and a cloud of dust made seeing his son difficult. "What, Sim?"

As they all busted out and back onto the main floor of Ward House, Simi rounded on his father.

"We need to get to the Clown Room!"

Abe tried to protest.

"Please, just *trust* me."

Simi turned to run and Mags and Daisy both followed him. With little choice or any valid objection to make, Abe decided to join the train up the corkscrew to heaven. He vaulted after the others, his manikin leg resting in wait on a shoulder—for the battle still to come.

FORTY NINE

Screeeeeeeech.

Abe and Daisy pushed the dresser in front of the door. Simi plucked the clown doll from its position on the floor and placed it in front of the window.

"Get away from the glass!" Abe screamed.

"Abe—" Simi tried to get a word in.

"Onto the bed, off the floor, away from the door—"

"Abe!" Simi screamed.

His father stopped directing and looked at him. "Sim, why are we *here*?"

A few clawed feet tapped by the door, pacing back and forth. A shadow swung past the window, but did not linger. There was an audible crashing and multiple sets of bodies wrestled overhead on the roof, but nothing touched the door. There was no opening from beneath nor was there an oozing of green. The Malevolent Nevers were not attempting to get inside the tiny, crowded, space.

Simi pointed at the doll. "I don't know why but, I think they're afraid of that—or—afraid of this room. Something in here is keeping them away." When Abe looked at him quizzically, Simi added, "Remember last night? That thing could've easily attacked us, but wouldn't cross the threshold. I don't know why but there's something—"

"Simi, that's nuts. How can this place be—?"

"Abe! He's right." Daisy's interjection caused the other three to look at her. "Just *listen* to him, Abe."

The discord and ransacking of Ward House continued outside of the room, but none of the beasts were making any sort of attempt to get in at them. Abe peered at Daisy and whispered, "D. What the hell are you talking about?"

She closed her eyes, rubbed her forehead, and seemed to be trying to force an old memory back to the surface. "I—I don't know. Not, exactly, I mean. Elma, she," Daisy looked around the small space. "She spent a lot of time in here. Always adding something, adjusting something else. Straightening and—" she hesitated. "*Whispering* to that... thing."

Mags gulped. "Why—what is it about this room?"

Daisy shook her head. "It was clearly special to her and she—she said this was the place mentioned in the song." Simi and Abe both stared at her, perplexed. "You know, the nursery rhyme?"

Only partially paying attention to her, Abe put up a hand to his ear and pressed it against the door. Something crashed to the floor in the hallway and he jumped. Carefully, he listened again and when nothing further sounded, he spoke. "Song? You mean…"

She nodded.

Abe started to sing, quietly, begrudgingly, trying to recall all of the lyrics.

"From the depths of me 'art, to the pit of me soul, with ne'er a breath nor need for a hole,
O' Malevolent, Malevolent Nevers.
Here they wait for all our evers,
O' Malevolent, Malevolent Nevers.
Our demons to bear.
Our demons to share.
O' Malevolent, Malevolent Nevers.
Sometimes they be locked away, where no one can see 'em, outter sight.
Sometimes they be a droolin' face, starin' in through 'yer winder, in the dead of the night!
O' Malevolent, Malevolent, Malevolent, Malevolent, Malevolent, Malevolent NEVERS!"

He trailed off. The others were all staring at him. Simi looked like he didn't even recognize his own father.

Abe ignored his son's ogling. "But there's no mention—anywhere in that song—of a *room*, D."

She shook her head. "You're forgetting a verse, Abe." He started to argue, but she continued. "The only reason I haven't is because she would sing it—the whole damn song— in here."

Simi looked down at the bed, at the clown in the window, and at all the mirthful accoutrements that adorned the surrounding walls. "How did it go?"

Daisy closed her eyes, clearly focusing. Her temple seemed to be burrowing into itself and, as she opened her mouth, the words tumbled out.

"When all is lost, and the demons do come,
And nighttime hath falln' darker'n some,
And your blessed 'art is tired and numb.
They can't getcha, in the embrace of Sanctum."

The corner of her left eye trembled and the last line she squeaked like an 'amen'.

"...O' Malevolent, Malevolent, Nevers."

Simi pulled his black hoodie tightly around his head. Fiddling with the zipper he looked up at her. "Sanctum? But, that doesn't mean *this* is—"

"She called it that. Elma did." Daisy stared back at him and then Abe and then Mags, daring any of them to challenge her. "*Sanctum*. Sometimes it was this room and sometimes—" she looked to the stiff, circus freak by the window. "Sometimes it was that thing. I don't know why, but she saw some sort of power here. Some sort of safety."

Abe scratched his chin, lost deep in thought. "It was always my room. Growing up, it looked exactly the same. And even then, she was always puttering around in here. I don't remember that particular verse or the—" he shivered. "The name. You might be right but, it doesn't make this any less nuts." He too looked at the doll. "Why clowns?"

Simi looked to each of the other's faces. No one, not even Daisy, had an explanation. He started speaking without any thought. "It might not be anything so mystical." Everyone, surprised by his assertion, waited for him to proceed. "Think about it. These creatures... faceless, for the most part. Void of expression. Walking emptiness. Isn't a clown sort of like... the *antithesis* of that? Those big, white, painted faces—pinwheels of color— could be—I dunno—*horrifying* to a being that's entire existence is darkness."

The others were silent until Abe spoke. He was smirking and leaned into Daisy. "Smart kid, huh?" he said.

She folded her arms. "Better explanation than I could've come up with."

Proud of himself, Simi puffed up. "Cool. Let's—uh—go with that then."

A large smash through a downstairs window jolted the group back to reality. Something groaned overhead—

metal being bent past the point it should have been—and they all looked up.

"The weathervane," Abe said. "Sounds like they're trying to rip it off."

Simi looked to Daisy. "So, any idea how long we're safe here?"

Her mouth hung open and she shrugged. "No clue. You think I majored in clown shrines? The totality of my knowledge on all of this shit stems from the disjointed ramblings of a hundred-year-old woman. Gimme a break, okay?"

And then, just as quickly as the anarchy had begun, everything suddenly went completely still.

All was silent, except for the—

"Rain," Mags whispered. "It's starting to rain." She moved cautiously toward the window, emboldened by the clown barrier. "Like, a lot."

"Do you see anything out there?" Simi asked.

She shook her head. "Just a lot of wet. Think they're afraid of a little water?"

Daisy put her ear to the door. "Everything's quiet out in the hall too."

Too quiet.

They all stood listening, tense, waiting for the next crash, growl, or scamper.

Abe cleared his throat. "Okay. We may only have a small window of time. For whatever reason—rain or otherwise—they're not out there at the moment." He steeled himself, visibly. "And I think I finally am ready to do what I should have six days ago."

FIFTY

This has gone on long enough.

Abe was convinced. He brought his hands together and cracked both knuckles, taking his time to deliver the idea so that it'd not come as a huge shock to everyone else.

"I can't believe I'm suggesting this, but I know what we need to do."

The other three stared blankly at him and he immediately recognized their confusion.

"We need to dig Elma up."

Mags appeared to choke on her own saliva. "I'm sorry—" she turned, whispering into Simi's ear. "What did he just say?"

"Tonight," Abe said, as if Mags hadn't uttered a word. He stared at the floor. "We need to do this *tonight*. The rain seems to have bought us some time. No idea why, but it has. We go now—can hop in the truck even, to go that little stretch of road. We'll all pull up to the burial ground and then—"

"This is what Mr. Halden was trying to tell us, isn't it?" Simi blurted. "Why didn't you listen to him—?"

"Because it's sounds—well—it sounds *bonkers*, Simi. Even after you told me you'd seen photos of that ritual, even then I couldn't believe it. I loved that woman, you know? She was the closest thing I had to a parent for most of my childhood. And I'm not supposed to even question any of this? The first old fart that tells me I need to feed my great-aunt's body to these—shadow elves—er—these wretches from the wood—*whatever* they are—you're saying I should have just instantly agreed to this lunacy? It's nuts. Come on, man."

Simi still wasn't ready to let him off of the hook. "Okay, so why are we getting' nuts now then, huh? You wouldn't do it then. Why now?"

Abe's bloodshot eyes widened and both Daisy and Mags stepped out from between the two Wards. "*Why* now? Holy shit, Sim. Look around you! We've been under siege—these things are trying to kill us. We're quite literally being attacked. I'm running out of time and options."

There still wasn't any alert or sign that the monsters were returning, but Daisy's unease was growing. As the father and son bickered, she wrung her hands and—more than once—shot a glance out the window.

"Guys—" she attempted to cut in.

"Well, it took you long enough." Simi continued to pile on. "We could've ended up dead, but your stubborn, excruciatingly-deliberate, ass couldn't get with the program. We've been harassed by these things since day one. So glad you finally woke the hell up. But I guess I shouldn't really be surprised, should I? You always were late to the party."

You're gonna go there now, Sim?

"And what the hell is that supposed to mean? I've been trying my best—"

"To what, repair all the damage you caused by missing the first fifteen years of my goddamned life? Hey, well guess what? You failed at that too. Maybe if you hadn't dragged me up to this actual hellmouth—"

"Enough!" Daisy bellowed over the both of them. They both looked at her. Mags sat down, out of the way, on the bed. "I'm sorry, it's clear you two have a ton to work on. And my sincere hope is that someday, who knows, maybe you'll get to rap about this again. But now—*right now*—is not the time. You said yourself, Abe, we might not get another chance. This small window of opportunity ain't gonna last, right? Well? Time to run, Assholes."

Abe looked to Simi and his son returned the glare. "Right," Abe said. "Help me move the dresser." He and Simi pushed it to the side. "Daisy's speaking the truth. Now's our shot. Let's run straight for the truck. Don't stop, for anything. No matter what. I'll drive us to the graveyard and then—well, then we'll figure out the rest." No one said anything and he wrapped his hand around the doorknob. "You all ready?"

They all nodded, but—just before he pulled it open—Mags yelped. "Wait!" She raced to the window and grabbed the stuffed clown. "I just realized something. His name," she pointed at the patch on the jester's chest. "Barachiel. I know that name. Wasn't he—I mean, biblically speaking—wasn't he like, the chief guardian angel? Or something? Am I remembering that correctly? Been a while since Sunday school."

Abe, Simi, and Daisy all fidgeted awkwardly. "Probably not your best sources for that sort of things, Mags," Simi mumbled. "Sounds good, though."

She blushed. "Okay, well. In any case... probably should bring—ah—Barachiel here with us. Right? Considering the whole *Sanctum* thing."

Will that even work outside of this room?

Ignoring his inner doubt, Abe raised his hand to hers and she high-fived it. "Good thinking, Mags." He turned back to the door. "Bringin' the damn doll with us. Alright. Ready or not. On three. One... two... three!"

He threw open the door and dashed into the hallway. Abe could hear footsteps behind his own and took it for granted that the others were following him closely. As he jumped down the spiral staircase, past the painting of the flower-covered gate, he tried not to pay too much attention to the destruction around him. Glass everywhere. Gaping holes in floors, walls, and ceilings. Green stains smeared across furniture. A steaming pile of something foul in a corner.

It's just stuff, Abe told himself. *We can fix stuff.*

The front door was open wide and he leapt, clearing the entire front porch and the front stairs, landing ungracefully on the cobblestone walkway. He turned and to find Daisy and Mags still managing to keep up with him. Simi was nowhere to be seen.

"Wait—" Abe choked as the two women climbed into the truck. "Where's Simi?"

Before either of the other two had a chance to respond, the front door burst back open. Simi catapulted himself onto the front lawn. In his arms, he cradled a small bundle.

"What were you—?" Abe stammered, trying to pull his son toward the vehicle.

Simi undid the knot in the dirty piece of fabric and threw it to the ground. In his hand he held the stained dagger, its green gem eyes catching a glint of light from a nearby lamppost.

"Thought this might come in handy," he smirked. "No time to get the rest of the weaponry in the shed, but remembered you'd stashed this one in your room. Pest control, right?"

"How'd you even find—?"

"Really, Abe? It was just sitting there on your bedside table. Not exactly a secret hiding spot."

Without any time to continue the conversation, Abe shrugged. "Get in," he grunted. "We need to move." Simi did as he was told—gripping the dagger tightly in front of himself as he did so—and Abe inserted a key into the ignition. The truck roared to life and he patted the steering wheel, jubilantly.

From the passenger seat, Daisy urged him on. "Go, go, let's go. Faster, faster, must go faster."

The truck was facing the wrong way on the road, so quickly Abe turned it into the driveway, backed out, and steered the vehicle in the correct direction down Brown. He hit the gas and they peeled out, Simi and Mags flopping back into the small window of the cab.

"Here we go, here we—"

As they came around the corner and beyond the trees that often blocked Ward House from a more direct view of the burial grounds, lights—blue police lights—lit up the small stone markers.

Abe hit the brakes.

"What the—"

Shit, shit, shit.

Daisy leaned closer to the windshield and wiped at the condensation developing on the glass. "That's Sheriff Candler's jeep."

They all stared, waiting for some sign from Foxborough's chief law enforcement officer. The town vehicle was parked, haphazardly on the side of the road. One if its doors was wide open, providing easy access to any would-be, nighttime prowlers.

Not a good sign.

Abe swallowed. "He did have that shovel. I wonder if he was headed—"

A figure, about a hundred paces down the medium—directly in front of the truck—stumbled out into the road. The shape was backlit by the blue flashing lights and the truck's occupants couldn't make out anything but the person's silhouette. Whoever it was, waved their arms wildly.

Daisy rolled down her window. "Will?" she shouted into the night. "You alright?"

Abe copied her action and stuck his head out. "Sheriff Candler?"

They all waited for a response. A muffled cry emanated from the figure, who fell to one knee.

"Hey," Mags whispered to herself from the backseat. "Anyone else notice it stopped—"

"Sheriff Candler!"

"—raining?"

The man tried to rise again and this time got off a full-throated scream. He pried something from his face and struggled to lift it above himself, high in the air. The demon thrashed and grabbed for a hold of the sheriff's head.

"Helllp!" he begged. "Please, help m—" his plea was suppressed again as the creature latched back on.

Abe leapt out of the truck and turned to the others. "Stay here!"

Again, Sheriff Candler managed a yelp and began to weave— running about—until he cracked his shins on a guard rail and fell, tumbling, into the ditch behind it. They all watched helplessly as he disappeared into the blackness.

"Sheriff—"

Daisy was out of the truck too. She put a hand to her eyes and tried to see where he'd gone. "Will!" she shouted. "Talk to us!"

The man went silent. There wasn't even the sound of a scuffle or the slosh of his boots from down in the muddy embankment.

Abe and Daisy stood out in front of the truck's headlights, their hands hanging limply by their sides.

And then the entire road shuddered.

"Guys—" Simi called.

Both Abe and Daisy were knocked off of their feet. The pavement, almost in perfect alignment with the yellow line, cracked wide open. Once more, green sludge began to froth and foam from the hellish mouth. Blackened fingers poked out from its edges.

The grisly cleft ran directly under the pickup.

"Time to go!" shouted Mags.

"Now, Abe!" screamed Simi.

The adults climbed back to their feet. They were making a move for the truck when the cab door on Mags' side was ripped clean off of its hinges. She shrieked.

Dark talons dugs into her thigh and yanked her from the vehicle.

"Mags!" Simi wailed.

The giggling sprites pulled her down the road. Thinking fast, Simi grabbed the stuffed clown —and the dagger—and followed after her assailants. Mags was putting up enough of a fight—landing punches and writhing about—that the creatures weren't moving her all that quickly and Simi was easily able to run ahead of them. He held the doll out to the three manhandling Mags and two of them immediately hissed, dropping her and scattering into the woods. The third continued to bear down on her leg and the saliva from its chasmal mouth began to pool on her flesh as it pulled itself closer. Simi slashed out with his blade at the creature's face, puncturing one of its glowing green eyeballs.

The demon squealed. Wisps of black sludge began to sizzle from its orbital socket and the creature fell to the ground convulsing.

Simi placed his armaments—Barachiel and the skull knife— onto the road, needing both hands to lift his girlfriend. The beastie continued to wail and he forced Mags onto her feet. As he started to lead her away, the Malevolent Never let out one final, painful, croak before bursting into a puddle of boiling goop.

Abe ran to them and shouted back to Daisy. "Start the truck, D!" He lifted Mags into his arms and ran with her, Simi close on his heels. Daisy rolled up to them in reverse and, just as Abe was lowering Mags into the backseat, he and Simi were both rocked back out into the road.

Another ripple—like a black, stone, wave— rolled down the street.

And then, the onslaught began.

The noise was deafening. Between the ululation of the demons, and the chorus of their clawed feet clacking up and out of the crack in the pavement, it was nearly impossible to hear anything else. The flood of featureless bodies and glowing eyes descended on them.

Simi leapt for the open door of the truck, but Abe was swallowed up in a tide of Malevolent Nevers. They bit and slashed at him and, though he tried to fight back, could not bring himself to a standing position or any closer to the others.

"Go!" he cried as a shadow hand found its way into his mouth. He spat it out. "Daisy, go!"

"No!" Simi protested. "Wait, we can still—"

"Go!" Abe screamed again, "Please, G-" and then he disappeared under a tidal wave of the wicked beings.

Daisy blinked once and then pressed her foot to the floor. As they drove off, somehow evading the giant split in the road, Simi looked out back through the tiny window. All he could make out—that pointed to where Abe had been—was a slight bump in the river of snapping jaws and green eyes.

"Abe!" he roared again, as Daisy took a violent, gut-wrenching, turn up North Street.

Fifty One

"Mags! Mags!"

Her eyes fluttered and Simi attempted to shake her awake.

"Unngh—" she moaned. "—it hurts, Sim."

He tried to reposition himself so that he could better prop her head. "Where's it hurt, Mags just tell me—"

Oh my god.

And then he saw it. A large gash on her upper thigh. Flaps of skin, intertwined with light blue thread from her jeans, floated in a lagoon of blood. Warmth spilled over his hand as he tried to cover the gaping wound.

She looked up at him, squeezing tears from her eyes. "I don't feel great, Sim."

A shudder ran through her and Simi yanked his hoodie off, throwing it over her shoulders.

'Simeon," Daisy called from the driver's seat, her eyes

facing forward. "You need to stop that bleeding. You need to—"

"I know, I know," he silenced her. "I'm just trying to figure out what I can use for a—". Without another word, he removed his t-shirt and tied it off as tight as he could just above her injury. Daisy fished around in the glove compartment and tossed back a handful of fast food napkins.

"Here. It's all we've got. But you gotta apply pressure. Now".

Simi did as he was told and Mags howled.

"Sorry, Mags. It won't be long now. We'll be there soon—" he stopped himself. "Wait, Daisy, where are we going?"

She looked in the rearview mirror, as if something might still be following. "I don't know. Just driving. I'd take you to a hospital, but—"

They all looked out the windows as the town of Foxborough flew by. Shadows pounded and clawed at each home that flickered past. Shapes hurled themselves through windows and on nearly every corner, and under the illumination of flickering porchlights, people were being dragged out into the night. Green eyes descended chimneys like St. Nicholas, greeting citizens of the community with the rotten stench of the swamp. Muffled screams tried in vain to get the attention of their speeding truck, before they too were silenced by the demons.

There's nothing we can do. We're too late.

As their party approached the rotary at the center of town and moved beyond the town hall, they drove by a building entirely engulfed in flame.

"Shit," Daisy breathlessly whispered.

Simi had to squint to keep looking at the single-floor building. Even through the car window, the heat from the conflagration was too strong and he was forced to lean back. "What was that?"

"The old video store," Daisy groaned. "Bastards." She hit the gas and they sped onto the roundabout. As she did, the 'P' in the lettering above Clay's Video Palace fell into the bonfire, causing a belch of white-hot plume to erupt into the street.

Simi shook his head.

What the hell did we do? Abe, why didn't we just—?

As if she'd heard his thoughts, Mags lifted her head and spoke into his ear. "It's not your fault. How were you, or Abe, supposed to know any of this was real? That any of this would actually happen?" Simi sniffed and she wrapped her arms around him. "He saved us, Sim. We got out of there, because of him."

He buried his face into her shoulder. "It's just so stupid. Such a waste. If he just—and now he's—"

She rubbed his back. "Don't say that. We don't know yet if—if—"

There was a large *thwump* against the hood and the truck crunched over something.

Daisy again looked in the rearview mirror. "Well. Got one, at least."

Simi cleared his throat, unfazed by what'd just happened. "We need to go back for my dad."

There was more screaming to their right as someone ran from the local liquor store with a few of the demons on his heels. The man fell to the ground with the swarm on his back, his case of craft beer smashing tragically into the road.

From behind the town library, three other shapes sprinted across the street. Simi watched as the wild-eyed, terrified, teens burst in through the back entrance of a local hardware shop and a deluge of the green-eyed mutants clambered in after them. The boys' excruciating screams and pleas for aid were quickly drowned out, the fading image of a pair of bloody lobster-pants burned into Simi's mind as his convoy lurched to life once again.

Daisy swerved around the person in the road and his ruined IPAs, shaking her head. "No. Not yet. Need to get you two to safety first. He didn't just do all of that for nothin'. He allowed us to escape. Once we are someone safe, then I'll go back for him."

"But, Daisy—" Simi protested.

"No!" she snapped. Simi hid his tears in Mags' shirt and Daisy softened her voice. "No. First, we need to get Mags some help. She's in rough shape, Simi. There's got to be somewhere to take her. Any ideas?"

He lifted his head again and looked at his girlfriend. Mags, who only seconds earlier had been consoling him, had her eyes shut. He couldn't tell if she was asleep.

"Only one."

Daisy caught his eyes in the mirror. "Where?"

Simi held her gaze and she seemed to read his mind. "You're not thinking—?"

He nodded.

"Christ in a cornfield."

She took the last exit off of the rotary and, before long, the truck was making its way down the twisting, unlit, back roads. Sunrise Pond was silent as they pulled up alongside it and the small, ivy-covered, house across the street was even quieter. There wasn't a light on inside and the bedlam that'd enveloped the rest of the town hadn't yet seemed to have percolated so deeply into the secluded neighborhood. Cautiously, Daisy kicked open the driver's side door and it squealed into the night.

She winced. "Sorry."

Simi forced his door open. Mags' eyes were half-open. "Where are we?"

"Come on," Simi said, pulling her outside. "Can you stand?"

She nodded, but put almost all of her weight onto his shoulder. She was pale, no doubt a result of the blood that'd continued to flow—unabated—out of the laceration on her thigh.

"Lemme help," Daisy said, throwing Mags' other arm around her. "And let's be quick."

They'd taken a few steps toward the small white cottage when there was a loud *kerplop* in the water behind them. They all froze in the middle of the road.

Even in her weakened state, Mags followed the other two in slowly twisting her head around. "What was that?" she whispered.

"Shh," Daisy begged, arching her neck. She turned her entire body to face the pond. "Something is—"

There was a sloshing not far from where they stood, like sodden, galoshes were suddenly slapping up onto the rocky shore. A green glow began to spread underneath the surface of the pond and the waters churned. A small whirlpool formed and—emerging from the void—were more of the wailing, faceless, demons. The creatures' eyes beseeched the three cowering in the street and hissed in unison as the humans began, once more, to run.

"Go!" Daisy pleaded. "Hurry!"

They arrived at the doorstep as the hordes began to materialize and come into view on the opposite side of the road. The shadowy devils, reaching for prey that wasn't close to being within reach, galloped across the street. Rivulets of greenish water poured off of the monsters in sheets, and many gurgled and spat through the streaming fluid as they laughed. The cachinnating Malevolent Nevers mocked and marked their desired kill. Simi held Mags, while Daisy pounded on the door.

"Halden! Open up! Please, we're—" Daisy looked over her shoulder and realized how close they were to being overwhelmed. "*Shit*. Mr. Halden! Please! Open up!"

Simi began to holler alongside her. Shielding Mags from the approaching onslaught, he tried to kick at the door. "Mr. Halden! It's Simi Ward!"

As the creatures closed ground in between the house and swamp, each of their steps splattering and leaving a sickening sludge in its wake, the depraved managed to infiltrate Simi's thoughts.

Thou, there!
Ward!
"Mr. Halden!" he screamed, again.
This way, this way.
What is owed.
What is owed.
What is owed.
With his free hand, Simi covered an ear. "Leave…"
Ay, yes.
"…me…"
What is owed—
"…alone!"

The door was wrenched open and they all topped inside. Ulf Halden slammed it shut, just as a wave of Malevolent Nevers crashed into it. The old wooden slab seemed to shift a few inches under the weight of the bombardment, but held.

"Downstairs!" Halden called, leading them. "Into the bunker!"

There was a light guiding their party directly toward the basement and then, within the cement enclosure, a small hatch in the floor. It lay open and a Lilliputian set of winding stairs awaited them.

"Inside! Fast as you can."

With Simi and Daisy practically lifting Mags the entire way, the four eventually found themselves down in the cramped room. There was a single mattress on the floor, and shelves of canned goods.

Ulf busied himself fastening a series of bolts and large metal bars. He didn't speak or breathe until his task was complete. Once done, he rounded on the others.

"Now. What in ever-living hell have you brought down upon me? Didn't I tell ya—?"

"Mr. Halden," Daisy said, pressing both of her hands together. "Please, we had nowhere else to go. Abe he—well, he—" Overwhelmed, she collapsed to the floor.

"Abel?" Halden suddenly realized he was missing. "Jesus. That fool. Thought he had all the answers, he did. I tried to warn him." He looked to Simi. "I'm sorry, Son."

Ignoring the statement, Simi continued to tend to Mags. "You have a first aid kit down here? She's…" he left the rest unsaid.

Halden nodded. "Right." He snatched a white box off of a shelf. "This should do for now. Everything you will need. Bandages. Alcohol wipes. The whole shebang."

Daisy took the plastic container from him and she and Simi began to uncover and clean Mags' wounds.

Simi looked up at the man. "Thank you, Mr. Halden. You saved—"

"*Horseshit*," the man grunted. "Done nothin' of the sort yet." He looked up toward the hatch over his head and listened as the hellions tore through his home. Their chortling and merry-making caused his jaw to stiffen and he gritted his dentures. "Not yet."

Fifty Two

Ward!
Foolish to shun us.
Thou were warned.
Slumber awaits.
To feast.
To feast.
'Tis what's owed.
What's owed.
Our time does call upon's, fool.
Blood of thy veins.
Blood of the Ward
Blood of—

Abe's eyes flew open. Where the voices had only just lived, ringing now took hold. The pain in his ears was overwhelming, but he could not lift his arms toward them to offer any sort of relief. Nearly every inch of his body was bearing the weight of a Malevolent Never. There were a few gnawing on his shins, struggling to pierce through his jeans. An untold number clawed at his shirt, their talons scraping at his flesh with each slash. Two others pinned his head to the blacktop; one was straddling his neck and the other his forehead. Their blazing lime oculi peered down at him, heads cocked in wonder, and drips of saliva fell from each of their open voids into his own. Their long, squishy fingers pried at his mouth, forcing it wide. He gagged on the vile bile pouring into himself and—as his vision became clearer and he began to more fully regain cognizance of the torture being imparted unto his being— he willed himself to fight.

Abe tried to roll to one side and the creatures forced him back, flat on the ground, once again. As more of the froth was poured into him, the voices inside his head became more emboldened, louder, closer.

Ward!
Fool to fight, Ward.
Posset of us, thou shall.
Ingest us, thou hast.
Fool to fight us.
Fool to fight—

"No!" Abe screamed. Somehow, he was able to wrench one of his arms free and belted the imp sitting on his throat. With a sickening thud he connected with the side of the creature's head and it fell, harmlessly to the ground beside him.

"Alright, you sons-of-bitches," he choked through the sludge in his throat, "Let's go."

He swung his fist again, this time at the cretin perched atop his bald head. "Get... off!"

Crack.

The little devil squealed and he heard it smack to the pavement.

Abe sat up and, in doing so, drew more attention to himself. The damage he'd inflicted did not go unnoticed. Scampering down the road toward him—all while he continued to bat at the creatures chewing on his legs and belly—was another crush of Malevolent Nevers. The throng snickered and, as they approached, Abe managed to jump up to his feet. There were still a few clinging to the back of his legs and shoulders and—with time running out before the next gang reached him—he had to think fast. There was a telephone poll only feet away and, with all of his remaining strength, Abe ran backward, at full speed, into the tall, wooden, post.

There was a loud *splurch*, followed by the flopping of three lifeless demon bodies, as he pulled away.

Without another moment to congratulate himself, he knew he needed to do something before he ended up back on the ground again.

And then he spotted it.

Lounging, forgotten, a few paces away, was Barachiel. The guardian-angel-clown thing.

Sanctum, Abe wondered. An itch of uncertainty fluttered to the surface of his thought. He batted the doubt away and cracked his neck, readying himself. *Sanctum*.

He ran for it, just as the flood of chattering, mucus-spewing, hellions hit. Diving, Abe landed directly on top of the clown at the same instant the snapping, howling, cascade of sprites flowed over him. He rolled to his back, somehow able to do so even under the crushing weight and the slicing that seemed to inflict itself upon every last inch of his body, and held Barachiel over his face and into the eye of the revolting storm.

Almost instantly there was an enraged wailing as every last one of the shadows on top of Abe—in unison—

threw themselves away from him. Away from Sanctum. They hissed—some leaping over the guardrail on the side of the road and back down into the swamp and others merely backing away, still keeping tabs at him from a safer distance.

Abe stood up and, in doing so, something *crunched* under his foot. He looked down and groaned at the sight of the crumbled dagger blade. He'd previously seen the tool as a formidable weapon, but years of neglect and rust had proven the opposite.

Well, so much for that family heirloom.

He spun around, looking for some sort of an exit or escape, but found none. While the creatures had no desire to come closer to him, they retained a circular wall, preventing him from making a run for it. The beasts continued to hiss at him; occasionally one would spit in his direction and even come close to reaching him with the spew that continued to leak from each of their faces. Green eyes watched—uncertain of what the human might do—and followed every step he took as he paced back and forth.

Ward!

The cry invaded the deepest recesses of his skull. Abe started to fall to a knee, but stopped himself. It was what they wanted. He couldn't allow them to regain control. If the Malevolent Nevers could fully wrap themselves around his mind and muddy all else, even Barachiel might not be enough to save him.

"No!" he bared his teeth in response. "I won't let you—"

Oh, yet thou shall, Ward!
Thou shall!
That trinket thou bare is yet a child's plaything.
We are forever
We are lasting.

Hark to us.
We bid thee to—
"No!"
Enter the gate.

Unable to fight the rising tide of voices—scrambling over one another for his attention—Abe collapsed, finally, to his knees. He dropped the clown doll to the ground and screamed, knowing there was nothing he could do to block the turbulence from spilling into his ears nor the imminent cataclysm. The drooling horde advanced.

"I'm sorry, Sim," he managed to say, "I'm so, so, sorry and—"

Hoooonnnnnkkkk.

A car horn blared from behind him. Abe spun and was immediately blinded by a set of high beams. Still unable to remove his hands from the sides of his head, Abe squinted into the brilliance.

And then he heard a familiar voice. "Move! Out of the way!"

Abe threw himself to one side, just as an old, black, Cadillac with a silver skull on the hood pulled out in front of him, colliding with the crowd of shrieking Malevolent Nevers.

Through a crack in a rolled-down window, Ulf Halden cursed at him. "Bloody hell, Ward! Get in the damn car, you idiot!"

Staggering to his feet, a hand still over one of his ears, Abe managed to leap for the passenger side door, scooping up Barachiel with his free arm in the process.

He slammed the door and Ulf hit the gas, crushing a crowd of yelping devils in the process.

Abe, gasping for air, immediately turned to the old man. "But how—how the hell did you know I would—?"

"The kids. And your lady friend. They're back at my place."

"Are they—?"

"Safe and sound in my bunker. Nuthin' getting' in at them there. Not even these bastahds. Trust me."

He turned to Abe and winked.

Abe, still struggling to slow his breathing, and nursing a series of wounds, tried to sit up straighter. "So, what do we do now?"

Ulf cackled. Even with all the terror and insanity filling the streets of Foxborough on that evening, the centenarian was somehow still able to find amusement. "Now?" he laughed again, as if the life was only just returning to his bones for the first time in decades. "Now, we give these bastahds what they've wanted all along." He scowled and turned the steering wheel hard. The Cadillac spun a full one hundred and eighty degrees. "And this time—hah—*this time*, God help me, there ain't gonna be anymore dickin' around."

There was a light in the old man's eyes that, *right then*, started to blaze. His pupils reflected the glare of the moon, which had decided to finally make an appearance. Peeking out from behind a few reticent clouds, its rays caused the skull ornament on the hood of Ulf's Cadillac to glow, bathed in lunar effulgence—like a lighthouse guiding their way through the grisly, blood-stained, night.

Fifty Three

Dust, likely left undisturbed for centuries, sprinkled down onto the three heads huddled in the claustrophobic bunker—originally intended for only one. There was a large crash from upstairs as something massive toppled to the floor. Malevolent Nevers squawked and scrabbled at the hatch in Ulf Halden's basement, the glow from their eyes faintly seeping around the edges of the heavily bolted, trap door.

Simi brushed at the soot and grime that showered over his face and covered his mouth, coughing. Daisy searched the room for something she might be able to wield in defense of herself and the two teens—should the need have arisen—though she'd already done a few laps without anything other than a dented can of cream of mushroom soup to show for it. Mags' eyes were closed as Simi finished tightening the gauze around her upper thigh. She didn't flinch or react throughout the cleaning or wrapping of the wound, even though the gash was ragged and had to have been painful. She appeared to be unconscious.

Too much blood lost. Simi looked to Daisy. "I'm not sure what else to do."

There was another loud thud followed by a primal giggle from above. Daisy winced and then seemed to realize she'd been spoken to. "Not much you can do right now, Pal, 'cept make her comfortable and keep her warm. The bleeding appears to have stopped, which is very good news. Possibly looks worse than it is. In any case, let's be on the safe side and keep her wrapped up. Don't want Mags going into shock." She gestured toward Simi's bare chest. "You okay? Gonna get cold yourself real fast if you—"

"I'm fine," he reassured her. "The air is thick down here anyway."

She nodded as if that was enough of an answer, her eyes again locked on the rattling hatch. "Well, good. 'Cause, I think we might be staying put for a while. That is, if that door even holds. Mr. Halden knew what he was doing—a serious craftsman in his day, you know— but these things—" she gulped. "I'm worried they aren't going to stop until they get down here. Until they get to us."

Simi's followed her apprehensive stare. "We can't do anything about it, either. We may be safe, for now, but we're also trapped. If we pull that thing open—"

"We won't," Daisy said, just as much for herself as for him. She slid down to the cement floor, her back flat against the cool wall. "All we can do is wait and *hope.*"

Wait and hope, Simi thought. *And what exactly are we waiting and hoping for?*

Daisy seemed to sense his question. "I think Mr. Halden—I think he has a plan. We just have to believe he's got a little left in that rusty tank."

Simi sighed and realized he'd been combing his fingers through Mags' dreads, one of which—to him—looked like it'd been recently shredded, most likely during her abduction. He picked it up, absentmindedly, and tried to smooth everything out. As if the image—something so incredibly beautiful to him—represented the full weight and true destruction they'd all experienced that evening—Simi began to cry. He wiped at his eyes with the bedraggled lock of hair and then caught Mags smiling up at him. Her stare had a bit of a hazy look—as if she were trying to see him through a fog or a steamed-up mirror—but it was also warm and familiar. Her bright green glasses hung, crookedly, and she attempted to straighten them.

He sniffed. "Well, hey there, Beautiful."

Mags tried to sit up to kiss him, but didn't seem to have the strength. She cried out and he forced her to lay back down. Simi bent over and kissed her on the lips. "Hey there, yourself," she said, after their lips parted ways.

"You shouldn't be moving, Mags. You're still hurt. I think we cleaned you up pretty good, but you've lost, like, *a lot* of blood. You need to rest."

Her grin broadened. He couldn't tell if she'd processed what he was saying. "Been missing that," she said.

"Been missing..." he struggled to figure out what she was talking about. "Oh, the kiss?"

She nodded, too weak to speak any further, and she silently mouthed. "I love you."

As her eyes began to close again, he whispered back to her, "I love you too."

When he sat up, Daisy—her hands hanging over her knees—was smirking from across the room. "Cute," she said, her eyes teasing him. "Brings me back..." she started to say, but something prevented her from completing the sentence.

Simi wiped some dust out of Mags' hair, but squinted at Daisy. "What do you mean? Brings you back to when?"

Daisy closed her eyes and tried to wipe away the memory before it could take form in the middle of her forehead. "Nothing. It's just—well, your dad. He was sort of like that too, you know. When he was your age."

Simi let himself rest back against the wall behind the bed. "Like, what?"

There was a sparkle in D's eyes. Something from her past trying to shine through into her present. "Struck."

There was silence for a minute or two, while Simi considered her surprising moment of nostalgia. He tilted his head to her, curious to know more about his father and eager to find something to distract himself from the tumult and constant bombardment from the floor above. "Struck? What does that mean?"

Daisy wrapped her arms around herself and stared wistfully into the wall beyond Simi, unable to stop herself from clutching at a scene from her youth. "By me," she said, finally. "He was struck—*by me*. At least, that's how I always felt. It was almost like, every time he'd see me—every time we'd meet or run into one another—I could sense, and sometimes even actually *feel*, how much he was blown away by—well, me." Simi looked at her quizzically and she laughed. "I know it must sound super weird, but it was an incredible feeling. To have someone who was so amazed by my every action, someone who hung on each of my words as if it were gospel. I felt—sort of special, you know? Like, why me? He was like that, all the way up until he…"

When she seemed incapable of continuing, Simi did so for her. "Until he left you. Right?" He shifted carefully, so as not to wake Mags. "Trust me, I get it. Been there. Done that. He's, uh—"

"Complicated," Daisy jumped in. Simi nodded, mutely, and they both sat treading water in their own remembrances for a while.

After a time, an idea suddenly came to Simi. "Hey," he said, quickly garnering Daisy's attention. "Hey, I feel stupid for not suggesting this before, but—cell phones. I have mine, Mags has hers—"

"I've got one too."

"Right," Simi continued, frantically reaching into his pocket. "We can call for help."

"Simi—"

"We can call the police," he talked over her. "Maybe someone can—maybe they can get us out of here and—"

"Simi—"

He looked up at her, dejectedly. "No signal." He reached for Mags' phone and in seconds, threw it down on the bed. "Hers too."

"Simi, I've been trying to tell you. I looked at my phone when we first got down here. There's no way we're getting any service in this concrete hole in the ground. Nobody's coming for us."

He groaned through his teeth. "This is so frustrating. We need to do something. We can't just sit here while Mags—"

"Simi?" Mags' eyes were open again. "Would you shush? I'm trying to sleep."

There was a twinkle there, deep inside in her pupils, that warmed him. He relaxed and took a long, slow, breath. "Okay, Mags. Okay, I'll try."

The door above his head shuddered again. The cries of the sludgy swamp spawn were becoming increasingly more agitated, more frenzied, more desperate to tear the door from its hinges. Simi looked up at the trembling square, wrapped his arms tightly around his girlfriend, and squeezed.

Fifty Four

"What is it about the rain?"

Ulf had just pulled up in front of the burial ground when the skies opened up again. They were parked behind the sheriff's jeep, its blues still flashing—illuminating the droplets in a way that gave the illusion too-bright blueberries were being dumped onto them from the heavens. The rain was torrential and it was difficult to see all the way up the hill. The stone markers— dark shadows waiting, judging from above— remained steadfast guardians of the mostly empty graves, even as the sudden monsoon spilled down over their cracked, ancient heads.

"Huh?" Ulf said, stopping before stepping out into the deluge.

"The rain!" Abe shouted to make sure the man could hear him over the pattering on the Caddy's hard roof. "This is the second time it's started and then they—those things— scatter. Why? They can't possibly be afraid of getting wet?

Coming from the swamp and Dead Rock River? I mean, they seem to have emerged from the marsh, right? Why would they—?"

Ulf's glare stopped him. His bloodshot eyes were wide and frightened, but— as he leaned toward Abe— his confidence and strength exuded a healing elixir that Abe absorbed through each of his pores. "Listen to me, Son. Don't you try and make any sense'r all this. Ya hear me? Them things do what they do, when they wants to do to it. Capeesh?"

Abe craned his neck out the window to see better. "Yeah, but they're—they're just gone. It doesn't make any sense."

" A'course it don't make no sense. Neither does diggin' up yer ancestors and feedin' 'em to these brutes. But we're here now, ain't we?" His face hung looser as he evaluated Abe's continued unease. "Look here. These cretins… they're *animals*, right? Animals, well, most of 'em are dumb as shit. Somethin' falls from the sky and they—who the hell knows—maybe they fancy themselves a bit of Chicken Little action. You understand? Let 'em be afraid of whatever they decide to be afraid of. Regardless of their reason, it's bought us a bit of time and we got a shit ton of shit to dig. Now, you with me or not? I'm too goddamn old to do this m'self."

Abe white-knuckled the door handle. "Okay. Let's get this over with." He was about to step outside when Ulf grabbed his shoulder.

"You forgettin' somethin', Son?"

Abe looked down at the console in between the two of them. Barachiel stared up, merrily gawking back at him, apparently oblivious to the calamitous evening they'd survived through up to that point.

He grabbed the doll and nodded at Halden.

They threw open their doors and stood in the downpour. Instantly, both were soaked. The old man's white locks hung heavily from underneath his little hat, like white, sodden, worms. He growled through the water. "There's a shovel in the road." Abe looked to what could only have belonged to the now-missing Sheriff. "You grab that one, I'll get the one in my trunk."

Abe did as he was told. He hefted the dirtied spade onto his back and Ulf produced an even more worn, more oxidized one from his car. The elder chap led their small ensemble up the steep incline, grunting through each step. Abe walked backward, facing the swamp, with Barachiel clutched against his chest.

This rain won't last forever. Keeping you close by, Sir, in case—

"Abel!" Ulf screamed down to him from on top of the plateau. "Get your ass up here! Stop lollygaggin' or whatever it is you're..." the man's voice trailed off as Abe reached the climax with him.

Ulf already had a shovel in the ground. Abe watched him wrestle with a few scoops. "I'm not sure I can do this, Ulf."

Halden stopped, leaning on the handle grip. The rain continued to dump over them and the wind seemed to howl even more in the small clearing. Ulf's hat started to creep off his head, but he grabbed at it before it flew out into the night. "A 'course you can, dammit. You *must.*"

Abe moved a hand over his head and skimmed the water off. It spilled over his face and into his eyes. He blinked a few times. "This feels wrong."

Exasperated, Halden stormed over to him and stood just below Abe's nose. He poked him hard in the belly with a bent index finger. "Now, look, Son. I loved her too. Way back then, those many years ago. God knows I did, if he were ever listenin'. And, I told m'self I'd never get involved in this mess again… but, now it looks like I've got no choice. I'll be damned if I'm gonna stand here and watch you let this all continue to spiral off, out of control, until there's nothing left to save. You couldn't do it yerself and neither could I. Together though—" he looked at Elma's gravestone. "Together, I think we can. There's a lot of love for that woman standin' right here, right now. Besides, it's your damn family that's brought this down on us. It's your duty. Your birth-rite or some shit."

Abe looked at him sideways through the rain. "Why does this fall on us—my family, I mean? Why do the Wards bear this awful curse?"

Ulf hacked something wretched from his throat. He was shivering slightly, the cold seeping slowly into his paper-thin flesh, over his creaking bones. "You fool. Haven't figured her out yet, have ya? Ha!" He coughed again and spat something greenish onto the mossy bed of earth. "Don't you know? You're the gatekeepers. The *wards* of this unholy hellmouth!"

A flash of lightning sizzled from high above. Abe stared back, his mouth working, wordlessly. "I—I—"

"You don't need to say nuthin', cause it won't change what is. See, these things—" he pointed back across the street, toward Ward House, toward Dead Rock River, toward the bog. "These things, right—the way I understands it, at least—they stay at bay while the gatekeeper lives. Waiting. Sure, Elma fed 'em. It was in her nature and, for all I know, maybe the feedin' were even part of it all. Shit, I'm glad I didn't get deeper'n this to find out all the specifics. But, what I do know—"

Abe stepped closer to better hear him through the rain. Ulf took his hat off and wrung it out before returning it to his head and continuing.

"—what I do know is that once their Ward is gone, they get to feast. That's the deal, you see. The contract, er—oh hell—what's the damned word?"

"The covenant," Abe whispered.

Another bolt of lightning cracked across the sky and both men reflexively covered their heads.

"Right," Ulf exclaimed, clapping Abe on the back. "Yes, the *covenant*. They've waited, what, seventy years for this one? Made this deal written in the blood of yer ancestors, they did. And now, it's time to pay that piper, Son." He smiled and his yellowed teeth caught the glint of a few transient strands of moonlight that'd found a way through the thick clouds overhead. The rainwater pouring over his mouth only made him appear even more diabolical. "They're hungry."

And with that, just as Abe turned to pull his first shovel from the ground, the rain stopped. Like a switch had suddenly been flicked, everything—including the two, oddly paired, men—seized.

Almost immediately, the woods across the street lit up, both in an electric shade of green and with the yelps and battle cries of the charging bog goblins.

"You dig!" shouted Ulf. "I'll be right back." He grabbed Barachiel and lurched toward the street.

"Wait!" Abe tried to stop him. "Where're you going?"

As he stumbled down the hill, Ulf called back. "My gun, it's in the truck. Don't stop what yer doin' and for godsakes don't worry about this old man. Hurry up with that, will ya?"

Abe turned with a reckless abandon and an energy that seemed to sprout forth from some long-forgotten well and wildly began to remove earth from Elma's grave. Clumps of heavy wet dirt flew into the air and *flopped* into a nearby pile as he worked. Abe's arms screamed, not familiar with that sort of manual labor, but he refused to slow. He'd already made good work of his aunt's final resting place when Ulf arrived again, pulling himself slowly up the hill. His back faced Abe and he placed Sanctum down in front of himself, in the path of any who might choose to attempt an ascension into the little, timeworn, highland citadel in the sky.

"You keep digging," Ulf said, before Abe could ask anything else. "I'll do all the shootin'." He dropped a cartridge into the shotgun and made sure it ended up in the chamber.

The snarling got louder and a wall of the demons, within seconds, bordered the burial ground. Ulf raised his gun. Though none of the creatures advanced, it wasn't the old man's weapon that made them hesitant. Barachiel, sitting confidently in front of the two men, beamed a jolly grimace toward the intruders and they hissed in his direction.

"Almost there!" Abe said, through shovelfuls of dark soil. The fresh dug earth was soft and the rain made the going even easier for him. "Almost—"

Thunk.

"That's it!" cheered Ulf, as Abe cleared dirt off the solid object. "Now get that old bat outta there! We're runnin' out of time."

All around them, Malevolent Nevers breathed patiently, inching closer with each passing moment.

"Such a shallow grave. It's almost like Burt Barney knew we'd be digging her back up—"

"Je-sus H. Are you still on this? Of *course*, he knew, ya bloody fool!"

The forest all around them was coming alive and Abe felt his heart might soon spring free of its confinement.

"But, don't these things know I'm doing what they want? Why are they still—?"

"Oh, who the hells knows, Abel. You took so fantastically long to do it, maybe they don't even care anymore. Maybe the little suckers don't believe you will actually see it through. The covenant and all, right? You didn't deliver like you were supposed ta. You pissed 'em off!"

Abe jumped down into the hole and began reaching for a handhold. Elma's coffin was a simple pine box and, without much effort, Abe managed to wrench the nails out of the spaces in which they'd only recently been hammered. "Got it!" he screamed, but hesitated before pulling the sarcophagus open.

Ulf looked at him and nodded.

Abe prepared himself. "I'm sorry, Elma. But, I think this is what you wanted."

He lifted the lid.

Elma Ward lay inside, peacefully asleep. Her arms were still folded over her chest and she wore her favorite flowered dress (Daisy's idea). Abe held his breath and put his arms underneath hers. She felt soft and brittle, but also quite light, and Abe easily—and gently—lifted her onto his shoulder. In doing so, her spongey cheek caressed his own and her smell caused him to gag. It was an immediate reminder that Elma's final wishes had stated she was not to be embalmed.

He turned and looked up and out of the hallowed crater. Ulf Halden stared down at him—his shoulders sagging, his bottom lip beginning to tremble, ever so slightly—and let his gun drop to the ground.

He sniffed and offered Abe a hand. As he pulled the newest guardian of Ward House out of his self-made hole, the old man's whimper was just audible over the increasingly loud cries of the Malevolent Nevers.

"Oh, Elma," Ulf said. "It's time to go, Dear."

Fifty Five

"You sure you guys don't hear that?"

Simi was on the ground, with his ear pressed firmly to the finished cement.

Mags sat up and Daisy stood over the youngest Ward. She squatted beside him and brought her own head closer to the floor. "What're you hearing, Sim?"

He listened. "Humming. Singing. Sounds like a child. A girl, I think." The other two stared, blankly, at him and he sighed. "Like what we heard out behind Elma's house, Mags. Remember? Just before... well, everything started. You don't hear it this time?"

Mags shook her head. "Nothing, Sim. Maybe you're just tired?"

He still hadn't changed his position. "It's almost like she—like *they*—are singing to me. Calling to me."

Daisy's eyes widened. "Simi, get away from the floor."

He tilted his head up toward her, but didn't otherwise

move. "But, why? They can't get through this." He knocked on the ground and then grabbed at his knuckles, wincing. "Mr. Halden said this is, like, six feet of solid foundation. They're not getting in that way." He returned the side of his head to the cool ground.

Daisy bent over and pulled at his elbow. "Sim, listen to me. This is—I dunno—it's some kind of trick."

He lifted his head again. His eyes, looking as if they carried the weight of the day, were noticeably drooping. Simi yawned. "Huh? What kind of *trick*?"

"I mean, this voice—whatever it is you're hearing—it's a disguise of some kind. It almost worked at getting you to follow them out into the yard, right? Now, you're hearing it through the floor. They're duping you into letting down your guard. If they can get you to do that, then they can—"

Tap. Tap. Tap. Tap.

"You hear that?"

Both women shook their heads.

"Simi, I think you should listen to Daisy. Why don't you come sit—?"

Tap. Tap. Tap. Tap.

"There, again. Something's down there." Simi leapt to his feet. His hands trembled and he attempted unsuccessfully to interlock his fingers. "Maybe it's not as deep as he says it is. Maybe there's—I dunno—a room or something down there."

Siiiiimiiii.

Simi shook his head as if a fly were buzzing in his ear.

Daisy put her hands on Simi's back and tried to lead him toward the bed. "Let's just—"

Siiiiimiiii.

He wrenched himself away and started searching through the shelf Ulf had bolted to the wall. "No!" he screamed. "She's down there. I've got to find something to—" At the foot of the shelf, in a dark corner of the room, was a simple hammer. He snatched it up and spun back into his original crouching position.

"Wait for it—" he whispered.

"Simi, please, put that—"

Siiiiimiiii. Help ussss.

"There!" he smashed the hammer down into the floor and grey chips flew up into their faces. The earth below them growled and—as if his swing was that of a demi-god—the entire floor of the bunker split into two pieces. In an instant, the crack widened and spider-webbed under their feet and beneath the bed. Mags screamed and Daisy tackled Simi to the ground, away from the opening.

Simi struggled as Daisy attempted to pin his arms down. "But, we need to help her!" he whined. "Get off me!"

Daisy knocked the hammer out of his hand. "Mags, get it! Hurry!"

Grabbing at the wrap on her leg with one hand, Mags hobbled to the ground and lunged for the tool with the other. In a panic, Simi thrashed and inadvertently kicked it into the crevasse. The hammer disappeared forever into the gaping wound that he'd somehow managed to inflict on Ulf Halden's— purportedly impenetrable—fortress.

"Dammit, Mags!" Simi continued to fight to get out of Daisy's hold. "What're we gonna do now?"

And then, just as before, the gurgling rupture belched upward a torrent of pulsing slime, intermixed with the searching, twitching, claws of the Malevolent Nevers.

Simi dove toward the abyss, reaching into its depths. The ooze covered and climbed his arms as he linked hands with those that stretched out to welcome him.

"No!" Daisy squealed falling onto the back of his legs,

just as he was dragged forward. Preventing his descent into the effulgently emerald, goop-filled, hell-bowels, she called again to Mags. "Mags! Help me!"

At first, Mags gawked, in shock at what had become of her boyfriend and at what was attempting to devour him. The howls and jeers of the demons mocked her hesitation and, though shaking, she too fell onto Simi. "Simi, please!" she shouted. "Please!"

With a strength that didn't belong to himself, Simi kicked his feet backward into the faces of both women. They each flew through the air and crashed into the wall behind them. With tears in their eyes, they whimpered as Simi turned his head.

Mags gasped at the sight of him. "Simi!"

Simeon Ward's mouth was stretched far too wide and his eyes flickered green. He leaned his head back and howled. His spine arched, like a cat cornered by another predator.

'Down, down, down. This way, this way. What is owed. Ay, yes." He giggled and puss bubbled at his lips. There was an unnatural cracking sound as his body's posture became increasingly more feral—bones breaking with each jerked, spasmodic movement—and he bit down hard, grinding his teeth together, sending shards of ivory dancing into the air.

'Simi!" Mags screamed, trying to reach for him. He laughed in her face and spat a black sludge into her eyes. She collapsed into Daisy's arms, gagging. Daisy held her close and hastily wiped the girl's vision clear. Simi's breathing became, suddenly, more rapid, and the two stared—slacked jawed—at the undomesticated shape seething at them both.

"This is the way," he cackled through the puss and back gunk spilling down his chin. "We hast obeyed." He twisted his body and hung his face out over the surging chasm. "'Tis *my* turn."

And then, without another word, the youngest of the guardians—the youngest Ward—fulfilled his family's colonial covenant with the swamp scourge and toppled forward into the sickening embrace of the Malevolent Nevers.

Fifty Six

Tree branches like claws and claws like passing tree branches, thwacked and grabbed at both Abe and Ulf as they hurried down a small embankment beside the burial plateau and through the throng of snarling demons. Ulf, albeit slowly, led the way with Barachiel held out in front of himself. The act parted the spritely seas just wide enough for the two men to sneak through, but Abe—in particular—bore the brunt of the demonic slashing as he took up the rear, with Elma's corpse dangling from his back. Ulf huffed from his position at the bow of their invisible bulwark as he made his way across the street.

Toward the Ward House.

"This way!" he roared without looking back to Abe, careful to keep his focus on the path ahead. "Stay close! We need to get her to the rock!"

Abe could barely hear him over the howling and taunting of the polluted spirits. Their voices pried at his mind and scraped at the surface of his consciousness with long dirty, invasive, talons. He barreled forward and squeezed his eyes shut in an attempt to block them all out.

"Ulf—" he tried to get the old man's attention. "I'm not sure if I'm gonna be able to—"

"Yes, you will, dammit!" The miser croaked back. "One step and then the other." He threw Barachiel—*Sanctum*—in front of his face as a particularly large Malevolent Never leaped from an overhanging branch. The demon squealed before making contact and skittered into the shadows. "Just keep moving! I can't get 'er there m'self!"

Ward!

"No!" Abe screamed batting at the air. Elma's arms flopped at the same moment, as if she too were fighting off the meddlesome voices. "Ulf, I can't—"

"Don't stop!"

"But, I can't—"

We hast taken him.

Thou are too late.

Failed us.

Failed the covenant.

"No!"

Failed thy blood.

Abe fell to his knees, dropping Elma's body to the ground. Ulf didn't immediately notice and continued pressing onward.

"Simi!" screamed Abe.

Ulf spun, realizing Abe had fallen behind, just as the monsters descended on the un-warded Ward. "Off of 'im, you rancid bastahds!" He staggered to Abe's side, the clown doll the only protection between them and the circling, shrieking, horde. "Get your ass up!" he called into Abe's ear, making sure to be heard. "We need to—"

Abe grabbed at his arm, wild panic showing itself in his wandering, erratic, gaze. "It's Simi. I—I don't know how but, I think they may have him."

Ulf, still holding the doll in between the two of them and the thrashing, charcoal limbs of the encroaching enemy line, grabbed Abe under the elbow. "He's fine, he's in my bunker."

"No! They have him!"

Ulf forced him to his feet. "I doubt it. If they did, would they still be coming at us like this? And, even so— even if they *do* got him— maybe there's still a chance to take him back." He looked down at Elma's peaceful, somehow-still-undisturbed, face. "There she is. Your only goddamn chance. Now, let's get this done, before we can't no more."

Abe gritted his teeth and scooped Elma back up. "Alright," he said throwing her once more onto his shoulders. "Lead the way!"

Halden staggered with his clown buffer across the road and onto the outer boundary of the Ward property. He looked up at the waiting, cast-iron, eye peering down from its safe perch above the old homestead. He winked at it and in the same motion, kicked a dark shape biting at his heel. "Hurry, Abel! He said, shifting the shotgun strapped to his back. "There's an old rowboat stashed down at the bottom of the hill. Things lasted practically forever. Hidden under some brambles behind her shed. Run to it and don't stop. Now!"

Abel did as he was commanded and heard Ulf fire off a couple of shots, giving him cover. True to the old man's word, there was a metallic glint interred under a pile of leaves and yard waste, right where the manicured lawn met the forest. A few more steps down the slope was the ominous glimmer of Dead Rock River.

Abe put Elma on the ground and began to pry the boat free. Just as he'd almost completely uncovered the nearly fossilized watercraft, a searing pain sliced itself in between his shoulder blades.

"Aggggh," Abe cried out. He grabbed at his back and his hand sunk into the murky shape that'd plunged its hooks into his flesh. A fanged mouth wrapped itself around Abe's fingers and clamped down hard. Blood trickled down his tattooed forearm. Abe screamed and flung his fist toward the closest tree, punching clean through the face of the chomping pariah. With a sickening *sploosh*, the monster's head cracked open like an egg, and blackish-green yoke sprayed up into Abe's eyes.

Without cleaning himself, he turned to heft Elma's body into the boat. She clunked stiffly into the metal bottom and he began to lift the craft toward the river. He was pushing the boat into the water, just as Ulf and Barachiel careened down the hill. The centenarian—

Moving remarkably well for his age, Abe noted.

—joined in pushing from the stern until the sludgy swamp reached over their wastes. Abe climbed aboard and then, grabbing the man under the armpits, pulled Ulf in beside himself. They both tumbled into the rocking dinghy.

"Row!" Ulf growled.

Abe did, his back to Dead Rock.

From his knees, Ulf reloaded his weapon and pointed it out over the still waters, into the night. From the shore, the miserable cries of the demons lamented the departure, but their wails gradually quieted as the craft moved further from the yard.

There was a splash to Ulf's right and he, reflexively, turned and fired.

Whether or not he hit anything was impossible to

know in the almost complete absence of any illumination. A few sets of green eyes lurked under the surface and from behind some river weeds.

Unblinking. Watching.

"I don't think they're following us," Abe gasped. "I think they're letting us go."

Ulf laughed and looked over his shoulder at the rower. "Hah! Bullshit. You really think that they'd just let us go?" He lowered his gun, momentarily taking his sight away from the watching neon spheres. "You just keep goin', don't stop until you get—"

A shadow exploded from the oily, lily-pad-covered waters just beside the boat. In one fell swoop, it engulfed Ulf, tackling him cleanly into the murky river. So quickly it'd all happened, the man hadn't even time to offer any sort of vocalization or exclamation. Before Abe even had a chance to lunge for Elma's old beau, Ulf Halden disappeared beneath the caliginous ripples of Dead Rock River.

"No!" Abe moaned, instinctively lowering his face to the boat's edge to look beneath the surface of the water. There was no movement. All was still.

He waited before calling again. "Ulf! Mr. Halden!"

There was no response. Abe was alone—save for the grinning visage of Barachiel. He picked up the clown and sat the odd smirking fellow in his lap, in an attempt to avoid the same fate brought unto Ulf.

Just keep going. Don't stop. Get to that damn rock.

Abe nodded to himself and again wrapped his shaking hands around the two oars.

Row dammit. Row.

Again, he did. The rhythmic slapping of the blades announced his intention and he saw, out of his peripheral vision, glowing green orbs lining the edges of the river.

The swarm had caught up to him once again, forced Abe to dig in. He bore down and felt himself speeding along the cramped channel.

Thunk.

Abe turned around. The white, jagged, monument— an immortal, fresh-water, Moby Dick— stood, awaiting his arrival. He grabbed for Elma, just as the waters around him began to churn. Little green flashlights swam by and the beasts who'd long held a pact with his ancestors once more scorned him. He covered his ears as he dragged Elma onto the chalky, stone, pedestal.

Ho, Ward!

Thou hast arrived.

"Come on—" he panted, pushing the body closer to the precipice of the boulder. "Almost— there."

With a gift.

A gift?

Yet is it too late, sirrah?

"No!"

Blood of the ward must be spilled.

Tonight.

Tonight.

Fill the chalice of our covenant.

"I am!"

Fill it with the blood of thy blood.

"She's here!"

Deliver us!

"She's here!" he screamed over the voices in his head, over the chanting emanating from all corners of the surrounding wetlands. "Take her! Take her now!"

But still, the water began to bubble and the creatures—their shapes lifting themselves into the night air, furls of steam escaping from their shadow-flesh—rose toward the stars. Abe spun in a full circle. Malevolent Nevers were everywhere. Bursting through the long, brittle grasses of the bog. Erupting from the flatulent, decaying, mudflats. Clambering over and into the rowboat.

"What do else do you want! Please! Just take her!"

The figures continued the abominable blitz. And then, Abel Ward heard their song.

It wasn't a language or tongue he spoke and yet, he *understood.*

The beasts pushed past him, knocking him into the rocking boat. He froze, waiting, beside the unmoving, unwavering, smile of Barachiel. Carefully, he raised his head, in an effort to witness the ritual.

The slithering shapes surrounded the body of Elma Ward. Their song continued for what seemed like an eternity. Abe groaned, propped up on his arms, wishing for the entire episode to end.

Just take her. What are you waiting for?

The demons sniffed around the rigid, serene, corpse. Her dead white hair flowed down over the even paler Dead Rock. And then, gradually, the sprites began to wrap their ghostly grips around her. Together they lurched, receding into the eternal, filthy, tomb from whence they'd all come. In an instant, Elma Ward was gone forever, and—in that moment—so were the Malevolent Nevers.

Abel Ward—the next in line—collapsed onto his back, into the rowboat, and sobbed.

And Barachiel—Ward O' the Wards, Protector O' the 'Borough, and Sanctum from the Unholy Wretches of Dead Rock River—beamed.

Fifty Seven

The shuddering stopped. The tear in Ulf Halden's basement ceased its widening. Daisy and Mags huddled in a corner gulping air, arms flat and bracing against the cement block wall. Both stared toward the opening, terrified to look, fearful to see what might be awaiting them in the bowels of the now muted, now lifeless, void.

Daisy tried to hold Mags back, but the girl threw her off.

"Wait, Mags—" Daisy rasped, in a half-hearted, futile, bid to stop her.

With tears streaming down her cheeks, Mags Downing bellowed down into the yawning rift. "Simi! Oh, God, Simi, pl—"

And then she saw him. Lying there, looking back up at her. His expression was blank, absent any sort of recognition. His eyes were open and, for an instant, she couldn't tell if he were alive or dead. Daisy scrambled up beside her and, upon seeing the gaunt figure, gasped.

They both stared, waiting for any small sign from him.

"He's breathing," Daisy said. "And look his—"

"I know, I see," Mag sniffed. "His eyes. They're *his* again." She buried her face in her hands. "That's my Sim."

And then, Simeon Ward blinked. Twice.

Daisy pulled Mags' face back to the hole. "Look, look. He's—" frantically, she pointed at him and forced the girl to peer again into the crevasse.

Mags stared. "Simi!" she cried. "Simi, can you hear me?"

He blinked another couple of times before nodding and then rolling onto his side. He heaved and vomited a black oily substance out next to himself. Wiping at his mouth, he looked back up at the two gawking down. "I can hear you," he trembled. "Is—is it over?"

Daisy looked around the room before answering. "I don't know for sure," she said. "Sure seems like it is, though."

Simi struggled to a seated position. He was a good six feet below them, on a small outcropping of foundation and sediment. "Well," he spoke carefully. "Wanna help me outta here?"

The three spent the next few minutes devising a plan to extricate him from his basement mausoleum. Together, Daisy and Mags reached down and, each grabbing one of his hands, they managed to yank him up and back into the bunker.

Mags squatted in front of Simi as he rested with his forehead on his knees. "Sim, are you okay? Does anything hurt?"

Simi looked up at her. His face was covered in dust and grime, streaked by whatever greasy fluid had only recently been pouring from his orifices. His stringy dark hair was disheveled and his bare chest was covered in long, streaks of red; uneven claw marks which showed just how much the creatures' barbs had overwhelmed him, partially obscuring his treasured lightning bolt chest-tattoo. He chuckled, but his voice was unsteady. "Everything hurts, Mags." He looked up into her eyes and the tears pooled. "I don't know what that was. What *I* was. I wanted to go with them. Wanted them to take me away. *Forever.* I knew you were both there, screaming at me, pleading with me to listen and to stop. But, somehow, I—I—"

"Simi," Daisy stopped him with a hand on his shoulder. "It's okay. We know that wasn't really you. Those things, they found a way inside—a way to control you—and there wasn't anything you could do to fight them off."

Simi hung his head. "I was weak. I gave in to them."

Mags wrapped her arms around his neck. "All that matters is that you're here now. You're okay. *We're* okay."

Simi cried. "But, I hurt you both. I could have—I mean—I could have really—"

"But you didn't," Mags said and then planted a gentle kiss on his cheek. "You didn't."

For a while, they all sat, none of them certain of what to do or say next. Eventually, Daisy looked toward the hatch and stood up.

"Waddaya say we go check it out up top?" She shrugged. "Can't stay here forever, ya know."

Mags nodded and, after a moment, so did Simi. They helped him to his feet.

Daisy led the way and the three climbed back into Ulf's trashed house and exited through, what was at one point, his front door. After the visitation by the mangy marauders, nothing more than a few splintered planks of wood hanging from a hinge remained.

Outside, all was still. The truck sat, patiently waiting, at the base of Ulf's driveway. Its windows were completely shattered, but it otherwise appeared unharmed.

Nothing's ever gonna take that sucker down, Simi thought.

Silently, they limped toward the old reliable and Daisy got behind the wheel. Simi and Mags both squeezed into the cab and he put his head onto her shoulder. The truck rumbled to life and, without a word, they headed back across town.

Back to Ward House.

Within minutes, Daisy was steering the vehicle into the driveway and, without hesitating, pulled it all the way around back. She left it facing the shed and swamps, with the engine running. They sat quietly, peering out through the few remaining daggers of windshield. Exhaust rose past their line of sight and in through the razor-sharp opening. None of them coughed, for they all were holding their breath—waiting for any sort of warning or harbinger for how the remainder of their evening would go.

"Look," Daisy spoke abruptly, pointing out toward the bog. "Right there. You see it?"

The other two squinted. "Is that— a rowboat?" Mags asked.

Simi nodded and jumped out of the truck. He was shouting even before he'd started running.

"Abe!" he called. "Abe!"

All the way to the water's edge he ran, before a slumped form in the boat stirred. The moon bounced off of the shiny head of the shape that'd suddenly sat upright. "Simi!" Abe called back. "Are you alright?"

Simi fell to his knees. He tried to get the words out, but was overwhelmed with relief. He sobbed, bringing his face to the earth. The sloshing of oars soon enough announced that Abe was approaching and Simi sat up. "Abe!" was all he could manage.

His father leapt from the boat before it'd even reached the shore. He waded up the last trickle of Dead Rock River and splashed up onto the ground beside his son. They embraced and cried into the other's shoulder.

"Are you okay?" Abe asked again.

Simi's mouth was pressed into Abe's flannel shirt and his response was muffled. "I've been better but… yeah. You?"

Abe pulled his face away and kissed Simi on the forehead. "Been better. But, I'll live." He looked up as Daisy and Mags approached them both. "We all will." He looked behind himself, toward Dead Rock, suddenly remembered the one still missing. "Well, most of us will."

Daisy covered her mouth. "Mr. Halden?"

Abe looked at her, the corners of his eyes quivering, and shook his head. "But he saved us. And now, it's done."

Simi took notice of the clown doll nestled in his father's arms. Somehow, he hadn't seen him carry it out of the boat. His gaze traveled down to examine the smiling face and then back up to Abe's exhausted simper. Abel Ward, absentmindedly, squeezed the stuffed toy so hard that blood escaped from the skin on his cracked, taut, knuckles.

For now, thought Simi. *It's done—for now.*

Fifty Eight

Dayum, that's a good cup of coffee.

Abe placed the Styrofoam cup back into the holder beside him in the truck and pulled away from the coffee shop at the center of town. He turned the wheel and drove back down Main Street in the direction of the common. Though all was relatively quiet—it was still early in the morning, the sun having only shown itself a couple of hours earlier—those he had seen out in front of their homes appeared to be willing themselves back to reality. An elderly woman swept glass from her front porch, a man pried some nailed boards away from his basement bulkhead, and a few businesses—the coffee place, Burton Barney and Sons Funeral Home, and a local used bookshop— unlocked their doors on time, just as they always did.

Abe wasn't sure why he'd walked out the front door that morning, or what he'd been in search of, but he certainly hadn't expected to find the people of Foxborough hustling back to normalcy so quickly. In fact, from what he'd seen thus far, most who were already awake were reacting no differently than if there'd been a bad Nor'easter overnight. They picked up broken mailboxes and bloody shreds of clothing in the same way—and with the same energy and purpose—they cleaned up fallen tree limbs and excess leaves. Though there was one gentleman with a red-soaked bandage over his head walking a dog, Abe wondered if he would have otherwise recognized anything was amiss if he hadn't just lived—and truly survived—through the tragic events of the previous evening.

He rolled down the hand crank of his window to allow the fall air to waft over him. It swept across his head and he, for just a second, closed his eyes and imagined the breeze blowing through the luscious locks of his youth. Abe took another sip of his black coffee and this time kept the cup in one hand as he drove confidently with the other. Beside him, in the passenger seat, were three more coffees and an assorted box of donuts. Energy for anything else was nonexistent and he wasn't even certain the others would be around to enjoy his offering when he returned. Simi and Mags were most assuredly still sleeping. He'd heard them up and talking into the morning hours—he hadn't left the living room, hadn't allowed his eyes to fall closed—and knew, once they'd gone quiet, that the remainder of their day was probably all for naught. They were exhausted, broken, and he wanted to let them rest.

God knows, I wish I could.

The third cup of brew jiggled in the grey holder and Abe put his own coffee down, reaching to steady it before any of the hot beverage spilled over. Daisy had kept him company until the sun rose, but then too decided she needed to head to bed. Back at her place, she'd insisted, and—

after a bit pointless pleading with her not to leave on her own—she'd won the argument. She'd promised to return after a quick power nap so that they could "talk". He knew that could mean a whole host of topics or business, but the truth was— if their dialogue was to consist of a rehashing of the previous night's events—Abe wasn't sure there was anything more he'd have to contribute. One thing was for sure, though. When it came to being available to Daisy— present and ready to listen whenever she needed him— he was determined to be better. He'd whispered as much to her, before she'd walked out the door that morning, but her weak nod told him she wasn't ready to fully trust him again.

Lots of repair work still to do there, he told himself. *Baby steps.*

Abe's truck pulled all way around the town rotary, passing the library and the old theater. He turned back down North Street and, as he happened by the Town Hall on his left and the burnt-out husk of Clay's Video Palace on his right, he noticed a limping creature closing the driver's side door of his jeep.

Abe slowed to a crawl past the man. Bandages wrapped both of his arms and he balanced, clumsily, on a makeshift crutch. Noticeably, he'd shed his uniform for a blue and green flowered shirt.

Abe put a hand to his mouth and called out, stopping his truck in the middle of the road. No other cars were waiting behind him—though North Street was typically quite busy— the after-effects of Halloween Night having left many starting their day a bit later than usual.

"Sheriff Candler!" Abe waved.

Startled, the man looked up. He scowled and quickly hurried, one crutched stride at a time, back up the front steps of the town hall. Before hobbling through the main entrance, he took one more glance back at the idling, antique vehicle.

"Took you long enough, Ward!" he hollered and then— stumbling into the building— slammed the massive slabs of wood behind himself.

Abe sighed.

"Glad to see you're okay too," Abe muttered.

He let his foot off of the brake and started rolling again back toward Ward House. As he moved further down North Street, he saw much of the same scene he'd witnessed closer to the center of town: citizens of the old New England community picking up the fragmented detritus after a night of freakish anarchy. In front of one house, a child played outside with his dog, while a parent sat on the front porch sipping his joe. Abe lifted his cup in a commiserating salute and the gesture was returned with a smile. They'd all been through an ordeal and the pieces would—in time—be put back together again.

As Abe arrived back on Brown Street, he drove over an already splatted jack-o-lantern in the middle of the road. It was symbolic of the catastrophic Halloween Night—one which he hoped would not repeat itself when the trick-or-treaters arrived next year.

If they arrive next year.

He pulled his truck up to the front of the old Victorian manor. Still leering at him from above was the awful eye, which had seen a lot of shit go down only hours prior. Abe sighed.

Gonna see about getting that damn thing removed. Can't have people thinking they're walking into Mordor when they show up on my doorstep.

He blinked.

My doorstep. He scratched his chin and looked toward

the front stairs. *Well, we'll have to wait and see about that.*

He got out and slammed the door and, after taking only a few steps up the cobblestone path, he paused. There was a package awaiting him on the porch, sitting just underneath the wide-mouthed gargoyle knocker.

Gotta get rid of that crap too. Jesus, Elma.

He strode up the steps and kicked at the parcel, as if it might bite him if he weren't careful. Even that, however, made him chuckle.

Been bit more than enough in the past twelve hours. Think I'll pass.

When the wrapped box did not leap up at him, ooze, or snarl, he quickly hefted it under his arm and unlocked the front door. With a nod to the knocker—whose eyes appeared to almost twinkle as he walked past—Abe slammed the entryway shut behind himself.

He listened. All was quiet and he smiled.

"Good," he said. "Still asleep."

Ignoring the still lilting and scarred painting of the gate that passive-aggressively cautioned him over the stairwell—even more of an eyesore since it'd been graffitied in demon gore—Abe walked into the kitchen and sat at the table, plopping the package down in front of himself. For a while, he just stared at it. There was no return address and the handwriting was written in a scrawl unlike any he'd ever seen. It reminded him a bit of calligraphy in how ornate and flowy it was—

Using the technical terms, huh Abe?

—yet, it was also written in a dark, splotchy, ink, as if it'd been scratched out with a quill or an antiquated fountain pen. There was also, quite unmistakably, a faded red thumbprint stamped onto the bottom right corner.

Abe adjusted his position in the chair so that he could

get a closer look.

Red didn't necessarily mean blood—he knew that—but he couldn't help but wonder what else it might've been. He shrugged and took out his keys, dragging them over the packing tape that tightly sealed the mysterious contents inside.

Just as he was about to tear the box open, he looked up. He sensed someone was watching him—just a feeling, nothing more—and spun quickly around. Sitting in the living room, on the couch where he'd been tossed carelessly hours earlier—was Barachiel. His posture remained rigid and he appeared to be watching—*waiting*—amused by Abe's sudden paralysis. Abe ignored the doll's stare and return to the parcel.

He tore it open.

Inside there was—well, not much. A single, unmarked, white envelope and a set of rusty keys, which hung from a white-skull key chain. The eyes of the disembodied skeleton face held two emeralds, which each reflected the sunlight streaming in through the sliding porch door. Abe didn't hesitate. He grabbed the envelope and ripped through the seal.

There was a yellowed piece of paper, typed on what could only have been an old-timey, honest-to-God, type-writer of some kind.

Abe read through the document quickly and then dropped it to the table. He rubbed at his face and then looked at the slip of paper a second time, to make certain he was reading it correctly. It read, quite simply:

Be it known to all persons that <u>Abel Ward</u> is the owner of:
Ward House, 12 Brown Street, Foxborough, Massachusetts
On this date of <u>November 1ˢᵗ, 2021</u>.

There was more—mostly legal jargon—but he got the gist. At the bottom, Abe ran his finger over the signature, which was likely left years prior in the event of the writer's death.

Elma Ward

He was about to place the document back in its box when he noticed a small inscription, handwritten in very tiny letters under her autograph. The note read:

Congratulations to the newest keeper of the gate.
The new Ward.
xoxo

Sitting back in his chair, Abe inhaled the—not exactly earth-shattering—news. The official confirmation that Elma had, in fact, left her home in his care wasn't the most jarring bit. The estate attorney had assured him of as much. What unnerved him was the timing of the deed's arrival, the almost archaic presentation of the document, and her final message to him. Abe read it again.

Congratulations to the newest keeper of the gate.
The new Ward.
xoxo.

He smiled, unnaturally wide, and looked back over his shoulder at the clown quietly musing, laughing back at him.

"Okay, Elma," Abe sighed. "You got me."

Fifty Nine

Simi felt Mags squeeze his hand.

"You okay?" he turned to her.

"Yeah," she sniffed "It's just sad, you know? He didn't have anyone else. We're all that's here."

Simi looked up at the two others standing around the plain stone marker. Abe and Daisy held hands on the opposite side of the granite slab. The name at the top was engraved in large block letters.

HALDEN

"It looks nice," Simi said, making eye contact with his father.

Abe smiled through tears. "Yeah, well. They gave me a good deal. I told them it was for a local hero. A *legend*."

Daisy put her arm around him and looked around the old burial plot. Rows of Ward headstones stared back at her, the space beneath each void of even a single bone. None were the actual resting places for the souls memorialized above. "He would have wanted to be here, I think."

Abe nodded. "In the end, he went out just like all the rest of them did. Ripped into the swamp, beneath the water, at the hands of those—those—"

Daisy shushed him. "Just leave it. No need to go there today."

Simi watched his father and Daisy. She was leaning on him, his bald head resting on top of her thick ponytail. Something told him they need a few minutes alone, so he grabbed Mags' hand and they began to walk back across the street, making the kitty-corner jaunt toward Ward House.

They stood, leaning against Abe's truck, until he and Daisy traversed the road as well. Abe approached the rusty pickup and looked to Daisy, who was already making her way up to the top step, in front of the porch. She sat down and smiled at him.

"Okay, D. I expect it's time for me and Simi to get Mags back home to Georgia. Her parents have given her up to us for longer than they bargained for, I think. You gonna be okay?"

Balancing her elbows on her knees, she rested her chin on folded hands. "Oh yeah. Think I can hold down the fort for a time."

Abe squinted. "I dunno. This is *some* fort. You sure?"

She waved at him. "Haven't we been over this? Nothing's happened for weeks. I put food out and there isn't anything coming to eat it. Course if anything changes, I'll call. You do still answer your phone, right?"

He winked at her. "Okay, okay. Fair enough. I can be back here in less than a day if you end up needing me."

Daisy stood up and walked back down to the sidewalk. She hugged both Simi and Mags tight and then turned to him. "I won't." She hesitated as if she were considering kissing him, but then turned toward the house and walked back inside.

Not quite, thought Simi. *Not quite.*

The door shut behind her and the space where the creepy gargoyle knocker had once been glared back at the three standing by the road—its absence obvious to anyone who'd ever before stepped foot on that unholy stretch of bogland.

Abe pointed at the truck. Mags got in without another word, but Simi hesitated.

"What about all of this, Dad?"

Abe cocked an eyebrow. "Dad?"

Simi punched him in the shoulder. "Hey, well, let's not make a thing of it. I'm trying something out."

Abe ruffled his son's hair. "Cool. Well, I like it. If *you* do, that is—"

"I said let's not make a thing of it. Chill, Old Man."

Abe put his hands up. "Okay, I get it. I get. 'Nough said."

Still didn't answer my question, though.

Simi tried again. "So, this place. All of it. What's gonna hap—"

Abe yanked open the driver's side door, taking his position within the cockpit, and Simi, reluctantly, climbed in beside Mags.

Exasperated, he started to speak again. "Dad, I—"

"I heard you, Sim," he whispered. "I guess I just hadn't thought we'd broach the subject so soon. Got a lot of driving to do today. Figured we'd have plenty of—"

"Dad."

Abe sighed. He turned around and both kids were staring back at him disapprovingly.

"Not you too, Mags."

She folded her arms. "Hey, you're the one avoiding the man's questions. Answer him already."

Abe turned back around and started the engine. It rumbled to life, but he didn't pull out of park. Ward House stood to his right, and he stared up at it, wishing the conversation he was about to have would come more easily.

"Well," he began. "The truth is—that is to say— I'm not sure I'll ever be able to fully leave. Not entirely."

Simi heard himself gulp, but didn't say anything. Mags folded a hand around his and he grabbed hers in return.

Abe continued when no one else spoke. His hands were tight on the steering wheel and he looked toward the door Daisy had just disappeared through. "There's a lot keeping me here, guys. Making me feel like—well, like I'll need to come back. And, I know what you're thinking. It's not just D. She's, of course, part of this all but, well..."

Simi leaned forward. "What?"

Abe swallowed. "I can already... *feel* it. They don't want me to leave, Sim."

They.

Simi struggled with what he was hearing. "But does that mean you have to—I mean, like, do you really need to?"

Abe nodded and reached over, patting his son on the knee that'd torn through his worn, black, jeans. "Yes, Sim. I do."

Simi scrubbed at his eyes, his face getting red. "But, when? Like, how long until you—?"

"Figure we'll get back to Georgia and then, once your mom returns from her 'vacation', then—well—then I'll need to—"

"But, that fast?" argued Simi. "She'll be back—shit—maybe as early as tomorrow. That soon?" He wiped his tears again. "Dad?"

Abe sighed. "Yes."

Simi put his hands on top of his head. Mags tried to comfort him but he shrugged her off. "And then what? You'll move here? For how long? For good? For—forever?"

Abe nodded. "Don't see how that can be avoided, Simeon. Great thing is, we're living in the twenty-first century. We can Facetime and all that jazz."

Mags giggled. "Did—did you just say, 'Facetime and all that—?"

"Okay, enough from you," Abe laughed and thought he could see a smirk from the corner of Simi's mouth. "And, well—Mags has already figured out the bus route. Should be easy enough for you two to visit me and D as much as you want."

Simi sniffed, but seemed to be brightening up rather quickly. "You and D, huh?"

Abe put the truck into drive. "Well, guess I'm getting a bit ahead of myself. Wishful thinking maybe."

Mags kicked the back of his seat, playfully. "Yeah, maybe."

They pulled away from the curb and Abe cleared his throat. "You know just—I dunno—maybe don't tell your mom *everything* that went on here. I wouldn't want her to—"

"Don't worry, Dad," Simi stopped him. "The Ward Family secret is safe with us and—well—with this whole godforsaken town too. But, we'll never tell."

Abel Ward's truck chugged away down Brown Street, toward Plainville, and away from the obscenities that hibernated in the morass of Foxborough, Massachusetts. In his rearview mirror, Ward House stood stoically, watching him leave, knowing he would return…

…and somewhere, someone quietly—and perhaps knowingly—sang a haunted rhyme. A child's verse, it giggled innocently past the ears of the unwitting, ignored by the unwilling, lifting up, prancing amidst the rising marsh fog, tickling the ears of all who dared to listen...

From the depths of me 'art, to the pit of me soul, with ne'er a breath nor need for a hole,
O' Malevolent, Malevolent Nevers.
Here they wait for all our evers,
O' Malevolent, Malevolent Nevers.
Our demons to bear.
Our demons to share.
O' Malevolent, Malevolent Nevers.
Sometimes they be locked away, where no one can see 'em, outter sight.
Sometimes they be a droolin' face, starin' in through 'yer winder, in the dead of the night!
O' Malevolent, Malevolent, Malevolent, Malevolent, Malevolent, Malevolent NEVERS!
When all is lost, and the demons do come,
And nighttime hath falln' darker'n some,
And your blessed 'art is tired and numb.
They can't getcha, in the embrace of Sanctum.
O' Malevolent, Malevolent, Nevers.

Acknowledgements

I never thought I'd write one book, never mind four.

My trilogy, which came first, was something I'd been building for the better part of a decade. Once that scampered out into the world, I finally found space to jot down some of my other nightmares.

Malevolent Nevers is the first such nightmare, but it's also one which stemmed from some real-life events. We did actually hear terrifying noises out in the swamp behind our home. We did actually find pieces of a number of creatures scattered about our property (including the head of a fisher cat). We did actually have a professional drop by to investigate.

But, most everything else is made up.

Mostly.

I would like to thank:

My family: KC, AC, and ET. I know you don't like scary things in the way that I do, but you have always been so supportive of my writing. Horror is a genre that you'd otherwise prefer not like to think about, but your joy for my books (mostly your joy for my joy for my books) is what makes me want to keep writing them. I heart you three.

Gemma Amor: you are so talented and I am so lucky that you agreed to create the artwork for this cover. You truly brought my Malevolent Nevers to life. Cheers.

Shadow Spark Publishing: Specifically, Jessica Moon and Mandy Russell. I was one of your first authors and I am thrilled that you're still eager to read what I'm writing. Jess, your cover design (as always) was amazing. And Mandy, I can't tell you how much it means to me that you were so genuinely excited about Ulf. Sorry about that.

Okay, well. Off to write the next nightmare.

Love, Tom

October 2021

Also By Tom Rimer

The Glowing Trilogy:
The Glowing #1
The Glowing #2
The Glowing #3

https://shadowsparkpub.com/tomrimer

Tom Rimer lives in Foxborough, Massachusetts with his wife and two children. He is the author of *THE GLOWING* (an epic sci-fi trilogy) from Shadow Spark Publishing. His short story "Clown" was published in 2016 as part of the horror anthology, *13 Tales to Give You Night Terrors*.

Right now, he's probably lost in an old bookshop. You can find him on Twitter, musing about what he finds funny and talking about all bookish things @RimerTom.

photo credit: Laura Gustafson

Made in United States
North Haven, CT
09 December 2021